THE CROSS OF SINS
Copyright © 2010 by Geoffrey Knight

All rights reserved. No part of this book may be reproduced or transmitted in any form or by any means, electronic or mechanical, including photocopying, recording, or by any information storage and retrieval system, without permission in writing from the publisher.

This book is a work of fiction. Names, characters, places, situations and incidents are the product of the author's imaginations or are used fictitiously. Any resemblance to actual events, locales, or persons, living or dead, is purely coincidental.

Published in Australia
ISBN: 978-1456566999

First Edition published in the U.S.A by STARbooks Press 2008

Second Edition published 2010 by Geoffrey Knight
in Association with Dare Empire eMedia Productions

Cover Art © 2010 Dare Empire eMedia Productions

THE CROSS OF SINS

THE CROSS OF SINS

GEOFFREY KNIGHT

For Maximus

I

THE ISLAND OF KAHNA TOGA, SOUTH PACIFIC

The naked flame of his torch swept the wall of the tunnel, illuminating rock and clay so dense and dry it looked as though it had been baked in a furnace. The young man wondered how long it had been since these caves had seen life. How long since they had known the stir of human breath, or felt the wary tread of feet pressing onward, inward, further, and deeper into the mountain. He guessed the answer was over a century, when the treasure he now sought was first hidden here.

If the legend was true, then these caves hadn't seen a living creature since 1899.

Since then, nothing had ventured inside. There was nothing here but stifling heat and suffocating darkness. And fumes. Like gas from a burst main. Hissing up through the pitch black. Through tiny crevices in the rocky ground and walls.

It was the earth's cocktail of poisons—sulfur and methane—that told him he was getting close.

From the seismic maps and geologists' reports that kept him awake during the plane trip to the island, the young man knew that soon the cave would open out, and he would be looking over a river of fire that oozed up from the center of the earth and streamed away into several deltas, churning and searing and slowly eating away at the belly of the volcano.

One week earlier, Jake Stone had received the following telegram.

To: Mr. Jake Stone. STOP. The Devil of Kahna Toga is no longer a myth. STOP. Wherever there's a will there's a way, wherever there's a priceless treasure there's someone who'll pay. STOP. Yours truly, P. Perron

He had received the message while in the expanse of his crumbling warehouse apartment back in New York. It was a sparsely decorated abode. In the middle of the space sat an ancient travel trunk resting on the floorboards with sleeves, jeans and cargoes draped down the sides. A worn and torn backpack hung from a hook on the wall. In one corner, there was a bathroom with no walls, just a tub and a toilet with a curtain and a few rusted exposed pipes running up the wall. And lying on the floor at either end of the warehouse space were two mattresses, both empty with messed-up sheets strewn over them. One was Jake's, the other belonged to Sam, a street kid who sometimes crashed at Jake's, ate his food, then vanished again.

Jake scribbled a note.

He stuck it on an old nail that had been hammered into one of the warehouse's old pylons.

He opened the trunk, pulled out a few items of clothing and stuffed them inside the backpack, then left the apartment, which was tucked away in the backstreets of New York's meatpacking district. He was on a plane to Paris within the hour.

The sender of the telegram was one Monsieur Pierre Perron, a wealthy French trader and fanatical collector of rare jewels, priceless treasures and objects of impossible beauty. He owned a villa in the south of France, an old tobacco plantation on the island of San Sebastian in the Caribbean and a mansion on the Grand Canal in Venice, each of which he had turned into his own private museum. For some years now, he had been compiling data from geological surveys submitted by the small but surprisingly efficient Kahna Toga Land Commission, which indicated that the temperature of the ground on Mount Kahna Toga—located at the north end of the tiny and remote Pacific island of the same name—was rising at an exponential rate. Crops at the foot of the mountain were failing. Vegetation was dying. Wildlife was slowly abandoning the region. Perron had in his possession enough scientific research to deduce that the mountain was getting ready to erupt. Of this he was absolutely certain. The only question was when.

Jake met with Perron in a suite at L'Hotel Lyon in Paris at 8:00am on a simmering Tuesday morning.

"I always forget," Perron smirked, one eyebrow raised suggestively, admiringly, as Jake was ushered into the suite by a one of Perron's goons. Although the offer had never directly been made, it was no secret that Jake himself was a treasure that Perron longed to possess.

"Forget what?" Jake asked, keeping his distance from Perron as the fat Frenchman stuffed a buttery croissant into his mouth and slurped it down with a bowl of coffee.

"How handsome you are. What must you do with all the money men like me pay you? What must it be worth to risk that pretty face of yours time and time again?"

Jake smirked. "What I do with my money is none of your goddamn business. Now did you ask me here for the pleasure of watching you stuff your face, or did you get me here to talk about the Devil of Kahna Toga."

Perron laughed. "That's why I like you so much, Mr. Stone. You're not just a cute ass; you're a smart ass, too. And straight to the point. No time for bullshit." The Frenchman finished off his croissant and polished his fingers with a cloth napkin. He pulled a cigar out of a sterling silver cigar case and flipped open a lighter. He lit his own cigar before offering one to his guest.

"They're from my own plantation. I'd be insulted if you didn't have one. You know I haven't even named these cigars, yet.

I could name them after you, if you like. Stone Cigars. It has a ring to it, you know."

"Are you trying to flatter me?"

"Perhaps, although I'm not sure why I even bother. You're always keeping me at arm's length. It's so unfortunate that our contact is limited to the number of transactions I make. Have you ever noticed that? You spend all your time trekking through God-forsaken countries, chasing riddles, digging in the dirt, searching for yourself. Yet if it's money you want, I'm sure you have so many other talents you're yet to explore. Talents I'm more than willing to pay for."

Jake promptly changed the subject. "The Devil."

"Ah yes, the Devil," Perron smiled, pretending to have forgotten the reason they were here. "The Devil of Kahna Toga. What's it worth to a man like you? What's it worth to be the one man to find the Devil of Kahna Toga? To take it from the mountain. To rescue it from that angry place before it blows. What's that worth? $40,000?" Perron grinned, trying on charm. "What would you say to that?"

Jake didn't say a word.

In the rich light of the Paris morning streaming in through Perron's balcony doors, 28-year-old Jake Stone cut a classic figure, with a set of fine shoulders branching wide and solid atop the firm trunk of his torso. He was sweating a little. Wet patches dappled his shirt, under his arms and down the middle of his chest. His white sleeves were rolled up and bunched high, revealing the veined forearms of a man who was no stranger to toil. His face was empirically handsome—dark skin, piercing green eyes, short black hair that perhaps had been combed earlier in the day, but now in the hot summer wind had been swept into a natural mess. In fact, it appeared his only physical flaw was the crease in his brow that etched an angry mark in his forehead at the price Perron had just offered him for the job.

Whether or not Jake looked like a New York catwalk model or a treasure-hunter for hire, he was by no means the kind of guy who would stand there and be met with the type of offer Perron had just made.

Finding the Devil of Kahna Toga was worth at least twice that amount. Without saying a single word in reply, Jake Stone simply turned and exited the suite.

"Wait! Wait!" the Frenchman shouted, suddenly surprised and angry—and a little panicked.

But Jake had already vanished.

"Wait a minute!" The infuriated Perron dropped his cigar into an ashtray on his desk, lumbered out of the hotel suite and cut Jake off at the elevator at the end of the hall. "I'll be damned if I've spent the better part of three years trying to find the Devil of Kahna Toga and have it slip through my fingers, just because of some egotistical thrill-seeker!"

"Then I suggest you go find it yourself."

"I'm not one for apologies," the huffing Frenchman snorted.

There was a soft, electronic chime, and the lift doors opened.

"And I'm not one for long, sad goodbyes." Jake stepped into the lift.

"You want to see it as much as I do. You want to hold the Devil in your hands as much as any man. Don't tell me it's not true."

Jake said nothing. He knew Perron was right, but he also knew if he gave in now, if he let Perron screw him down on price, then the Frenchman would never stop screwing him over. Hell, there was no guarantee that Perron wasn't already hatching his own wicked little plans to get his hands on what he wanted. But that's what this game was all about—getting your hands on the treasure. Perron wanted the Devil. Jake wanted the money.

And the lift doors began to close.

"Wait," Perron was getting desperate. "I'll pay you double."

Jake smiled as the doors continued to slide shut, but shook his head. "You blew it, pal."

"Triple!" Perron cried. "That's my last offer."

Jake's hand slammed against the rubber-cushioned rim of one of the lift doors. Perron held his breath.

Jake eyed him sternly. "Two hundred thousand—U.S.—deposited directly into my account before I leave this building."

Perron squirmed visibly. The thought of parting with so much money was obviously killing him inside. "One hundred thousand now," he offered, "the other hundred thousand when you bring me the Devil."

Jake forced open the lift doors and extended his hand to Perron. "Done," he said with a firm shake.

Back in Perron's palatial suite, the Frenchman loaded up a glass of scotch and ice. It was still early, but this was no ordinary conversation taking place on any ordinary day. "Forgive this dull suite, won't you. Damned striped wallpaper, paintings of vases and fruit. Normally, I like to surround myself with art that's a little less—how do you say—restrained." Perron took a gulp of his drink then unlocked the top drawer of a bureau in the suite's parlor and unfurled a handful of maps and graphs across the coffee table in front of Jake.

"Mount Kahna Toga?" Jake asked, trying to read the scribble of geological data.

Perron nodded. "I've spoken to the locals. On my last trip, I met a man—116-years-old—claims to know the location of the Devil. He was only a boy at the time. He says he followed the elders into the volcano on that day back in 1899, followed them to where they placed the Devil, inside a small alcove in the heart of the mountain."

Perron looked at Jake as he pored over the maps. Casually, he leaned across Jake, his hand brushing against the young man's shoulder and resting there. "That was just after the first eruption—"

"I know," Jake said, still poring over the charts. "It devastated half the island. Killed most of its inhabitants. The people thought they'd brought a curse upon their land, so they made an idol. The Devil. A twelve inch diamond statue forged from the volcano's own rock and hardened lava. They took it to Mount Kahna Toga, into the caverns, deep within the tunnels of the volcano. It was an offering, so that destruction and chaos would never again rain death and fire upon the island."

"Faith," Perron chuckled. "It's the same all over the world. So well intended. And yet so delusional."

"There are some who would argue," Jake countered.

"I have no doubt," the Frenchman said. "But in this case, science is about to give faith a lesson in reality."

Perron turned away from Jake and the charts. He walked over to the open bay doors that led out onto the balcony of the suite. He didn't step outside, but simply gazed upon the reflection of the hot sun bouncing off the jutting, slated rooftops of Paris. "Mount Kahna Toga is going to erupt. Perhaps tomorrow. Perhaps next year. Perhaps at this very moment. If the Devil is inside the mountain, as the old man claims it is, then it won't be for much longer." Perron crossed back to where Jake stood. The Frenchman took another sip of his early morning drink.

Jake stood back, narrowing his eyes at the silhouette of Perron looking out the window. "Why me? What makes you think I'd risk my life venturing into a volcano for something that may be nothing more than a village legend? An old man's tall tale? An island ghost story?"

"Because you're the best. Because I like you." Perron turned, a broad smirk on his face. "Because it's what you love, isn't it?"

Jake said nothing. He did not move a muscle.

By noon that day, he was on another plane, this time flying out of Orly on his way to the South Pacific.

*

As soon as he arrived on the island, Jake hired an interpreter and met with the ancient Kahna Togan that Perron had spoken of. He made a tape recording of his interview with the old man and played it back over and over, until he knew the trail into the volcano, step-by-step. He made drawings. He etched out a map in his mind. If the old man was wrong, if he had been lying or imagining the entire story, then Jake knew he would be walking into a fiery hell.

But if he was right—

If the diamond Devil really did exist—

Then Jake Stone would be the first person beyond this island paradise ever to lay his eyes, to lay his hands, sures of the South Pacific.

And he knew that was worth a hell of a lot more than $200,000.

—Or was it?

So far, the old man had been right.

Jake had entered the mountain behind a waterfall that flowed into a beautiful, sulfurous, milky-green lagoon. Sulfur bubbles popped and burst on the surface of the water. Once he was inside the waterfall's cave, he pulled a match from the pocket of his cargo pants and lit his torch. A large flame ignited. He repositioned the wire climbing cable, looped tightly over one shoulder, and started his descent into the mountain.

As the drumming of the waterfall faded behind him, so did the light of day. Soon he was guiding himself along by nothing more than fiery torchlight and the memory of a 116-year-old man. Down through the cave of shimmering pools, he made his way, along the ridge of gleaming stalagmites and into the steaming tunnel. Jake followed the cave along for almost an hour, heading steadily downward, journeying deeper and deeper into the heart of the volcano. At the base of the cave, he looked around for a rocky step formation, just as the old man had described, descending down even further. He found it, hidden behind an enormous fallen rock; a tremor must have knocked it loose from the ceiling of the cavern.

By now, the heat was becoming unbearable. His throat felt thick and tight, his lungs felt as if they would cave in with the pressure of the fumes. Sweat ran in dozens of tiny rivulets down his face. His clothes were drenched and heavy. He was losing mobility with the weight of the sweat-soaked material, so he hauled off the coiled wire cable and stripped off his shirt. It slid groggily off his skin and slapped against the rocky floor. Jake replaced the cable and squeezed between the fallen rock and the cave wall before heading cautiously down the rock steps.

When the earth leveled out once more, the ceiling of the tunnel lowered significantly, and Jake found himself crouching low to move. He quickly realized that with its smooth rounded walls he had entered an ancient hardened lava tube—a flawlessly formed passage once chiseled out through the interior of the mountain by a jet of lava.

As if to remind him of his own mortality, a low rumble suddenly ripped through the mountain. The ground beneath his feet quaked. The torch fell from his hand and the flame went out. He quickly dropped to his knees to steady himself, ready to jolt into action should the lava tube suddenly open up beneath him or fill with another stream of fire. But Jake Stone was tough. He was scarred, but he was a survivor, and if nothing else, he was certain he could claw his way out of this volcano should hell rise up to meet him. He had seen hell many times before, and every time he had lived to tell the tale.

Seconds passed. The earth soon quieted down and the tremor rippled away, but the warning sign was enough for Jake to push on as fast as he could. He jumped to his feet, and that was when he saw it.

A soft, red glow reflecting off the walls far ahead.

A radiance dancing across the distant ceiling.

A slow incandescence filling the dark void of the earth.

The old man had called it the well of fire, and as Jake took a deep breath and walked determinedly toward the glowing red light, he realized why.

The tunnel opened out onto what could only be described as a medieval vision of the Inferno. The well of fire was a giant cavern that dropped fifty feet into a smoldering moat of molten lava circling a huge, dome-like island in the middle. Enormous gas pockets ascended through the thick churning river of magma and exploded on the surface, spitting globules of liquid rock forty feet into the air. The heat was so intense Jake felt every inch of his flesh tighten. The sweat on his body formed a mirror of the cauldron, the taut muscles of his smooth, hairless chest and glassy, ridged stomach glistening bright orange. Veins stood out like cables beneath his searing skin.

His keen eyes quickly sized up the cavern.

Over one section of the lake of lava stretched a narrow rock bridge crossing to the large central island. Jake noticed now there was a crater in the middle of the island. This was the place. According to the old man, the Devil of Kahna Toga was hidden inside that pit, in an alcove midway down the interior of the crater wall. Jake would have to cross the rock bridge and lower himself in through the small opening of the crater to reach the alcove inside.

Only then would he know if the Devil truly did exist.

Only then would he know if his quest was a brave risk

or reckless gamble.

He edged his way slowly around the thin rim of the cavern and stopped at the foot of the rock bridge. It was a precarious formation, suspended fifty feet over a fiery death, its width tapering in at the middle to what looked like mere inches.

Jake lifted his right foot and eased it out onto the bridge. Small stones, unmoved for decades, centuries, perhaps even millennia, trickled away from his boot and rained into the lava below, turning instantly to fluid on impact. He pushed his left foot out over the bridge, and suddenly he was over the magma sea. He tried not to look beyond the bridge at the lava below. He tried to focus on the stony ledge ahead of him and the rocky bridge beneath his feet. But the glow of the lava was so bright it was impossible not to be drawn by its hypnotic shimmer.

"One step at a time," he assured himself steadily. "One step at a ti—" But before he could finish his sentence, it began to hail.

He felt the rocky debris from the cavern's ceiling pelt his bare arms and shoulders before the rumble began. When the sound of the tremor hit the cavern, it echoed like thunder. The walls and ceiling seemed to shatter like glass, the lava pitched and lapped ferociously below as the entire mountain shuddered.

Jake managed to hold his balance for one second before he was rocked from the bridge. As he tumbled his arms went wide. His fingers reached desperately. His nails caught onto the jagged edge of the bridge, enough for his fingertips to latch onto a craggy sheet of rock. As his body swung, his hands held firm. The lava splashed and swept up the banks of the lake, sending massive balls of magma shooting up through the air around Jake.

He tightened his hold and hoisted his legs up to the rock bridge. He got a foothold. The mountain chamber was still quaking violently. Great chunks of rock plunged from the ceiling. Jake pulled himself up onto the bridge, pressing his stomach against the hot rock, keeping his center of gravity as low as possible. He glanced upward to see a giant boulder break loose from above and plummet directly toward the middle of the bridge. Jake knew that when it hit the bridge, it would take the whole walkway into the bubbling lava with it. He had a second to decide—back up fast, or run for his life and pray he'd make it to the other side of the trembling bridge before it was smashed to pieces.

Jake Stone's legs exploded underneath him, pumping into action.

He sprang from his belly and charged across the bridge like a cougar in the heat of the hunt. As the boulder bore down upon him, Jake put on all the speed he could manage. The giant rock missed his back by inches before smashing into the narrow bridge. Rock pulverized rock. With still fifteen feet to go, Jake looked beneath his feet to see the entire length of the bridge splinter apart. He launched himself into the air, getting just enough push from the rocky foundation of the bridge before gravity sucked it into the molten river below.

He sailed through the air, clearing the jump to safety.

Just.

His stomach crunched against the edge of the island's rim, knocking the wind out of him. Below, pillars of fire spewed upward as the lava devoured the falling bridge. Despite his locked lungs and the razored flesh of his abdomen, Jake managed to haul his legs up and over the edge of the island an instant before a pyre of flames sailed up the wall and winged its way toward the cavern's ceiling.

As the flames vanished in the air, the tremor, too, began to subside.

Jake gave himself a second to recover. He forced air into his lungs. He touched his fingers to his battered ribs, but felt no breaks. With a groan, he sat up and looked around. He was now stranded on the rim of the dome-like island in the middle of a lake of burning orange liquid.

If there was a way out, he could not see it from here.

All he could do now was find the damn Devil of Khana Toga or die trying.

The island arced to a central point, like a beehive. At the top, a small opening led down into its core. Jake climbed to the top and stepped warily along the thin crust of the rim and peered in through the opening. Immense heat funneled up from inside. There was a drop of twenty feet, maybe thirty. Beyond that, Jake could see nothing but the blinding orange glow of lava.

Seconds later, he was lashing the wire cable tight around a giant rock that had dropped and come to rest near the edge of the moat. He made sure the knot was tied firmly, then wrapped the other end of the cable tightly about his waist. He trailed it out behind him as he returned to the opening, then slowly, carefully, Jake lowered himself into the oven of the crater.

The first thing he noticed were the walls of the cavernous dome, sloping away from him in every direction. The further he lowered himself, the further he was from the relative safety of the walls. The second thing he noticed was the lava below. Some magnetic pull, some strange physical law had set it in motion, circling the well of fire in a slow, surreal, unsettling whirlpool of lava.

The third thing he noticed was the alcove.

About halfway down, one of the walls of the crater gave way to a small vent, just wide enough for a person to climb through. Jake couldn't imagine how the Kahna Togans could possibly have managed to get this far inside their mountain. Perhaps they had called upon their gods for help. However they had managed it, Jake, himself, was going to have to rely on nothing more than a length of wire cable and some clever guesswork to get to the fissure.

Slowly, he lowered himself to just below the height of the alcove and began swinging his body weight on the cable.

At first, there was no momentum whatsoever, but gradually, as he built up speed and inertia, he was swinging like a pendulum. As he pitched to and fro with ever-increasing strength, he managed to steer his movement toward the alcove. He cut though the boiling air and sent hot pockets and currents swirling through the rising steam. With greater speed, he reached closer. And closer. Until eventually, with his chipped nails and cut fingers, he hooked the edge of the alcove. He held himself there for a tense moment, pulling against the weight of his own swing as it tried to pry him off the wall. But with all the might of his burning biceps and bulging shoulder muscles, Jake managed to haul himself into the vent of the alcove.

It was small and smoldering inside. There was practically no air. There was very little light seeping in through the narrow entrance.

But there was, however, propped against the far wall, sitting alone in the dark, smothering space of the alcove, something perfectly out of place.

Something shimmering.

Something sparkling.

Something made from the diamonds of the mountain itself.

With the cable still tied firmly around his taut waist, Jake took one step forward and reached one hand toward the glittering fabled Devil of Kahna Toga.

But Mount Kahna Toga had other plans for him.

At the precise moment his fingertips touched the glass-like surface of the idol, squatting on its priceless haunches, flickering its glimmering forked tongue at him, the mountain let out its mightiest roar yet.

From the pit behind him, lava began to erupt in sporadic, blazing bursts.

The whole of the island shook, and as it did, virtually the entire ceiling of the cavern outside the alcove slid from above and toppled into the boiling lava, taking with it half the crater's rim—and setting the boulder—around which Jake's cable was tied—into motion.

Bombarded by the sudden avalanche, the huge boulder tipped off its broken shelf and tumbled backward, away from the beehive crater, back into the lake.

Jake's fingertips brushed the sparkling diamond Devil, then suddenly—whoosh!

The cable, still tied around his waist, yanked him out through the opening of the alcove. The skin of his torso was torn and shredded as he was ripped away from his treasure and swept up into the air.

The cable slithered upward, out through the opening of the crater and down the other side where the rock to which it was tied slapped against the surface of the lava and began to sink. The wire cable turned red-hot, the lava eating through it at a veracious rate.

When the rock hit the lava, Jake, on the other end of the cable, jerked to a sudden halt and was left dangling over the lava inside the beehive crater. He felt his bruised ribs strain, but he had greater concerns. The bubbling magma below him began to rupture and rise, the cavern began to break apart all around him, and his best hunch told him that his cable was caught somewhere between a rock and a very hot place, with very little hope of remaining intact for much longer. He had seconds—if he was lucky.

In a reflex action, Jake's fingers quickly unhitched the knot around his waist. His body dropped free, but his hands held tight to the cable. As the lava continued to gush and flare, rapidly filling the crater, Jake realized he had one last shot at the alcove.

Still clinging to the cable, he pushed his body through the air, swung backward with all the force he could muster, then catapulted himself forward and let go of the cable, leaping haphazardly at the crater wall. He soared above the rising lava, his hands thrust out before him, and slammed into the crater wall with a hard thump.

Behind him the sizzling wire cable dropped into the lava like a snake on fire.

Jake clung to the wall for a perilous second before feeling the opening to the alcove just below his feet. He looked down. The lava was splashing up toward the fissure. He clambered down as fast as he could, swooping into the vent and crash-landing inside the alcove. Swiftly, he seized the diamond devil in both hands.

As he did, lava surged up and over the entrance to the alcove. It streamed inside. Jake glanced over his shoulder at the scorching magma flooding furiously toward him. He lifted the Devil high above his head.

For a second, he hesitated.

He was bargaining that the crust floor of the alcove might be thin enough to break through. If he found a weak spot, it could lead him to a way out. It could also lead to a pool of seething lava, waiting to explode beneath his feet. It was a risk. Not to mention what he might do to the statue, which he was now using as a sledgehammer. A single flaw in the Devil, a single imperfection in the idol, and it would shatter into a million worthless shards. For the sake of his own life, Jake could only pray the Devil of Kahna Toga had no flaws. Right now, all he could do was take his chances.

The lava was guzzling into the alcove now. It formed expanding puddles that inched toward Jake's feet. The leather of his boots began to melt. His laces spontaneously ignited. He held the idol high and danced around the magma, finding the highest possible ground. Then, with all his might, Jake thrust the Devil of Kahna Toga at the ground beneath his feet.

There was a loud crack.

The ground beneath the idol shattered.

The crusted floor of the alcove split and opened wide, and suddenly the Devil of Kahna Toga vanished.

As did Jake Stone.

As well as a river of lava that flooded into the alcove and swiftly followed him, flushing down into the newly formed chasm.

Jake fell into the darkness for what seemed like minutes. When he finally hit a surface, it was smooth and sloped and sent him into a treacherous tumble. He picked up speed fast, turning and toppling uncontrollably until he managed to twist himself onto his back and stay that way, sliding feet-first at a breakneck pace down what appeared to be a dangerously steep lava tube. Ahead of him he could make out the gleam of the diamond Devil, still in one piece, barreling down the perilous descent. It made a heavy, bashing, crashing noise as it toppled head over heel, echoing thunderously all the way down the tube—

—Until another noise rapidly filled the tunnel.

Tearing along at lightning speed, Jake managed to turn his head to see what was coming down the chute behind him: a giant, roaring, ravaging wall of lava, storming down the hole at a speed greater than his, consuming every inch of the lava tube with an insatiable appetite.

Jake turned back quickly to face forward. He jammed his feet together like an arrow and laid as flat as he could, trying to pick up even greater speed. The diamond Devil rambled and ricocheted off the walls of the tube ahead of him. Behind him, he could feel the heat getting closer; feel the torrent of fire bearing down on him, hungry and determined to wolf him down whole.

Suddenly, somewhere far ahead, he glimpsed daylight streaming into the tube, speeding toward him.

The torpedo of lava behind him closed in. Out of the corners of his eyes, he saw bolts of orange streak the walls on either side. He felt the sting of fire spitting against his bare shoulders.

Then without warning, the diamond Devil stopped clanging.

Jake looked ahead and saw it shoot out into blinding daylight.

He held his breath, and suddenly he was jettisoned into the air, into the wide open, high above the dazzling blue of the Pacific Ocean.

As the mountain spat him out, he spun in mid-air and rolled into a dive.

Behind him the stream of lava spewed from the lava tube.

Jake saw the Devil of Kahna Toga break the water below him. He slapped his palms together and plunged into the ocean a split second later. Then he kicked. With all his strength. With every muscle in his legs. Furiously, he pushed himself as far beneath the surface of the ocean as he could manage.

When the jet of lava hit the water above him, there was a boom like thunder, as though the whole ocean was exploding. On the surface, the blast of boiling steam spread out in a shockwave that slammed the ocean cliffs and swept out to sea.

Beneath the water, small chunks of instantly solidified lava teemed down to the seabed, where Jake had already found the Devil of Kahna Toga nestled in a thatch of seaweed on the ocean floor. As the black hail of lava rock pelted him from above, Jake snatched the idol off the ocean floor. His lungs were bursting for air. He kicked furiously, heading into deeper waters, pushing himself away from the cascade of lava that was already forming a new coastline for the island.

Moments later, he broke the surface of the warm tropical South Sea. Behind him, the mountain exploded. A gigantic plume of ash and steam billowed down its slopes. Lava burst into the sky and streamed down the coastal cliffs below its rumbling peak.

"Some people make great entrances. Others make memorable exits. You, my friend, seem to do both."

The voice came from behind Jake, shouting over the rupture of the mountain.

In all the commotion of the eruption, Jake hadn't seen the ocean cruiser pull up behind him. He didn't hear its motors above the roar of nature's explosion. Now, as he turned in the churning waters, he saw Perron's grinning face looking down upon him. He heard his wicked, gleeful laugh. That's when he knew things were about to get even worse.

Before he could dive out of view, two men in scuba gear jumped into the water beside him. One of them tried to seize the idol, but Jake fought him off.

Then, he saw the spear gun in the second scuba diver's hands.

He felt the searing heat, the pain pierce straight through his side.

Then, he felt the warmth of his own blood, swirling all around him.

He felt the idol slip from his arms. He saw the two divers swim back to the boat, leaving him in the choppy red-blood waters. He heard the motors of the cruiser fire up, churning smoke and foam in his face as he struggled for air. But above all the noise—the roar of the cruiser, the rumbling of the distant mountain, the rush of his own blood thundering through his brain and oozing from his body—above it all, the one thing he knew he would never forget was the shrill caw of Pierre Perron's laughter fading in the distance.

*

He could still sense the motion of the sea. At first he thought he was imagining it. Then he realized he was on some sort of vessel. His eyes opened, just a little, and he saw a circle of light. A porthole, he realized. It was smeared, a combination of salt and grease on the glass and his own grogginess. He tried to sit up, but the pain shot through his body with a paralyzing bolt.

His first fear—that he had been taken onboard Perron's cruiser like some sort of prisoner—quickly subsided when he listened more closely to the whine and chug of the engines, as he squinted through his weary eyes at the cramped confines of his quarters and the dank and grime on the walls; as he smelled the stink of fish all around him.

This boat was not exactly the kind of vessel Perron would set foot on.

Jake saw his torn and tattered cargo pants hanging on a fish hook nearby, his boots stacked in one corner. He looked down to see a filthy blanket covering his body. He lifted it to see that he was naked. Blood had dried in dozens of lines—some thin and slender, some thick and deep—all over his body. There was a frayed and filthy bandage bound around his waist with a large crimson stain pin-pointing the wound he had received from the spear gun.

Just then, the door burst open.

An enormous unshaven Polynesian man in rubber pants and a thick shirt smeared in fish scales and dried guts stood in the doorway. In a gruff tone, he blurted something at Jake in a language he did not understand. Whether it was angry abuse or a piece of friendly advice, it was impossible to tell.

Jake was unsure of what to do or say. All he could manage was, "Thanks," in a weak voice.

In reply, the burly Polynesian gave a stern nod. Then, surprisingly, he seemed to speak in English with a foreign accent. "You're lucky we found you before the sharks did," he appeared to say, although the accent didn't sound remotely like that of a South Pacific Islander. In fact, it sounded Brazilian.

That was when Jake saw the second man, squeezing into the cramped quarters from behind the thick-set Polynesian. It was the second man who had spoken. As he moved into the small space, he knelt beside Jake.

"Try to relax," he said. His voice was soothing, his accent thick yet gentle. His face was handsome and brown, his eyes were like pools of dark melted chocolate, his short hair only a shade or so lighter. The sleeves of his shirt were rolled high and his arms and hands were strong and firm. "My name is Eden Santiago. I'm a doctor. You're on a fishing boat. These men were kind enough to fish you out of the water. But now I need to move you."

Confused and in pain, Jake watched as the handsome Brazilian produced a small medical pouch. He filled a syringe with fluid. Jake flinched quickly despite the pain. "Hey wait a second, buddy. I don't know who you are or where you came from, but back up with the needle. No offense, but the last guy who stuck something in me didn't leave me feelin' so good."

The Brazilian threw back the blanket that covered Jake, exposing his naked body and pointing to the tattered and soiled bandage wrapped about his waist. "I don't want to ask when that bandage was last used, or why, but do you know how quickly an infection can work its way into your body?"

Jake said nothing, conscious only of the pain and the exposure of his body to this Brazilian stranger. It seemed he had little choice but to trust the man. Lying there, vulnerable and wounded, he looked the Brazilian in the eye.

"You don't want to die on a fishing boat," the Brazilian said. He gave a reassuring smile. "Besides, the Professor needs a man like you. He's had an eye on your work for some time."

As the needle slid into his forearm, Jake managed to ask, "The Professor? My work? I don't know what you mean—"

"Perhaps work is the wrong word. Perhaps 'adventures' is more accurate."

Jake's head was spinning with questions, but the drugs were already sending him into a deeper spiral. The soothing voice of the Brazilian slowly began to slip away. "Close your eyes. When you open them again, you'll feel better. I'll look after you, I promise..."

II

SAN DIEGO, CALIFORNIA

Young Will Hunter leaned with both palms flat against the white tiles of the shower room and held his head under the rush of water, letting the cool cascade trickle over the bruise that was already forming around his left eye. With one hand, he gently massaged the tender cheekbone.

He was alone in the showers now. He'd been abandoned by his team. All the other guys left without saying so much as a goodbye to him. He'd screwed up, he knew it, and while his teammates were content with the old silent treatment, it was Coach Kelly who had laid it on the line.

"Another stunt like that and you're not only off the team," he'd shouted at Will as the young footballer hauled off his shoulder pads and jockstrap, "but I'll make damn sure you're kicked out of this school for good. And I don't give a damn if your ancient history professor defends you or how good your grades are. Another scene like that and your college days are over!"

Will wanted to tell his coach to go to hell. In fact, the way he felt right now he wanted to tell the whole world to go to hell. He wanted to tell the coach it wasn't his fault, that damn Sandy Banks, the quarterback for the other team, was a goddamn loose cannon. He was an asshole, and he deserved the right hook that Will had given him.

But then again, Sandy Banks would probably say the same thing about Will. It didn't help matters that after last year's Interstate Awards night the two of them had fucked. They went to bed drunk, woke up—awkwardly—as friends, and now after all these months, with not a single phonecall, not even a text between them, the two teenagers faced off as competitors on the field.

Too much testosterone.

Too much history—

—or perhaps not enough. Perhaps both boys wanted more than history had handed them.

Now the fight on the field was over.

And the game was over.

San Diego had lost, and everyone on his team seemed more than willing to blame Will for their defeat, whether the fight had anything to do with it or not.

"Hey!"

The voice came from behind him with such force it echoed through the shower room. Will spun about, expecting to see the coach back for another lecture, or maybe one of his teammates ready to teach him a lesson. But instead he saw the enemy himself.

Sandy Banks.

He stood at the entrance to the showers in his red letter sweater and gym bag hooked over one shoulder.

The first thing Will did was smirk at the bruise he'd left on Sandy Banks' handsome square jaw, despite Will's own eye coming up black and bruised.

"What are you laughin' at?" Sandy demanded.

"Your face. What are you doin' here?"

"To tell you off the field, face to face, that I think you're an asshole."

"The feeling's mutual. Are you looking for another fight?"

Sandy shook his head. "I also wanted to tell you I think you're the best player out there. But you're way too fired up."

Will let the hint of a smile slide across his face. "My life is—more complicated than you think."

"Whatever," Sandy shrugged, pissed, as the two nineteen-year-olds eyed each other through the steam drifting and swirling around the shower room. For a moment, Will tried in vain to suppress the physical feelings he'd felt all those months ago, but it was no use.

At the same time, Will watched as Sandy's eyes—voluntarily or not—wondered over Will's naked body: his muscular chest, his buff stomach, his thick legs, his hardening cock. Will didn't try to hide it now, why should he? On the field, Sandy was his worst enemy. But off the field, there was no denying the guy was hot, with his dark hair and blue eyes and chiseled young face. If Sandy had a problem with Will's increasingly evident appreciation of that fact, he could turn his back and leave now.

Instead, Sandy let his gym bag slide off his shoulder and onto the floor. "I waited for you to call."

"So did I."

"Like I said, you're an asshole. You're not the only one with a complicated life, you know."

Will smiled. Perhaps Sandy didn't quite get the entire gamut of Will's complications. But then again, with someone like Sandy Banks standing in front of him—now peeling off his letter sweater and the shirt underneath and kicking off his boots—Will didn't see the need to complicate things even further.

He could see the head of Sandy's cock before Sandy even got to the drawstring of his track pants. Will watched, letting the water cascade over his own body, trickling around his now erect penis, as Sandy dropped his track pants. The young quarterback's rock-hard cock flicked up, slapping against his six-pack stomach.

Will let Sandy come to him. He watched as he walked up to him, the muscles in his legs and arms still hard after the game. As he neared, Will reached out and wrapped his hand around the back of Sandy's neck, pulling him under the shower. Their mouths locked in a hard, ruthless kiss. Their smooth wet stomachs pressed against each other, their hard cocks stabbing at one another.

Sandy groaned, as though a lifetime of denial was suddenly escaping his body. Will grinned, treading assuredly, excitedly, on very familiar territory.

"I don't know why I'm doing this again," Sandy mumbled, looking into Will's hazel-green eyes. "I don't know why I came here. I just had to, I couldn't help myself. If we get caught doing this, I'm screwed."

"And if you don't get caught, you'll be screwed, too," Will grinned. "So why worry?"

It was all the convincing Sandy needed. He practically melted into Will, their hands groping and fingers clawing each other as if the two young footballers wanted to tear each other to pieces. Water cascaded all over them, splashing off their hungry faces, their broad shoulders, their frantic heaving chests. Within seconds, Sandy dropped to his knees and grabbed Will's cock in his fist. He devoured him, almost whole, with an appetite that, for a long time, had yearned to be satiated.

Will let out a cry of pleasure that echoed throughout the shower room. He seized Sandy's dark wet hair in both hands and controlled the thrust and lunge of the quarterback's mouth. Meanwhile, Sandy seized his own throbbing dick in his right hand.

Will could feel the ecstasy mounting inside him. He also knew that at the pace Sandy was pounding his own flesh, the young quarterback wouldn't last long. Suddenly, Will felt the muscles in his back clench tight, his back arched, and with the twisted locks of Sandy's hair in his clenched fists Will felt himself explode in the quarterback's mouth, turning the warm wet tunnel of his throat into a well of hot cum.

Sandy swallowed hard and fast, sucking, gulping, at the same time letting out a muffled groan as his own balls erupted.

Will felt the first jet of Sandy's cum hit the inside of his thighs and stick there. The second spurt shot even higher, splashing against Will's balls which were still pressed hard against Sandy's chin.

With his cock still in the young quarterback's cum-filled mouth, Will could see Sandy's entire body quiver with the ecstasy of the blow. He could feel his jaw clench and his teeth gently sink themselves into the shaft of Will's cock. Sucking every last drop of cum from Will.

Forcing Will's own body to quake and jolt.

His horny teenage lust sucked clean out of him.

Every last shiny pearl painfully extracted.

Every head-rolling gem of gism filling Sandy's hard, heaving belly.

Until finally, slowly, giddily, Sandy released his bite on Will and let him slide his gleaming, still hard cock from his mouth.

As Sandy slowly rose to his feet, Will smiled, the two young men still panting, their chests rising and falling almost in unison. "That probably wasn't too good for the bruise on your jaw," Will said.

Sandy had forgotten all about the pain. He stretched his jaw, touched his fingers to it and shrugged. "Probably not, but it was worth it."

"So was the black eye." Will reached over and turned the shower on next to him. He passed Sandy the soap.

Will gave a wink then—with his black eye—and winced at the pain. Sandy laughed, then leaned forward and kissed it better.

Sandy Banks left before he missed his team's bus. "They'll be waiting for me," he said, toweling off as fast as he could and pulling on his track pants and sweater. "The coach'll be totally pissed off."

"Fuck him."

Sandy threw his gym bag over his shoulder, and before dashing out of the locker room, he grabbed Will's shoulder and laid a quick kiss smack on Will's lips. He smiled cheekily, "I'd rather fuck you. Maybe next game?"

With that, he turned and dashed.

Will stood there, grinning from ear to ear with complete contentment, watching as the quarterback vanished. Lost in a lingering moment of bliss, Will didn't even realize his cell phone was buzzing frantically in his gym bag until it was almost too late to answer.

Snapping out of his daze, he rummaged through his gear, glanced at the caller ID and answered the call before it rang out. "Professor!"

On the other end of the line, a man responded in a gentle voice, a British accent, pronunciation so proper and precise it was almost Shakespearean. "Will? Are you alright?"

"Sure." Will tossed his fingers through his wet blond hair, trying to mess it dry. "Why do you ask?"

"I've been calling for the last half hour? Are you in trouble?"

"No, not at all. I just had a game on, that's all. A big game."

"How are your studies? Can you spare some time off?"

"Sure, I can cover things here. Anything for you. Is everything okay?"

The Professor didn't answer the question directly. "I've booked you on the first flight to Vienna in the morning," he said. "I've organized transportation for you—your favorite. I'll explain everything as soon as everyone's together."

"I'll be there. What's going down?"

The Professor paused a moment, then said quite matter-of-factly, "History."

*

Felix Frazer had a sixth sense when it came to the sound of young Master Will's Ducati tearing down the street. He could sense Will was on his way even before he heard the roar of the bike's engine. Personally, the boy's butler hated that motorcycle. It was noisy and dangerous, and young Will drove the monstrous vehicle far too fast. But it was Will's favorite thing in the world, and for a boy who had grown up barely ever seeing his widowed diplomat father, then who was Felix—the butler who had practically raised Will from childhood—to deny Master Will one of the few pleasures in his life.

Of course, looking around the beachfront house that Charles Hunter had so graciously given his son on his eighteenth birthday, one would assume that pleasure was something abundant in Will Hunter's life. He owned all the latest in technology, from computers to sound systems to visual hardware.

But, possession and pleasure were two completely different things.

Felix knew that Charles had given Will the house to keep him happy, to send him off on the road of life with a minimum of fuss and bother to Charles' own existence. After all, Charles' career and affairs—both professional and personal—had always taken priority over the raising of his only child.

That's what Felix was there for—raising Will.

He was employed to look after the Hunter household when Will was four. Will's mother, Amelia, became sick shortly after Felix began working for the family. She lost her battle with cancer when Will was six. Charles threw himself into his diplomatic career shortly after the funeral. In the thirteen years since the death of his wife, Charles Hunter had spent a grand total of eleven weeks at home with his son: three weeks in the spring when Will was eight; another month in winter with his son when Will was eleven, and another four weeks leading up to Will's eighteenth birthday when he bought Will his own house. Charles always told Felix how proud he was of Will, how he had grown into a handsome and strong-willed young man. Once, Felix asked Charles if he had ever told Will that himself.

Charles changed the subject.

It seemed strange that after fifteen years together, Felix and Will were complete opposites. While Felix was a peaceful, placid and very organized man, Will liked things perilous and unpredictable. He enjoyed loud music, made impromptu decisions and indulged in the type of sports where bones were often broken. Of course, Felix was well aware, and had been for some years, that Will was gay. When Will was sixteen, he came out to Felix over dinner one night, while making them both eat home-delivered pizza and watch football. Felix asked Will if he was going to inform his father.

Will simply shrugged and shook his head. "He doesn't give a damn who I am."

Felix felt saddened that night, not because of Will's announcement that he was gay, but because the boy was right about his father's attitude toward his only son. Yet, at the same time, Felix couldn't deny—or even feel guilty about—his overwhelming sense of pride that the boy he had often considered his own son, also considered him the closest thing to a parent he had ever known.

So, Felix and Will made for an odd family in a world where the meaning of family was constantly redefining itself, despite their differences.

Yet, there was a part of Will's world that the young nineteen-year-old had never invited Felix into—and that was the world of Professor Fathom.

Felix knew who the Professor was—vaguely.

Felix knew that Will would often forgo his college attendance and football games to visit the Professor. Once, while attending to Will's laundry, the boy's passport had slipped from his jeans and fallen open on the floor. Felix was stunned to discover that young Master Will had been to places Felix had never even heard of. Perhaps roaming the world was in his genes, perhaps it was something he'd picked up from his always-absent father. Although somehow Felix doubted that simple sightseeing was at the top of Will's travel agenda.

And as for Professor Fathom, he was indeed something of a mystery. But if Will did not want Felix to enter Professor Fathom's world, then Felix trusted Will enough to know that his reasons must be sound.

Now, as he turned down the heat on the oven and pulled the rump steaks off the plate, Felix untied his apron and plucked a central remote off the wall of the kitchen. From there, he could operate everything in the house, from the television and stereo to the garden lights and central heating. Being a fan of the twentieth century (Felix still sent mail using a postage stamp rather than the click of a mouse), it had taken him some time to conquer the tiny remote. But he had eventually done it and was rather proud of himself.

With a single selection and a click with his thumb, he now opened the garage door from where he stood in the kitchen.

A moment later, he heard the dreadful sound of the Ducati, coming down the winding roads to the beach house and pulling into the garage.

Seconds later, young Master Will appeared, pulling off his black motorcycle helmet and revealing a tumultuous tangle of blond hair that, in Felix's opinion, was long overdue for a haircut.

"Hey, Felix! How's it goin'? I can't stop long. Gotta pack. Gotta go, first thing in the morning. Do you know where my passport is? And my cargo pants, you know the ones with the zillions of pockets? Say, what's for dinner? Smells good."

And with that, Will vanished into his room, shouting more

questions as he dumped his motorcycle and football gear and proceeded to get changed.

Felix couldn't help but roll his eyes and smile. At least his life was never dull. Not whenever young Master Will was around.

III

TUSCANY, ITALY

The young Italian scaled the empty, ancient cobble-stoned street. The road—in fact, the entire village of Vita Sola—had been built before cars. It was so steep and so narrow he could almost stretch both arms out and touch the walls of the cottages on either side. He arrived at the crest of a hill and heard the clip-clop of a horse's hooves. An old man with a horse and a slim cart stacked with vegetables emerged from the other side of the hill.

The young Italian stopped. "Buon giorno," he said. The old man nodded, huffing and puffing after his trek up the desolate street. The young man said in Italian, "I'm looking for the house of Signor Brancaso, the artist. Do you know him?"

The old man managed a grin. "Yes, I know him, but not as an artist, at least not a good one." He pointed to a laneway veering off to the left of the street. "He lives down there, the fourth cottage on the right."

The young Italian's eyes followed the old man's finger. "Grazie."

"You can knock on the door," the old man said, "but don't expect an answer."

The young man smiled again. An answer was the one thing he was hoping for. And knowing Marco Brancaso as well as he did—or at least once had—he knew exactly how to get an answer out of him.

The sound of a bottle of Bulgarian vodka—no label, no brand, nothing but the potent forces of a peasant family's labor inside—makes a much different sound clanging against an eighteenth-century-old door than the knuckles of a man's hand. The young Italian heard footsteps inside somewhere, clambering down a set of stairs. The door opened. The face of a man in his late forties, unshaven, unkempt, but still—as always—in his own way handsome, looked up in sweet surprise.

"Luca? Luca da Roma?" Marco had dark brown eyes that seemed to deepen as he smiled at the sight of Luca. Gentle lines creased his forehead and the skin around his eyes. "I must be drunk!"

Luca, the young Italian, smiled back at his old friend and lover. "No, Marco." He raised the bottle of vodka. "But you will be soon."

For a moment, the two men stood looking at each other, smiling. "You've cut your hair." Marco reached out and ruffled Luca's medium-length brown hair. "It's been such a long time. Three years?"

"Five."

"You look good. You always did. Come! Come inside!"

Marco led Luca up an old set of creaking, cracked stairs, into a dusty old loft attic with large arched windows that overlooked the village of Vita Sola and the pale green plains that vanished into a white horizon. "The light," Marco said. "I love this place for the light."

"It's good light." Luca looked around the attic. There were canvases, dozens upon dozens of them, propped against every available inch of wall space. Luca noticed that not a single one of the canvases was finished.

Marco held the smile on his face, but he knew that Luca knew him all too well, and slowly the smile turned into a shrug. "Even if the work isn't, the light is good. Inspiration," he said. "It comes and it goes, that's the nature of the beast. You know, I had a muse once, someone who made painting easy, too easy, as though the mere sight of him moved the brush for me, and chose the colors, and so gracefully, so lovingly placed each stroke." Marco turned and began rifling through a stack of leaning canvases. He pulled one out. It was complete—old and dusty. With a gentle breath, Marco blew the age off and looked upon it proudly.

Luca couldn't see the painting, but knew Marco was looking at one of the portraits he had done of the young Italian. He could only guess which one—there had been so many. "The balcony in Florence, overlooking Il Duomo, am I right?"

Marco smiled and turned it around for Luca to see.

It was like looking into a mirror of time. Luca looked upon himself, standing naked, head down, one hand resting on the handle of an open door that led out onto a small balcony. Behind him, the famous dome of Florence stood against a cloud-clustered sky. Suddenly, the memory of that day came back to him in a swirl of small details. The coffee he had burned on the stove. The empty wine bottles from the night before still on the floor by the bed. Evidence that during the night, after they had made love, once they were sleeping soundly, a mouse had done his best to finish off the bread and cheese they had left on the table.

"It was the day after your twentieth birthday," Marco said.

Luca was twenty-six now. Where had the years gone? "It was the first painting you did of me."

"I hoped—still hope—there will never be a last."

Luca turned and helped himself to the cupboards in the small kitchenette in one corner of the loft. He found two mismatched glasses and wiped the dust off them with his fingers. He plonked the bottle of vodka on a small table that stood in the middle of the room. "You haven't asked me what I'm doing here."

"I didn't want to have to."

The two men each pulled up a chair at the table. Luca poured them each a generous glass of vodka. Marco took a gulp and smiled. "From old man Zabriski's farm," he commented approvingly.

"I kept a few bottles."

"So you've come to get me drunk. To take advantage of me. You're copying my old tactics."

"I need some information. You're the only person I can trust to ask."

"Are you in trouble?"

Luca raised his glass with a grin. "Not yet. But I'll find some."

Marco laughed. "I'm certain of it. That's what I miss, a little adventure. I thought I moved to this village to find myself, but I was running away. I craved inspiration, while all you craved was chaos. I miss that now. I miss your little games."

"Then let's play," Luca smirked. He clinked his glass against Marco's, and the two men polished off their first drink together in over five years. Luca put down his glass, took off his jacket and unbuttoned the top two buttons of his shirt, then filled up their glasses once more.

Marco raised one eyebrow. "Ah, the conversation game," he grinned. "My favorite. So tell me, what is it you're after this time?"

"A statue. Sixteenth Century. Have you ever heard of The Naked Christ?"

Marco nodded. "Heard of it, yes. But have I seen it? No. I don't know of anyone who ever has. It was lost, wiped from history. Just like Videlle, the artist who sculpted it."

"He was murdered," Luca said. "I know that much."

"Not simply murdered. He was tortured for what he did. They sliced out his eyes. They cut off his hands. And while he was still alive, they strung him up in the middle of Piazza della Signoria and disemboweled him. Creating an image of Christ on the crucifix, completely naked, who would dare! Christ with a cock! It was unheard of! It was a sin punishable by death. They condemned Videlle to eternity in hell for what he did."

"They, being the Church?"

Marco paused a moment and grinned. "The Church has many factions. It wears more than one mask. Faith has many faces." The artist raised his glass, and the two emptied their drinks.

Luca sat back and undid another button. Marco noticed the small silver crucifix at the end of a chain that hung around Luca's neck. It rested comfortably in the cleft between the young man's pectoral muscles. "You still wear that?"

"I'll always wear that. As you were saying, faith has many faces."

Marco tilted his head and gestured to the remaining buttons on Luca's shirt. "My handsome muse, if you want more information, it's worth more than a glimpse of chest."

The young Italian unplucked the remaining buttons of his shirt and peeled it away, fully revealing the tan mounds of his chest and a sparse forest of hair trailing from his pectorals down the ridges of his belly, disappearing into his jeans.

Another drink was poured and emptied.

"There is a secret arm of the Church that calls itself the Crimson Crown. Its members believe themselves to be soldiers of Christ. God's very own vigilante group. For centuries, they have killed and crippled in the name of God."

"And nobody stops them?"

"Nobody knows they exist. Except the Vatican, who turns a blind eye. Men of God do not judge men of God. They're far too busy judging everyone else."

Luca poured them both another drink. "What about Zefferino?"

Marco took a short breath. He smiled, realizing what the mention of that name meant. "You found one of the halves of the stone tablet?"

Luca nodded. "We think so."

Marco laughed, astonished and excited. He downed his vodka, poured another glass and downed that one, too. "Where?"

"This is a game, remember?"

Marco was happy to pull off his own paint-splattered shirt in exchange for an answer. He was strong and toned from decades of building frames and stretching canvases.

"Somewhere in Turkey. At an archeological dig. Yesterday, a man named Doctor Hadley stumbled across it at his excavation south of Ankara. He didn't recognize the markings on it, so he called Professor Fathom. He thinks it might be—"

"The code?" Marco whispered.

"We don't know what it says, yet. We won't know for certain until—"

"—Until you find the book," Marco finished for him. Another vodka vanished. "Well?" the artist said, plonking down his glass, sitting back in his chair and clasping his hands behind his head in a show of complete self-assurance. "Are you going to get those jeans off or do I have to come over there and do it myself?"

"So you know where the book is? You know who has it?"

"Maybe." Marco grinned teasingly.

Without hesitation, Luca pushed away his chair, kicked off his boots, unbuttoned his jeans and pulled them down. Below a dark brown thatch of pubic hair, he boasted a large uncut penis, one that Marco knew all too well. He'd missed it very much. The artist watched now, his eyes roving over Luca's muscled young form as he pushed his jeans down past his ankles and kicked them across the dusty floor.

Luca smiled, "So?" The thick head of his cock began to slide out from under its hood.

Marco poured the last of the vodka into a glass and launched himself drunkenly out of his chair. The bulge in his own torn and tattered painter's pants was more than evident. "So now," he said, "Inspiration takes hold."

With a passion he hadn't felt in a long time, Marco scurried about his loft, pulling a large blank canvas clear from the clutter. He pushed a bland unfinished landscape off his easel and let it bang to the floor, then spun the easel away from the window to face Luca.

He dragged the table across the room.

He took Luca by the shoulders. "What about the book?" Luca said.

"Do you trust me to tell you where it is?"

Luca nodded. Then, like a prop, like a possession, he let himself be guided into the arms of his ex-lover.

"I'll tell you soon," Marco whispered. "But first..."

The artist leaned Luca back against the table. "Put your weight here for me." He positioned one hand back, he pulled the other forward and laid it across his tight muscled stomach, tilted down. He spread the fingers just so, like arrows pointing down to his cock. Luca could feel himself harden at Marco's touch, at the tenderness with which he sculpted him into the composition he desired.

Luca almost felt as if he needed to apologize for the involuntary reaction. Marco spoke as though he could read his thoughts, "It's okay. I'm going to call this one, Eternal Muse. If I don't see you for another five years—if I'm unlucky enough to never see you again—this is exactly how

I want to remember you. Zefferino was a muse too, you know. His short black hair, his youthful body. He kept the fire burning in Videlle."

"Do I keep the fire burning in you?"

Marco touched his index finger to Luca's chin and guided his head up and to the left, just a little. Then he placed a single gentle kiss on Luca's lips and said, "Sometimes the embers are hotter than the fire itself. Now don't move."

The artist stood back and looked. The sun shone from a skylight onto the back of Luca's shimmering brown hair, forming a glow behind his beautiful face and body. He looked angelic, Marco thought. He looked like a work of art, even before the paint had touched the canvas.

"Perfect," Marco smiled.

*

The light was gone, the painting sat propped upon the easel, its glistening thick brushstrokes drying in the lamplight of the loft. A complete work. A product of passion. The most perfect painting Marco had ever created.

"My Eternal Muse," Marco whispered again, although his lips had trouble forming the words as they pressed hard against Luca's, their tongues pushing into each others' mouths.

With his hands, his forearms, his chest splattered with reds, browns, yellows and blacks, Marco pushed Luca flat onto the table, accidentally kicking the empty bottle of vodka across the floor, which hit the leg of a chair and smashed. Neither of them cared.

The paint from Marco smeared across the mounds and valleys of Luca's hard young body. While the artist took Luca's jaw in one hand and his hard heavy cock in the other, Luca himself struggled to get the zip of Marco's pants down. When he did, Marco's penis pounced, pressing into Luca's balls with a hot hard hungry greeting.

Luca groaned. Marco responded by shoving his own thumb and index finger into the young man's mouth. Luca sucked on them ravenously. Marco pushed the bulbous head of his cock harder into Luca's balls, pushing against his sack, and for a second, Luca thought he was going to burst. This early in the piece he had no choice but to shove Marco off him. He pushed too hard. Marco slipped and rolled off the table, landing on the floor hard and laughing hysterically as he did.

Luca quickly leaned over the edge of the table and looked down, concerned. "Are you alright?"

Marco responded by grabbing the young man by the back of the head and pulling him down onto the floor as well.

Luca landed on top of Marco awkwardly, winding him, forcing more laughter out of him. "It's been a while," the artist managed eventually, gasping and wheezing and panting as the air returned to his lungs. He scrambled to his feet and clambered over to a set of drawers in the kitchen. From the last drawer, he pulled out a packet of condoms and a bottle of lube.

Luca watched from the floor, his large stiff penis getting even harder still at the sight of Marco tearing open the condom packet with his teeth and rolling the rubber onto his cock. Marco massaged it with his lubed fist, making sure the fit was comfortable, before returning to Luca on the floor.

Luca instinctively lay flat on his back while Marco took his ankles and raised his legs in the air. He let go with one hand, so he could guide his cock inside Luca's ass, then smiled as the young Italian grinned, groaned, and slapped both palms flat against the floorboards, locking himself down and getting ready to take Marco in.

From past experience, Marco knew—and always loved—that once he was inside Luca, the young man was capable of coming without so much as touching himself.

Marco began to slide in and out of Luca's warm ass, slowly at first, but Luca prompted him to push harder. Faster.

Luca felt his stomach muscles contract as Marco crunched him up into a tight ball. He felt the pressure, the pleasure, of the intruding cock. His body sent signals of pain to his brain, telling him of the danger that there was something foreign inside him; his brain sent a signal back to his body, telling it that danger is ecstasy.

Luca felt Marco's balls rocking against his ass.

He felt the head of Marco's cock inside him, bulging. Getting ready to explode.

He saw the look on Marco's face. His eyes squeezed shut. His jaw dropped open. And then, as a rush of air escaped him, Luca felt the shaft of Marco's cock swell against the rim of his ass and felt the hot rush of cum fill the tip of the condom inside him.

At that moment, Luca clamped his eyes shut and felt his own balls erupt, forcing a flood up the vein of his shaft, a flood that erupted from his cock and spattered all the way up his body, covering his stomach and chest in cloudy pearls and vines.

Luca rocked and groaned as a delayed second spurt burst forth, shooting and dripping more cum onto his belly.

When he eventually opened his eyes, wide and glazed, he saw Marco's smiling, panting face looking down at him. "My God, I do love you. Even though I know you're going to walk out that door. I'll always love you."

Luca leaned up and kissed him. "I'll always love you too. And yes, you're right, I am going to walk out that door. But not before you tell me—"

"I know, I know," Marco said. "The book."

*

The convent of Santa Maria del Mare was a tiny whitewashed mud brick building overlooking the Mediterranean, half an hour's travel from the village of Vita Sola.

In 1919—the year after the Great War ended, when the convent was built—thirty-two young girls, widowed wives and village virgins became the brides of Christ and joined the convent in its honest and innocent mission to salvage peace and faith—through the word of God—in a world that had lost its way.

But as time moved on, fewer and fewer women joined the convent. Heaven claimed more brides than even God could provide.

Now there were merely four inhabitants of the convent Santa Maria del Mare: Sister Francesca, a sixty-two-year-old nun, who had come from a long line of olive growers, whose family had taught her the goodness of God and the toils of the soil; Sister Eva, a seventy-one-year-old nun, who devoted the majority of her time in the chapel, praying constantly for the lost and displaced souls of the world, for those tormented by war or ravaged by famine or taken into God's kingdom by the tragedy around them; Sister Margarita, a spritely forty-nine-year-old nun, whose sheer love of life meant that she sometimes had more energy and enthusiasm for sunshine and sport than she did for her prayers; and last but not least, a troublesome, free-spirited orphan who, twenty-six years ago, had been left in a basket on the convent's doorstep. There was a note pinned to the baby boy's blanket explaining that he had no name and was a bastard child, born in the ghettoes of Rome. Around his neck was a small crucifix on a silver chain. No markings. No engraving. No clue as to who this child could be.

When Sister Eva discovered him on the doorstep, the morning sun was shining on his face. So she took him in, and the three nuns named him Luca da Roma—a Light of Rome.

Luca was a good boy and a good student. He grew up helping Sister Francesca in the fields and the vegetable patch, praying solemnly with Sister Eva in the chapel, and playing soccer with Sister Margarita on the cliff top overlooking the sea—they had lost more than one soccer ball to God's great ocean over the years. As Luca grew older, he became interested in history and art, until the day finally came when Sister Francesca, Sister Eva and Sister Margarita drove seventeen-year-old Luca to the nearest train station—twenty-three miles away, bouncing along in a 1962 Fiat that had been left to the convent in the will of deceased local villager—where Luca bought a ticket to Rome to discover the world beyond the convent.

Before he boarded his train, it was Sister Eva, the eldest of the three, who had taken his hands in hers and said, "Remember one thing. Be courageous always. Courage brings fortitude. Fortitude brings character. Character will make you the man you will become. And that man, above all else, must believe in who he is. That is the greatest lesson I can ever teach you. Everything you do, do it always for courage." In the years that followed, Luca questioned his sexuality as many times as he questioned his faith. He was a handsome boy and made enough money to live, modeling for the struggling artists of Rome. There were times he did more than model and made more money. And there were times he doubted the presence of the Lord in his life.

But he never doubted the place the Sisters held in his heart.

As often as possible, he would return to that tiny convent on the cliff tops.

And the Sisters would always greet him with open arms. They kept his room tidy, they dusted the surface of his drawers and they washed the dusty sheets clean if and when they knew he was coming to visit, so that every time he walked through the doors of the convent and into that tiny bedroom, he knew everything would be as he had left it. He knew that this was his home. These women were his mothers. And he was the son that they had given up for God.

Today, Luca was returning home.

Even if it was only to pack a bag and take off again, the Sisters didn't mind. They loved his visits, no matter how fleeting or far between.

Luca had called ahead to say he would be there by two in the afternoon and wouldn't be leaving for his connecting flight to Vienna until seven the following morning. Sister Francesca had pulled her finest tomatoes, potatoes and pumpkins from her garden and was busy cooking up Luca's favorite soup. Once the broth was simmering, she pounded flour and water into a thick dough, which she baked into a luscious loaf, sprinkled on top with sprigs of rosemary. Sister Margarita had spent the time cleaning Luca's room, throwing the windows wide open to let the bright day flood inside. Meanwhile, Sister Eva had spent the morning on her knees in the chapel, praying for Luca's safe arrival.

It was Sister Margarita who first spotted the dust trail from the taxi as it made its way along the long deserted road leading to the convent. She called the others, and by the time Sister Francesca had untied her apron and Sister Eva had pulled herself up from her old aching knees, the taxi was pulling up in front of the convent.

Luca stepped out of the backseat, lugging a tattered old shoulder bag behind him and grinning at the sight of his beloved family.

Before he could even close the car door, Sisters Francesca and Margarita rushed toward him and wrapped their arms around him.

"It's so good to see you again."

"We've missed you so."

Luca kissed them both, first on one cheek then the other. "I've missed you all, too."

Slowly, with sore and steady steps, Sister Eva moved forward. She took Luca's face in both hands and smiled at him. "God Himself only knows where you've been. God Himself only knows where you go. But welcome home," she said in a quiet, loving voice. "Even if it is just for one night."

*

Before the sun went down on that day, Luca dug the root of a dead fig tree out of the garden for Sister Francesca. He challenged Sister Margarita to a one-on-one game of soccer in the open field between the convent and the cliff top, dribbling the flat old soccer ball without once kicking it over the edge. And last, but by no means least, he spent twilight with Sister Eva in the chapel. As she bowed her head in prayer, he knelt beside her, watching the stained-glass colors of the windows deepen with the setting of the sun.

That night, Luca nursed his over-full belly in his old bedroom on the second floor of the convent. He stood at the wide open window and looked out at the canvas of stars, gleaming like a million lazy candles in the sky. He took in a deep breath, enjoying the scent of the ocean breeze drifting in through the window and listening to the distant sound of waves crashing against the rocks at the foot of the cliffs. He felt so warm and safe here, everything in its place, everything where it had always been— the bed; the dresser; the wooden crucifix on the wall above his bed; the painting of Saint George slaying the dragon on the wall opposite, a classic hero for whom Luca had held a childhood crush for as long as he could remember.

Luca clutched his own small silver crucifix now sitting next to his heart. The silver was warm, soaking up the temperature of his body.

Sometimes he wondered if he would ever return here for good. Would he ever give up the adventure and surrender the fight? Deep down, he knew the answer, but it was nice to return—even if only once in a while, for only a short time—to take in a little peace.

Luca turned off the small lamplight on the old dresser and peeled the sheets off the bed, then pulled off his clothes and lowered himself down into the tiny bunk.

He lay on his back, naked, enjoying the whisper of the breeze on his bare body. He thought about his journey tomorrow to Vienna. By tomorrow night he would be at the Professor's chalet—his other home. Eden, Will and Shane would be there, too, as well as another. That's what the Professor had told him on the phone.

Luca thought about the stone tablet, broken in two.

He thought about the secret book, and the information Marco had given him—eventually—after they made love once more on the floor of the artist's loft.

Luca thought about Marco's naked body, covered in paint, panting with exhilaration and heaving with passion.

As he lay there naked on his bed, recalling the night spent with Marco, he let the tips of his fingers coast gently down the length of his own body, over his chest and along the vale that ran down the center of his stomach.

He felt like he was twelve again, secretly discovering himself beneath the roof of the convent. Caressing himself gently. And although, as a boy, Jesus watched from above—from the wooden crucifix hanging over his bed—Luca never felt as if Christ judged him. God made Luca in his own image. It seemed wrong to him, even as a boy, to take on any blame, or feel any shame, in feeling every emotion and exploring every sensation his body was made to experience.

Now, once again, he took himself quietly to the threshold of pleasure beneath the accepting gaze of Christ.

He felt the hot burst spill up his stomach.

He let his seed bake against his hot skin on that warm Italian night.

Then he drifted into a deep, deep sleep.

But his dreams were far from peaceful. His arms flinched, his legs kicked and his body jolted as his unconscious mind flooded with terrible visions of the torture and murder of the artist Videlle—his eyes being sliced open and scooped from their sockets, his beautiful artistic hands being severed at the wrist, his creative soul tumbling in coils and loops from his body as he was strung up and cut open like a pig.

In the dead of night, Luca sat bolt upright in bed, gasping for air, his eyes wide open, his body drenched in sweat. He turned suddenly, as though he was being watched, and looked at the wooden crucifix on the wall.

"Marco was right," he said to the cross above his bed, still panting and sweating from the nightmare. "Faith does have many faces."

IV

BROKE RIDGE RANCH, TEXAS

Shane Houston was asleep, slumped low in the front passenger seat of the limousine, one boot slung out the open window, his cowboy hat in his lap, his sunglasses sliding down his nose, the wind playing with his short blond hair.

When Gertie's driver, Sinclair, had picked him up at the airport, Shane asked the family chauffeur why his mother had requested his company so urgently.

Sinclair had explained he was under strict instructions not to steal her thunder. The comment had been followed by a roll of the eyes. Shane had fallen asleep in the front passenger seat a short time later.

The drive to Broke Ridge Ranch—the ten thousand acre property that had been in the Houston family for the last forty years—took a little over two hours. As the limousine veered down the road that led to the gates of the property, something inside Shane woke him. Perhaps it was instinct. Perhaps it was the gentle deceleration of the car as they approached the tall timber gates of the ranch. Perhaps it was the scent of the hay and the dust and the horses, drifting in through the open window.

Whatever it was, Shane knew he was home.

He opened his eyes, stretched, and saw the name of his family's ranch on the sign, swinging in the wind above the gate's threshold.

That's when he saw his horses, too—Arturo and Acacia, and the new colt, Jax—racing along the fence of the property, Jax's lanky young legs doing their best to keep pace with his parents, as though all three horses sensed that Shane was home.

Shane smiled at the sight of them. "God, it's good to be back."

"Enjoy it while it lasts," Sinclair muttered with a sigh.

Shane looked at his mother's driver. "Sinclair, what aren't you telling me?"

Always one to opt for a sarcastic gesture over the simple truth, Sinclair made an exaggerated zipped-lips sign. He emphasized the point by pretending to lock a keypad on his tightly-clamped lips then threw his invisible key out the car window—not his own window, but Shane's, for added effect.

Shane pulled his head back for fear of being hit by the invisible key. It annoyed him greatly that he still fell for Sinclair's melodramatic pantomimes. "Sinclair, what the hell's going on?"

They were already cruising down the long drive toward the majestic old ranch house, although since he had last visited, it looked more rambling and rickety than it did majestic. The eaves were dilapidated, the paint was peeling and the dry desert grass around the porch was overgrown and full of weeds and wildflowers.

That's when the front door opened and Shane's mother, Gertie Houston, emerged from the house, looking as beautiful and radiant as she ever did—a true Southern Belle—even if her house no longer matched her charm and grace.

Shane smiled, but his happiness quickly faded when he saw a man in his late fifties, with slicked silver hair and twirled moustache, step out onto the porch behind Gertie.

With a suspicious crease in his brow, Shane asked, "Is that—?"

Sinclair nodded unhappily before Shane could put a name to the face. "It certainly is."

*

"Claudius Welles," said the man with the silver hair, shaking Shane's hand vehemently on the porch. "Perhaps you don't remember me, son."

"Yes, sir. I remember you, alright."

"Well I'm glad you're here. And I'm happy to say I'm not afraid to shake your hand."

"Why would you be?"

"What?"

"Afraid to shake my hand?"

"Well, because you're—"

Suddenly Gertie jumped in, quicker than a coyote at dinner-time. "Why don't you two boys go grab a place at the table. I've fixed spare ribs from here to kingdom come, so I hope you're both hungry!"

With a grand wave of his hand, Claudius opened the door for Gertie and Shane to step inside their own house. Shane took off his hat and followed his mother inside, shooting Claudius Welles an uncertain, disapproving look as he passed.

Claudius simply smiled back.

Before he closed the screen door, Claudius noticed a flash of lightning over the mountains in the distance. Twilight was falling and rain was on its way.

At the dinner table, Gertie laid the spread and Claudius made himself very much at home by serving everyone their meal, just as the man of the house would. He loaded Shane's plate high. "Son, you look to me like you enjoy a good meal. You've filled out a lot since you were a littlefella. Why, I remember your mother and father used to invite me over for supper and you barely ate a thing. You were kinda scrawny back then."

"And you were kinda rich back then."

Outside, thunder rolled across the sky.

"Sounds like something's brewing," Claudius muttered sarcastically.

Shane ignored it and cut straight to the chase. "It's true, isn't it." It wasn't a question, but an accusation. "It's true you laid hundreds of networks of pipes nobody knew about so you could steal all the oil from your neighbors, including my father."

Gertie spluttered and choked on her first sip of wine. "Shane!"

Claudius stopped cold, a spare rib dangling from his serving fork. "I never did any such thing. You believed the words of liars."

"Are you calling my father a liar? He killed himself because of you."

"Shane! Stop!" Gertie insisted sternly.

But Shane didn't stop. "Gertie, he took everything from Dad. He took everything from us!"

"Shane Houston! That's enough! I will not have this discussion at my dinner table!" Gertie turned to Claudius and muttered a humble, embarrassed apology. "Claudius, I am so sorry!"

Claudius simply put down the serving fork and smiled politely, then reached across the table and patted the back of Gertie's hand. "It's alright, my dear. No offence taken."

Shane stared at Claudius' hand now resting on his mother's, quickly sized up exactly why he was here, then shot a furious look from Gertie to Claudius and point-blank demanded, "Are you here to tell me you wanna marry my mother?"

"Shane! I said that's enough!"

"Well why else did you ask me to come, Gertie? You said it was urgent. You said you had something important to tell me."

"I... I..." Gertie squirmed, unable to speak.

Claudius cleared his throat awkwardly.

The uncomfortable silence was all Shane needed to confirm his fears.

He threw down his napkin. "Gertie, can I please see you outside!"

Gertie threw down her napkin, nervous and defensive. "Why, yes you can!"

Shane picked up his hat and Gertie picked up her shawl and simultaneously mother and son stood, then both stormed for the door. Shane and his mother let the screen door slam and pounded the boards of the dilapidated porch, far enough away from the door so that

Claudius couldn't hear them.

As darkness fell and distant thunder echoed off the mountains, both Shane and Gertie started talking at once. But it was Shane who had the louder voice.

"Gertie, what the hell are you doin'? Has he asked you to marry him? After what he did to our family!"

"Shane, he did nothing to our family."

"Gertie, he drained the entire well. He bled us dry and made billions. And left Dad broke."

"What your daddy did, he did to himself. I don't know why you're taking his side, anyway. We both know he was a mean, angry drunk. You and he never once saw eye to eye! And stop callin' me Gertie in front of Claudius! He's a gentleman. And yes, he did ask me to marry him. And I said yes!"

"What! Why!"

"Because, dammit Shane, I'm lonely!"

"You've got me!"

"No, I don't! You've got your own life! Shane, I love you. And in a lot of ways I loved your father too, despite the things he said and the way he acted. But now I need you to understand my life too. I'm all alone, Shane."

She reached for him then and touched his arm. Her shawl fell from her shoulder down to her elbow.

"Honey, you know nobody will ever take the place of you. But Claudius, he makes me feel alive. And for an old woman—"

"Ma, you ain't old."

"I'm getting old. And since you left home, I get lonely too. And these days, when someone knocks on my door, I open it. And I ask them in for a cup of tea."

"Ma, I don't think Claudius is here for a cup of tea—"

"Hush!" scolded Gertie. "He keeps me company."

Shane sighed and wrapped his mother's shawl up around her shoulder. "He doesn't treat you bad?"

Gertie shook her head. "Heavens, no! Not at all."

"What can he give you?"

"He's got big dreams, Shane! He tells me he's working on something incredible! Something to do with new energy. Something that'll change the world. I don't know what it is, but he tells me he's cooking up a storm!"

"Yeah, but does he cook you dinner?"

Gertie laughed. "Goodness, I haven't met a man yet who can."

"Gertie, you need to meet more gay men."

Gertrude eyed him with a soft anger. "Shane Houston, I told you about that Gertie thing!"

Shane sighed. "Yes, Ma."

Gertie smiled and pecked her son on the cheek.

He wrapped his strong arms around her then. Either his arms and shoulders had gotten bigger than she remembered, or she'd gotten smaller. It didn't matter.

"Just be careful," he whispered into her neck as he hugged her tight. "I worry about you!"

As another bolt of lightning illuminated the distant sky, Arturo and Acacia galloped across the paddock toward the house. Shane could hear them. And he smiled.

Tomorrow he would take all three of them out—including young Jax—and let them run wild in the sun, trampling the earth, grazing the prairie, having fun. Just Shane and his horses.

"I'd better get these guys into the stable," he said now. "That thunder's getting closer."

"And I'd better get back inside and make sure Claudius is alright."

Gertie kissed him on the cheek once more and headed through the screen door.

Shane stepped down off the porch as Arturo and Acacia approached. He immediately sensed their anxiety. He saw their wide-eyed fear.

"Whoa, whoa, guys! You okay?"

Suddenly Shane realized that Jax was nowhere to be seen.

Riding Arturo bareback, with Acacia by their side, Shane and the horses thundered across the land as the sky thundered above them. They came to a halt, Arturo rearing upward, at the edge of a shallow ravine.

Shane jumped from Arturo's back and stood staring down into the dark.

He heard a frightened whinny, then, as lightning shot across the sky, he caught a glimpse of young Jax, trapped in the gully. He seemed unharmed, but somehow he had managed to fall or find his way down there and couldn't get back up.

Shane quickly sized up the steep ravine. "I'm comin' little buddy! Hold on!" Then he turned to Arturo. "Arturo. Rope! I need you to get me a rope from the stables. Rope! Do you understand?"

Arturo's head bucked up and down, his hooves clomping, and as swiftly as he raced across the ranch, he disappeared into the darkness.

At that moment the heavens opened and the rain came down in a deluge.

It turned the sides of the ravine into a muddy slippery slide as Shane scrambled and rolled his way down, his clothes soaked through by the time he hit the floor of the ravine.

Jax came bounding up to him.

"Hey, mister! You okay? You hurt?" Shane checked the colt's lanky legs, his hips, his ribs. No broken bones. Now all they had to do was find a way out.

Shane knelt in the pelting rain and stroked Jax's wet coat. "Okay little buddy, here's the deal. You're gonna be brave and let me sling you over my shoulders, okay? Then you and me are gonna climb our way outta here." He glanced up the wall of the ravine to see it quickly turning into a mudslide, then added, "Somehow."

With some effort, Shane hoisted Jax over his shoulders and felt the weight. "Damn, you're a growin' boy, ain't ya!" Then, with his fingers clawing into the mud and boots finding footholes wherever he could, the young cowboy started to climb his way out of the ravine.

He got six feet up when thunder cracked across the sky.

Jax squirmed nervously.

Shane lost his grip and slid all the way to the bottom again.

"Okay," he panted to himself. "Maybe this is gonna take a little longer than I thought."

He started clambering up the embankment again. Just then the rain got heavier. It poured over the brim of his hat. He had trouble seeing what he was doing, feeling his way, making a grab for a ledge or a sturdy-looking shrub with each flash of lightning.

Then the mud beneath his left foot gave way, the rocks in his right hand came loose, and Shane once again slid to the bottom of the ravine with an increasingly-frightened colt on his back.

That's when both man and colt heard Arturo's whinny at the top of the embankment.

Shane looked up and a coiled rope landed across his face. "Ow!"

Then suddenly he heard another sound.

Not Arturo's whinny from above.

Not thunder.

This was something altogether different.

A rush.

A roar.

Shane looked quickly up to the opened heavens, then left, where the ravine ran all the way up to the mountains. And all he could whisper was, "Oh shit!"

Quickly he hoisted Jax off his shoulders.

He ripped off his drenched shirt, the weight of it slowing him down.

He took the rope in both hands in seconds made a lasso out of it. "Arturo!"

The crashing roar—the sound of a fast-approaching flashflood—grew louder and louder. There was no telling how far away it was. Minutes. Maybe only seconds.

Jax gave a scared whimper and begin to trot in the opposite direction of the coming flood.

Shane dropped the rope and tackled him. "No, Jax. Stay with me."

With colt in one hand, Shane scrambled back to the rope. "Arturo! Are you there?"

Arturo's head appeared over the top of the embankment. Lightning broke the sky above him. Thunder belted across the night, setting the angry clouds aglow. And getting closer by the second—

—the rush of the killer flashflood.

Shane swung the lasso over his head and threw it hard and high. The loop landed over Arturo's head and slid down his neck.

Shane grabbed Jax and slung him over his shoulders once more. He tangled the roped around his wrists, looked up and screamed, "Arturo! Pull!!!"

As the mighty stallion backed up, the rope snapped tight, hauling Shane and the colt upward. Shane dug his boots into the muddy, collapsing wall as best he could, taking huge strides upward, trying to help Arturo as the horse pulled on the straining rope.

For the dark of the ravine, the roar became deafening.

The rope cut deep into Shane hands and wrists.

Still he pushed upward with every kick and stride.

Arturo pulled backward, his hooves slipping in the mud.

Lightning flashed, and Shane glanced left once more. That's when he saw the wall of water appear, destroying a corner of the ravine a hundred feet away as it tore its way toward them.

"Arturo! Pull! Pull!"

Arturo gave it all he had, sliding and stamping backward through the mud.

Jax saw the wall of water coming for them and began to kick and buck.

Shane held on tight.

Pushing and kicking higher and higher.

Mud sliding under his boots.

He felt the spray of water jetting down the ravine toward them. It smacked against his face, his arms. It would only be a matter of seconds before—

—the flood hit the base of the embankment and devoured it.

Everything began to slide downward as the rushing water rose. Fast!

The wall slipped into a mudslide.

Shane's footing went with it.

The torrent of water slammed into his feet, trying to drag them down as the flood quickly rose.

"Arturo!"

The rope lurched higher.
The flood took out half the wall.
It pulled down on Shane's legs.
Grabbed hold of his bare waist.
Jax kicked and panicked.
Arturo pulled as hard and fast as he could.
Shane felt the tangle of ropes around his hands and wrists begin to give.
Then suddenly—
—the edge.
Shane hit the edge of the ravine.
He threw Jax to safety.
He felt Acacia bite painfully into his shoulder, trying to pull him out of harm's way as Arturo continued pulling on the rope at the same time.
Dragging him clear of the hungry flood that ripped apart the ravine.

Flat on his back, heaving with fear, adrenaline, relief, Shane lifted himself on his elbows and in a flash of lightning saw Acacia sheltering a scared but safe Jax.

Then he felt Arturo nudge his shoulder to make sure he was okay. Shane let out a sigh and stroked Arturo's mane. "Thank you," was all he could manage before collapsing on his back in the mud.

*

He walked up the steps to the porch—drenched, shirtless, covered in mud—as Gertie rushed to the screen door.

"Shane! Where have you been! Are you okay! What happened?"

Shane shrugged. "I guess I had a little trouble gettin' the horses into the stable."

"Oh, that Jax!" said Gertie. "He's adorable, but such a darn handful!"

"Tell me about it!"

"Oh, and before I forget. Someone rang for you. A Professor Fathom. Such a polite gentleman. He wants you to call him back as soon as possible. He said he works on your geological survey team and that you have a new assignment."

"New assignment? Where?"

V

THE DESERT, SOUTH ANKARA, TURKEY

Visibility was all but gone. A sandstorm had turned the world into a chaotic white haze, whipping at the tents that surrounded the dig site. The sound of canvas flapping and cracking in the wind competed with the roar of the gathering storm and the hiss of flying sand.

The young man arrived on horseback, a frayed brown cowboy hat pulled down low and a scarf tied tightly over his face, covering his mouth and nose as if he was some bandit. It was not an unreasonable assumption. In these parts, in the craggy mountains and endless deserts of central and southern Turkey, bandits still plagued busloads of travelers and caravans of aid-workers, stealing money and medicine and sometimes the lives of those they robbed.

When the old man first glimpsed the rider, materializing through the storm, suddenly upon him, his first instinct was to run and warn the others, to hide his discoveries, to save the treasures. But part of him told him to wait.

Wait and see who this rider was.

After all, he knew all too well that Max Fathom's man was on his way. And quite frankly, the sooner he got here, the better.

Amid the sand blasting across the desert, the rider pulled his horse to a nervous halt next to the old man, and with a gloved hand pulled the scarf from his face. Even in all the chaos, under the brim of his hat, the rider's face was strikingly handsome. Blue eyes, as crisp as a desert sky in winter, glimmered out of the dust and dirt that had collected in a powdery horizontal stripe that ran from one ear to the other. Short thick tufts of honey blond hair, protruding from under his hat, trembled with the force of the storm.

"Doctor Hadley?" the rider shouted over the ferocious wind. The old man detected an accent. American by the sounds of it, although it was difficult to hear anything. "Are you Doctor Joseph Hadley?"

The old man nodded. He practically quivered with relief. "Are you Mr. Houston? Did Max send you?"

The rider dismounted. Despite the gale force conditions, he removed his hat and the glove on his right hand, as a gentleman would, and with a smile and a twang in his voice that came straight out of Texas, the rider introduced himself. "You can call me Shane."

*

"This is the worst storm we've seen yet," Hadley said as he entered a large tent, his voice still raised as the sides of the tent belted and billowed like the sails of a ship in the middle of a typhoon. Shane followed him inside. The space was filled with instruments and tools, with backpacks and blankets and bundles mysteriously wrapped. Artifacts waiting for shipment, Shane surmised. There was a table in the middle of the room, with maps unfurled and diagrams half-etched on parchments and papers.

Hadley, slight and nervous-looking, with gray stubble on his face and dread in his eyes, glanced anxiously at the internal tent poles, all of which were leaning on the same angle and bowing under the pressure of the wind outside. "I'm astounded you actually found us."

"Hand me the reins of a horse, and I can find just about anything. Either that or I'm just lucky, I guess."

"The desert might be a big place, Mr. Houston, but there's no room for luck out here." Hadley spoke with a stiff British accent.

"People die out here all the time. Or worse, they simply vanish forever. Sometimes the sand swallows them whole. Sometimes, the sun turns them into dust or the wind sweeps them away."

He made his way around the warping tent poles to the table, then pushed aside several maps to reveal a small item wrapped in a frayed yellowed cloth. "Then again, sometimes it's not just the desert that claims lives. Half the men here, I employ them to do a job—to dig. I do not employ them to be trustworthy or kind. I employ them to shovel earth, to move rocks. It's a sad reality that some of them would kill a man without hesitation or remorse. For food. For water. Sometimes just for the thrill of it. And sometimes for things much more precious. The moment this was unearthed, I hid it."

Shane raised one eyebrow, dubiously. "I don't mean any disrespect, Doctor. But you hid it under a bunch of maps? On a table? In the middle of the room?"

Hadley grinned. "The most obvious places always make the best hiding spots."

The Doctor picked up the small wrapped parcel. Delicately, with the patient hands of a man who had unearthed some of the rarest treasures in the world, Hadley lifted back the layers of the cloth.

When the last fold of cloth was pulled away, a thick black stone lay flat in Doctor Hadley's palm. It was more than ten inches long on each side, with the jagged right-hand side evidently the result of a breakage. On it, carved deep into the slate, were three rows of etched markings, each unique with its own curves and lines, almost Arabic or Egyptian in appearance, but not as elaborate. The markings disappeared into the broken edge on the right. Up the top were the letters "Z E F F E."

Hadley said, "I've never seen symbols like this. There are no records anywhere in the world to match these inscriptions. It's not a language, at least not the language of a culture. This is a personal language. A secret language." He stopped and looked at Shane. "That's why I called Maximilian. I suspect he knows the answer. I suspect deep down, we all do. And I can't think of anyone in the entire world who would make a better guardian of a treasure such as this, than Max."

Doctor Hadley held the stone out to Shane.

"Take it to him—with great care."

"I will," Shane said, with confidence, with certainty.

Shane's hands were so much larger and stronger than the frail archeologist's, this Hadley noticed. It somehow gave him faith in this stranger, to keep the tablet safe, to deliver it from harm, and with those large strong hands pass it onto his dear old friend.

"There's something more valuable than the stone out there," Hadley said, "and it's worth finding. The truth is always worth uncovering. One day, an archeologist just like me will dig up my old bones, and when they do, I hope they see the truth in me. I hope they learn something."

Taking as much care as he could, Shane wrapped the cloth over the stone tablet.

"I'd advise you against riding through the storm," Hadley said, "but you found your way through it once already, and I feel now that time may be of the essence."

Shane winked and placed the cowboy hat securely on his head. "The storm'll cover my tracks. I'll keep the wind at my back. I can't ask for anything more."

"Good luck."

"Thanks."

Hadley stayed in the tent while Shane returned to the savage storm. The young Texan reached his horse, slipped the wrapped stone into his saddlebag and tied it down as securely as he could. He steadied his unnerved animal, then hooked one foot in the stirrup and hoisted himself into the saddle effortlessly. He pulled the scarf up over his mouth and nose once more. Then with a tug on the reins, Shane Houston evaporated into the storm just as suddenly as he appeared.

*

The boy rushed to the tent as the storm began to die down. "Doctor, quickly, quickly!" he shouted in Turkish, his voice filled with what sounded like excitement. Or perhaps it was fear. "They've found something!"

Instinctively, Hadley grabbed his brush and chisel and raced out of the tent, following the boy who was already halfway to the excavation. The wind was settling quickly now, blowing the sand in harmless swirls. The sun was beginning to set. Darkness came swiftly in the desert, but as Doctor Hadley hurried as fast as he could down the path leading to the excavation, he saw a pool of yellow light deep within the dig site. It was the light from a dozen or so flaming torches, held by men in hooded robes, illuminating a well that some of Hadley's men had been excavating.

"What is it?" Hadley panted excitedly, his eyes focused on the well and the torches throwing light into it. "What have you found?"

It was only when he received no response from his men that he turned his back on the well and saw that of all the faces surrounding him—grinning at him menacingly from under their hoods—he did not recognize a single one.

Except for the boy whom he had followed here.

The one who now put his hands out greedily as three or four silver coins were thrown to him. He caught one of them and scrambled to gather the others from the sand. In a moment that Doctor Hadley hoped the boy would learn from and regret for the rest of his life, the brown-eyed child looked up and said, "I'm sorry."

And with that, he ran off, leaving Hadley surrounded by a dozen men in long robes and hoods and flaming torches in their hands, all of them standing over the well which was at least fifteen feet deep. This morning, before the storm, there had been an old wooden ladder leading down into that well. Hadley saw it now lying on the ground some distance away.

He swallowed hard, petrified yet trying his best not to show it. "Who are you?"

Three men stepped forward, two in black robes, the one in the middle in a crimson robe, all of their faces concealed beneath their hoods. The black-robed man to the left of the crimson leader wore a white sash around his neck; the black-robed man on the right was missing his left arm.

In a thick, Mediterranean accent, the man in the crimson robe said, "We are your fate. We are the messengers of your destiny. And we have but one question for you." Beneath the hood, Hadley made out a sneer as the crimson-robed man edged closer to him, forcing him to take a backward step. A step closer to the edge of the deep well. "Where is the stone tablet?"

Hadley stammered, "S-s-stone? What stone?"

The crimson-robed man gave Hadley a shove, and the archeologist stumbled backward a little further. "I don't think you understand the gravity of your situation. Perhaps, soon you will. I'll ask you once more, where is the stone?"

"I told you, I don't know what you're talking about?"

"There was a man on a horse."

"What man?"

"Your faithful young boy told us. There was a man on a horse who came and took the stone. You can either tell us where he took it—or you can die here tonight. A frightened old man. Another fossil. Another life that was never worth living."

Hadley trembled, but the words that came out of his mouth were very possibly the most courageous he had ever spoken in his life. "History will be the judge of that."

The crimson-robed man laughed. Then with one hard vicious shove, he pushed Doctor Hadley backward.

For a moment, the old man teetered on the brink of the well, his heels slipping out from under him, sending a small avalanche of stones and dirt cascading into the well. Then, with his arms flailing wildly, he began to tumble backward.

The hooded man stepped forward to watch, laughing.

Hadley's body reeled backward, falling into thin air. But his hands reached forward, and before he fell, his fingers brushed the hooded man's cloak, desperately trying to snatch at his robe, in the process snagging something around his neck.

The crimson-robed man knocked the archeologist's hands away from him—not feeling the gentle tug around his neck—and laughed out loud as the archeologist plunged into the well.

The old man's shadow blurred and distorted against the excavated walls as he fell.

When he hit the rocky bottom of the well, Doctor Hadley gasped in pain. He felt several bones break on impact, including his ribs. For a moment, he lay on the floor of the well, stunned that he had survived the fall, yet terrified by the fact that he was unable to move. His fingers twitched. His arms moved an inch or two. He still had feeling in his right leg; he could feel the snapped bone and the hot blood coursing over his shin, so he knew he wasn't paralyzed.

But, as he saw the hooded faces of his attackers peer over the edge of the well above him, he suddenly realized his best chance of escape, was not to attempt an escape at all. As the light of their torches shone down upon him, Hadley clamped his eyes shut. He held his breath and stopped breathing. He froze. He played dead.

As the blood coursed from him—as each and every broken bone sent shockwaves of pain through his frail old body—Doctor Joseph Hadley stayed completely still... until he heard the crimson-robed man's command from above. "Throw in your torches. Burn him."

In terror, Hadley opened his eyes and saw the first of the flaming torches descend into the pit, like a fiery comet from the skies, coming straight at him. All he could do was scream.

VI

THE CHALET, THE AUSTRIAN ALPS

Although his eyes could see nothing, the Professor stood facing the enormous floor-to-ceiling window that overlooked the valley and the mountain peaks on the other side of the forest. He stood as though he was watching something through the glass.

As the last of the day set beyond the far horizon, it turned the world a pale blue.

The Professor smiled, "Elsa, we have more company."

Fraulein Elsa Strauss, a stout woman in her early fifties, was setting the long oak dining table a few feet behind the Professor. She rushed to the window still clutching a fistful of knives and forks, and stood beside the Professor, looking out, squinting into the vanishing light.

"I see nothing," she said. She had grown up in a small hamlet on the border of Germany and Austria, and her accent was thick.

"There," he said.

Suddenly a pair of headlights appeared in the valley far below, blinking off and on through the trees, making its way up the winding mountain road toward the chalet.

The Fraulein rolled her eyes and made a noise under her breath. The Professor smiled at the sound she made; it meant he was right. "Don't think I'm going to humor you or even ask how you do that," the Fraulein muttered. "I have food to prepare! Your boys eat like hungry lions."

She scampered away. The Professor continued to smile. "Yes, they do."

His blind eyes continued to stare through the glass.

Then he sensed a third headlight coming up the mountain road.

*

Luca turned the wheel of the red 1976 Alfa Romeo and steered the car swiftly up the road, the forest pines passing in a blur on the high side of the road as he quickly gained altitude. Through the windscreen, he could see ahead of him the glimmering lights of the chalet far up the mountain.

Then something else caught his eye.

As the road straightened for a moment, he saw in his rearview mirror the bright beam of a motorcycle headlight, coming up fast—almost too fast—behind him. For a fleeting moment, he suspected danger.

Then a smirk spread across his face. "Will," he shook his head. "You should know better."

With that, he ripped through the gears on the Alfa, picking up speed with each throw of the shifter. The Alfa soared along the road, the suspension so smooth it seemed almost weightless, leaves and pine needles taking flight in its wake. But gaining rapidly from behind was the roar of a Ducati, bending perilously low on every curve and burning full throttle on the steep straights.

Luca crunched the gears again, spinning sharply around a bend and leaving a swirling set of tire marks along the road like an artist's signature.

And still the bike gained on him.

Taking each turn faster than the one before.

Leaning into the curves so aggressively that leather shrapnel shot from the rider's kneepads and splintered off into the air.

Up ahead, the lights of the chalet grew brighter and closer through the trees. Luca melted into another bend and lost the headlight of the bike behind him for a split second. And in that moment his heart sank. Where had his pursuer gone? Had he crashed? Had he spun off into the forest taking the corner too sharply? Luca immediately slowed the Alfa. His eyes scanned the rearview mirror, looking for any sign of the bike. Any sign of life behind him. He saw nothing, and pulled the car over to the side of the narrow mountain road.

Luca leapt out of the car and turned back down the road, when suddenly the blinding beam of the motorbike's headlight swung around the corner and roared toward him at top speed.

As Luca pressed his back hard up against the side of his car, the bike shot passed him at breakneck speed, revving through its gears. Luca caught Will's triumphant "Wwwooohhhoooo!" listening to the sound of the kid's voice changing frequency like an ambulance siren as he raced by.

"Just you wait," Luca said, shaking his head again and grinning at the same time. He straightened his hair with his fingers now that the wind from the bike had knocked it out of place, before getting back into the Alfa and continuing up the mountain.

At the foot of the chalet, Luca pulled up beside the black Ducati. As he stepped out of the car, Will appeared from nowhere—dressed in full leathers and carrying a shiny black helmet—and launched himself at the handsome Italian, greeting him with a full and passionate kiss, his tongue plunging deep into Luca's mouth.

When Will pulled back, his face was fixed with a mischievous grin. "God, I've missed you."

"First you try to race me out of the road, then you tell me you've missed me."

"Off the road, not out of the road," Will laughed. "Geez, dude, your English sucks almost as bad as your driving."

Suddenly a voice called from behind both of them. "Boys! It's cold!" Both Will and Luca turned to see Elsa standing in the open doorway of the chalet, a shawl wrapped tightly around her shoulders and a stern look on her face. "Quickly, come inside, before you let all the heat out! Before my schnitzels turn into icicles!"

"Elsa!" Will shouted, genuinely thrilled to see her. He raced over to her and gave her a giant hug, almost thumping her on the back of the head with the helmet still in his hand. Elsa's eyes nearly popped out of her skull at the strength of his big-hearted hug.

"Let go of me and get inside!"

Will kissed her on the cheek and did as he was told, disappearing quickly inside the chalet.

Luca smiled then and walked up to Elsa. "He's happy to see you."

"And I'm happy to see him, too. But I'll be happier inside where it's warmer. Now quickly." She wanted to shoo Luca inside, but he wrapped an arm around her affectionately.

"It's not so cold."

"Austria in the mountains is always cold."

Luca smiled and pecked her on the cheek. "I'm happy to see you, too."

Elsa started to smile, then snapped her hands together like a boarding school teacher. "Come, come. Enough hugging and kissing. If I stay out here any longer I'll turn into a snow-Fraulein. You get old, you get cold. Come, come!"

Luca chuckled and watched as Elsa headed inside, mumbling to herself as she disappeared up the stairs leading to the main floor of the chalet. He closed the door behind him and followed her.
Instantly, he felt the warmth of the chalet.

*

Jake opened his eyes. The first thing he saw was a face. A face that was at once familiar—yet foreign. It was the face of a stranger, a handsome stranger. Jake realized it was the last face he had seen—on the boat—seconds before he slipped into unconsciousness.

He squinted his eyes in concentration. In pain. Somehow, from somewhere deep inside his brain, a name returned to him. "Eden?"

The face hovering over him smiled. "You're awake," the handsome Brazilian said. "How do you feel?"

Jake nodded, then winced, then shook his head. "Like someone just chewed me up and spat me out. And I think his name was Perron."

Eden Santiago slid a needle into Jake's forearm. "It's a sedative. I've already given you morphine. For the pain. You'll mend, but it'll take time."

"Where am I?"

"Somewhere safe."

Jake seized Eden's forearm. It was not a gesture of hostility, Jake could not summon up that kind of strength, and he knew it. It was a plea, made in good faith; made with a measure of trust. "Where?"

Eden took Jake's hand in his. He gently cupped his fist, taking his hand safely in his grasp. "Austria," he replied. "You're somewhere safe—in Austria."

As the sedative took effect and the morphine took hold, Jake let his fingers ease into the cradle of Eden's palm. He surrendered to the drugs once more, knowing at this stage it was his only hope of survival. Almost instantly, he felt the pain subside. He watched that handsome face fade away yet again. And as he lost consciousness once more, he thought to himself in all his years of journeying, never once had he been to Austria.

As he slipped into sleep, a word softly escaped his lips.

"Sam—"

*

"He's sleeping. He'll be fine. He just needs to take it easy." Eden joined Luca and Will by the fire, taking the glass of red wine that Luca handed him.

"Who is he?" Luca asked.

The Professor still stood in front of the enormous window. He turned now and faced the three young men. "Let's wait for Shane. Then we'll talk. There's much to talk about."

"Jake said something," Eden told the Professor. "A name. Sam?"

The Professor nodded. "The homeless boy. He sees Jake as something of a father figure. He's old enough to look after himself. At least for the short while that Jake's incapacitated."

"What the hell's going down, Professor?" Will asked, distractedly stabbing at the fire with an iron poker. "Come on, give."

"I told you, I'll 'give' when Shane arrives."

"Where the hell is Shane, anyway?"

"On his way. With a very important package." The Professor suddenly smiled and turned his head, as though a ghost or an angel just whispered in his ear. "Ah, here he comes now."

Will crossed the room to the window and saw the headlights of a Jeep cutting its way up the mountain road.

The young college student grinned in astonishment and was about to open his mouth when Elsa entered from the kitchen, a stack of dinner plates and wine glasses in her hands. "Don't ask," she told Will, setting the glasses down at the table and shaking her head. "You'll give him an ego."

Will smiled. "I wasn't gonna say a word."

"Gentlemen," the Professor announced, "please take a seat at the table. Something quite extraordinary is about to come to light. At least it soon will, if we have anything to do with it."

The men took their places at the table. The Professor sat at the head. Luca and Will sat to his left, Eden to his right. Next to him, an empty chair awaited Shane. Fresh bottles were opened, wine was poured. Elsa vanished once more into the kitchen and returned with a large silver dish. A roasted leg of lamb was surrounded by mountains of steaming baked vegetables—potatoes, pumpkin, beans, carrots and parsnips. As she emerged from the kitchen, all the boys pushed out their chairs and moved to help her carry the dish. She barked them back into their seats. "Don't be stupid, all of you sit down. I can carry this. I carried the Professor up a flight of stairs once. You think I can't handle a little bitty dish?"

"You did not!" Will grinned, amused and impressed.

"You did not!" Will grinned, amused and impressed.

The Professor raised an eyebrow and leaned toward his youngest. "She was drunk and showing off. She had a hold of me before I knew it. And no, it wasn't an entire flight of stairs. The mighty Elsa managed to climb three steps before she dropped me. On my head!" The Professor turned to Elsa as she plonked the roast into the middle of the table. "If my memory serves me, you couldn't walk for a week."

"Pssh-pssh!" Elsa scoffed. "Silly details." Just then, the door opened downstairs. Elsa shouted over the table, "You better make certain that hat is off before you come up here, otherwise no dinner for you!"

Everyone turned as they heard Shane's footsteps bound up the stairs, three at a time. He burst into the room, a bag slung over his shoulder and his cowboy hat in his hand. "Give me a kiss, Elsa," he beamed.

He put down his bag, rushed toward her and scooped her up in his arms. Elsa let out a shriek but let Shane plant a kiss on her cheek nonetheless. "Now put me down!"

He did so. Elsa fanned herself with her apron, shaking her head as she trotted away. "You boys! You boys! I don't know what the Professor is teaching you but it's not manners, that is certain. I'm going to leave you to your business. I'll be in the kitchen. Where it's quiet. And peaceful."

"Thank you Elsa," the Professor smiled after her. The boys all called out thank you as well, but Elsa and her shaking head had already disappeared into the kitchen. The Professor turned his attention to Shane as the others all stood to greet him with warm embraces. "You found him alright?" Professor Fathom asked.

"Big open spaces are my specialty," Shane replied.

He reached into his bag and pulled out the treasure from Turkey, still wrapped in cloth. Gently, he placed it down in front of the blind Professor, then took the old man's hands in his and laid them on the object so he could feel it.

The Professor drew in a short excited breath, then smiled, then slowly—ever so carefully—began to lift away the layers of cloth. Shane took his seat next to Eden. All eyes were fixed on the object in front of the Professor as he peeled away the last piece of fabric to reveal the stone. The tips of his fingers traced the surface of the treasure so lightly, they barely made contact. But with one touch, the Professor knew exactly what the object was before them.

"Gentlemen," he breathed softly. "Behold, one half of Zefferino's stone."

Will looked curiously at the broken piece of stone on the table in front of them, at the small carvings etched into it, the intricate tapestry of a language Will did not recognize. "I'm guessin' whatever that is, and whatever it says, it's gotta be important," he said, "because I've never heard anyone use the word 'behold' before."

"Important is perhaps an understatement," Professor Fathom said. "Zefferino's stone is revered by some and scorned by many. This is one of two halves, dispersed by Zefferino himself after the execution of his master, the artist Videlle. According to legend, the two pieces of the tablet tell the secret location of Videlle's last work of art. A statue called The Naked Christ, known by some as The Cross of Sins. Luca, perhaps you'd like to shed more light on the subject."

Luca took a sip of wine and recounted the story of the artist Videlle. "Videlle was born in Paris in 1606 but moved to Florence when he was a young man to pursue a life of art. He painted feverishly, he sculpted figures so real, it was as though one kiss could breathe life into them. He was underrated, often snubbed by both critics and fellow artists alike for his unconventional compositions and inappropriate subject matter. Instead of saints he painted sinners. Instead of kings he sculpted thieves. Instead of virgins he portrayed whores and hags. He depicted vices rather than virtues. He created real life, but that's not how the Church viewed his work. They called it 'evil unpunished.' No morality, no heavenly salvation, no humility or respect for God. Videlle teased his critics by always signing his name upside-down, jokingly referring to himself as the anti-Christ of the art world. One fanatical faction of the Church in particular, the Crimson Crown, began to keep a watchful eye on him. It seemed the only person who appreciated his work was his young lover and apprentice, Zefferino. As the years went by, the constant rejection of his work turned Videlle bitter and reclusive. He began to shun the world, just as the world had shunned him.

He sent Zefferino to the market for food and wine and refused to leave the house. He boarded up windows. He became so paranoid of eavesdroppers and spies, he even went so far as to invent a secret language that only he and Zefferino could understand. He wrote a book of translations for Zefferino and told him to keep it in a secret place. Then one day, Videlle announced he was about to create his finest work ever—his last work. He went into his studio with a block of marble and his chisel and did not surface for three months. When he finally emerged, he was a different man. Almost as though he had been enlightened. Almost as though he had been set free. He took down the boards from the windows, he stepped outside the house, and he unveiled to the world The Naked Christ."

Luca stood from his chair and moved over to the fire, as though trying to shake off a chill. "The rest of the story is nothing short of tragic. The Crimson Crown, with all the strength of the Church behind it, descended upon Videlle like ravenous wolves. The moment he revealed The Naked Christ, he was ambushed. There on the street, in front of his house, they snatched out his eyes and cut off his hands and had him executed for all the world to see."

"What about Zefferino? And the statue?" Will asked.

"Zefferino was no match for the Crimson Crown, he knew that. He could not save Videlle from his fate, but he realized quickly that he could save The Naked Christ. While Videlle's tormentors were busy with their murderous crusade, Zefferino fled with the statue, hiding in the shadows of Florence, behind church columns, in the dark of sheltering doorways, until he managed to smuggle the cross out of the city. Nobody knows where he went, but as the legend goes, he carved the details of the statue's whereabouts onto a stone tablet using Videlle's secret language, then he purposely broke the tablet in two. He hid one part of the tablet in the back of a cart traveling east, and the other he smuggled on board a merchant ship heading west toward the sunset."

"So we're missing half the clues then," Will said. "One piece isn't going to lead us to the statue, right? And even if we did have the other piece, we can't read what's on it. Not unless we have—"

"The book," answered Luca. "Which is in an antique shop in London, run by a man called Elliott Ebus. Once we have the book, we can translate the carvings on the tablet."

"But we're still only half way there," added Shane. "What about the other half of the stone?"

The Professor smiled. "The key to that is in the other room."

"What is it?" Will asked.

"Actually," the Professor added, "The question is who is it? His name's Jake Stone. I've been observing Mr. Stone for some time now. He's infamous from Bombay to Brunei as a treasure hunter, a rogue with a taste for adventure and a talent for trouble."

"Sounds like he'll fit right in," Shane smiled.

"I hope so. I see great potential in him. Fortunately, Eden was at hand and managed to track down Mr. Stone in the South Seas after a run-in with a rather shrewd Parisian art collector."

"Art collector?" said a hoarse voice from a nearby doorway. "I've got a few other titles that'd better suit the guy."

Everyone at the table turned quickly to see Jake using the frame of the door to prop himself up. He was naked but for the bandage around his midsection and a bed sheet wrapped loosely around his waist. Just then, his eyes rolled back, and he began to fall.

Eden jumped up from the table and caught him just before he hit the floor.

Shane, Luca and Will rushed forward and helped Eden get Jake to the sofa.

The Professor stood just as Elsa came storming out from the kitchen. "What is all this fuss!" she demanded. She saw Jake. "Oh my. I'll get some water."

Through splintered vision, Jake tried to keep focus on the faces looking down at him. He recognized Eden's face almost immediately, but not the others. Then Professor Fathom appeared over him.

"What are you looking at?" Jake challenged groggily.

"Nothing," the Professor answered calmly. "I'm blind."

"Where am I?"

"I believe Eden has already informed you that you're in Austria. My name is Professor Maximilian Fathom. This is my home."

"Where's Sam?"

"Back in New York. My interest is not with Sam, it's with you."

At that moment, Elsa pushed her way through the men with a glass of water. "Here, drink!" she demanded.

"What is it?"

"What do you think it is? Water!"

"It's okay," Eden assured Jake.

"Who's she?"

Professor Fathom said, "This is Elsa, my housekeeper. And I'd advise you to do as she says. She has quite a temper." Elsa gasped indignantly before the Professor continued the introductions. "You've already met Doctor Eden Santiago, biologist, physician and genetic engineer. To my right, is Shane Houston, expert in cartography and horse handling. Beside him is Luca da Roma, my guiding light when it comes to all things artistic. And to my left is Will Hunter, currently majoring in ancient history at college in San Diego—although given his heroics on the football field his education may well be ancient history any day now."

"Enough with the formalities. Drink!" Elsa insisted.

Jake looked at Eden who smiled and nodded. Elsa pressed the glass gently to Jake's lips and wiped his mouth with her apron as he coughed and struggled to drink it.

At that moment, the phone rang.

Elsa patted Jake's mouth dry and excused herself to go answer the phone. Before Jake could ask another question, Elsa came hurrying back, her face twisted with panic and despair.

"Professor! Professor come quickly! It's Mr. Musa on the phone, curator of the museum in Ankara. Something's happened to Doctor Hadley! Something terrible!"

For the next few minutes, the room was silent as Professor Fathom was told of the shocking murder of his dear old friend, Joseph Hadley. "Whoever did this was looking for something," Mr. Musa said over the crackling line from Ankara. The Professor couldn't tell whether the line was breaking up or whether it was Mr. Musa's grief-stricken voice. "The camp was ransacked, the workers were driven into the desert. The police think it may have been nomads, but nothing was stolen from the site. Whoever did this didn't bother to steal any of the gold artifacts or silver treasures at the camp. They took nothing. Nothing but Doctor Hadley's life! Who would do such a thing?"

For a moment, the Professor said nothing. Then, in a soft and somber voice, he replied, "We'll find out. I promise you. I swear on Joseph's body, we'll find them."

Nobody said a word after the Professor hung up the phone.

For a long time, the only sound in the room was the spit and crackle of the blazing fire. Then, suppressing all the rage and shock and pain inside him, the Professor turned to the others.

"Freedoms have been lost. Lives have been taken. The time has come for truths to be told, and for secrets to be revealed. The Naked Christ is more than just a statue. It is a symbol of the fight against oppression. It's a fight we must win."

Professor Fathom turned toward the fire then, his face orange in its glow. He whispered into the flames, "My dear, Joseph. My poor, dear, intelligent, Joseph. I'm sorry."

"Professor?" Elsa appeared behind him, her face filled with sorrow for him, her hand resting tenderly on his shoulder. "Let me take you to your room."

"No thank you, Elsa. I'll be fine. I need to get to the bottom of this."

"But Professor," Eden said. "You need time to—"

"Time is a luxury we cannot afford!" the Professor interrupted. "Time is something Joseph no longer has. And it's something we too may run out of very soon."

Just then, he staggered backward a little. Elsa was there to steady him. The men hurried forward, and Elsa and Eden helped him back into his chair. "I'm alright, I'm alright," he told them all. "I didn't mean to raise my voice. But this is no time for an old man to be fussed over. I'll be fine. All that matters is we find the book before the murderers who killed Joseph find us."

"But what about the other half of the tablet?" asked Will.

"Have faith."

Professor Fathom had many strengths, the greatest of which was clarity of mind and his ability to form a sound plan, even in the face of adversity or, as the case might be, the terrible grip of grief.

Over the next few hours, Jake fell into a deep drug-induced slumber on the sofa, the food on the table was slowly eaten, even if it did go cold and was picked at randomly, and the Professor devised a strategy that would give them all the best chance of finding The Naked Christ.

By sunrise, the plan was underway. In three days time, they all agreed to rendezvous at the Royal Hotel in Vienna. In the meantime, Will left his Ducati at the Chalet and departed with Luca in his Alfa Romeo. They reached Vienna's airport several hours later and bought two tickets to London.

Eden and Shane left in Shane's Jeep, and the two of them also headed for the airport. By midday they were on a flight to Ankara.

Eden left behind medical supplies and instructions with Elsa so that she could adequately care for Jake in his absence. "He's as strong as they get. Just keep up the morphine and his body will heal itself."

"Don't worry," said the Professor. "We won't let anything happen to him. We need him."

Eden smiled before he left. "You do have a plan, don't you. Why doesn't that surprise me?"

The Professor kissed him on the cheek before he left. "Take care. We'll all be together soon. And we will find The Cross of Sins. In this, I really do have faith."

VII

NAPLES, ITALY

Vesuvius loomed large over the sprawling chaos of Naples, a city steeped in poverty and crime, with mountains of garbage alight on every street corner and guileless tourists having their wristwatches snatched by men on Vespas in every alley.

The handsome, dark-haired German walked along one such alley, his stride confident, his face cool and calm. He wore sunglasses, a perfectly-fitting black suit, white shirt unbuttoned down to mid-chest. Italian shoes clapping against the cobblestones.

Suddenly, from the other end of the alley he heard the wasp-like buzz of a motorscooter approaching, its unserviced engine straining, its wheels bouncing on the cobblestones as it raced up from behind. The German didn't turn his head to look. He simply smiled and kept walking, leaving his left arm exposed, Rolex on view, while his right hand reached inside his jacket pocket.

As the scooter droned up behind him, the driver reached wide, arm outstretched ready for the snatch, the watch an easy target.

But as he sped within two feet of his prize, the man in the suit spun about quickly.

Somehow the driver of the scooter managed to snare the watch.

At the same time he felt a thump against his ribcage.

The man in the suit had punched him. Punched him hard.

The bike teetered, wobbled precariously, then turned completely on its side as the winded driver fell. Momentum sent both driver and scooter crashing into the wall on the opposite side of the alley.

Engine still running, the dented bike spluttered smoke.

At the same time, the fallen driver spluttered blood.

He felt it splash and trickle down his chin. Confused he wiped his mouth. That's when he felt the searing pain in his ribs.

He glanced down at his side quickly and saw the pool of blood spreading out from under him. He put his hand of his side and felt the hot rush of blood. Suddenly he panicked. "Aiuto! Auito!"

With a calm smile, the man in the suit crouched beside the fatally-wounded man and wiped the blood from his switchblade knife onto the driver's shirt, before retracting the blade and replacing the kife in his jacket pocket. "Sorry, I'd like to help," he said in his thick German accent, snatching his Rolex out of the dying man's clutches and checking the time. "But you've already made me late for an appointment."

With that he made his way to the end of the alley and turned a corner, leaving the watch-thief to gasp and splutter and slowly die, alone on the cobblestones, sticky and black with blood.

*

The door to the rendezvous point was red.

The German knocked twice.

An old woman in an apron answered. She said nothing and simply pointed the visitor up a set of stairs in the decrepit street-front apartment.

Upstairs was a room, its curtains drawn, a table and two chairs inside.

A man sat in one of the chairs, his face concealed beneath a crimson hood. "You have the money?"

"Do you have his location?" the German asked in return.

The man in the hood gestured to the chair opposite. "Hans, please. Sit."

The legs of the chair scraped along the dusty floorboards and the German sat. He reached into the inside pocket of his jacket once more, but instead of pulling out his knife, he produced a thickly-packed envelope. As he slid it across the table, he said, "I thought your people were already rich?"

The hooded man put his hand on the envelope and slid it under his robe. Faintly the German could make out a smile beneath that hood. "In a world of give and take, you can never have enough money."

"So you've taken. Now give me his location."

"No," was the hooded man's calm response.

The German stood angrily and leaned across the table, the scraping chair slamming backward onto the floor. Now the knife was in his hand, blade drawn. "Tell me where I can find the son of Valentino!"

"I will," came another calm response. "But not yet. I need him."

Anger mixed with suspicion on the German's face. "You need him? For what?"

This time he saw the smile for certain. It was a wicked smile, lingering like a snarl beneath that crimson hood. "To find something that was never meant to be found."

VIII

PICCADILLY, LONDON

Red open-top double-decker buses and black taxis roared past a London policeman wearing a black bobby's hat and white gloves as he blew into a whistle and directed traffic. At the same time, Will and Luca walked down the crowded pavements of Piccadilly, arguing.

"You think a Ducati gives you style?"

"I think—correction, I know—a Ducati gives me speed!"

Luca shook his head. "You may be fast. You may be young and handsome and full of stupid tricks. But none of it makes you invincible."

"You're beginning to sound like the Professor," Will smirked.

Luca pulled him aside as a large group of fat German tourists waddled by with their cameras and maps.

"If I sound like the Professor, it's because I care. We all care. You're our little brother. You can't blame us for wanting to look out for you."

"I'm touched, really," Will grinned. "But I can look out for myself."

He took a step backward—a little too close to the street—and slipped on the curb. He began to fall backward, just as a bus packed with sightseers blasted its horn and careened straight toward him.

Suddenly, Luca's hand was there, clutching Will by the shirt and hauling him back onto the pavement, a mere second before the bus roared past.

Will stumbled against Luca, then quickly straightened himself, eyes wide. "That was close. Thanks."

Luca flashed a gleaming I-told-you-so smile. "Don't mention it."

He looked up and saw the entrance to the Burlington Arcade, a beautiful and ornate shopping strip filled with dozens of expensive and tightly-packed boutique shops. "This is the place," Luca said.

They found Elliott Ebus's antique shop in the middle of the arcade. It was a curious little place, dark and maze-like, crowded with cases and cabinets filled with old toys, dusty sewing machines and prehistoric grammaphones. When Will and Luca found the owner of the shop, Elliott Ebus, he himself looked like a curio.

"Can I help you gentlemen?" said the little man in a crisp British accent. He was short and bald, with thick round spectacles on his little rodent's nose.

"Are you Elliott Ebus?" Luca asked.

The little man nodded proudly. "Indeed, and this is my store. Are you shopping for a gift? Something for yourself perhaps?"

"We're looking for a particular book, a very old book."

"Well then," buzzed Elliott excitedly, "you've come to the right place."

Straightening his little knit vest and checking his bowtie was tied nice and tight, Elliott led Will and Luca to an aisle filled with towers and towers of ancient books. "Do you know the title?" Elliott's nimble little fingers began to dance along the spines of books, ready to knowingly seek out the treasure these gentlemen sought.

"No," Luca said, "but we know who the author was. An artist by the name of Videlle."

Elliott Ebus suddenly froze. His fingers stopped dancing. He seemed to stop breathing for a moment, and his right eye developed a rather obvious twitch.

"You okay there, dude?" Will asked.

"Yes," Elliott snapped nervously. "But I'm afraid I can't help you.

I've never heard that name before in my life. I know all my books. I know every item in my store. But that one doesn't ring a bell at all, I'm afraid. You'll have to look elsewhere."

"I had it on very good advice that this was the place to come," said Luca, "and you were the person to talk to."

"Whoever told you that was wrong? Now if you'll excuse me, gentlemen, I have an errand to run."

Elliott Ebus scurried quickly back behind the safety of his counter, pulled on a tweed jacket and plucked a Back in 15 Minutes sign out of a drawer.

"I think we get the hint," Will said. "Come on, let's get the hell out of here."

Luca handed Elliott a piece of paper with Room 212 scribbled on it. "We're staying at the Piccadilly, in case you think of anything that might ring a bell. Sorry to have bothered you."

Elliott Ebus mumbled something about it being quite all right—although clearly it wasn't—before shooing Will and Luca out of his store.

*

Steam rose from the open door to the hotel bathroom, forming sparkling plumes that collected near the ceiling. Will kicked off his shoes, fetched a beer out of the mini-bar and made his way to the bathroom door. He leaned against the doorframe, watching as rivulets of water made gleaming patterns down the length of the glass shower screen; watching as Luca stood under the hot stream of water, running the soap up and down his torso and arms. The small silver crucifix around his neck glistened.

"You still believe in Him?" Will asked. "Your cross, I mean."

"I believe one day I'll find the person who gave it to me. Then I'll finally know who I am."

"I hope you're not disappointed when you do."

"Why do you say that?"

Will shrugged. "I dunno. I guess sometimes knowledge doesn't necessarily bring you happiness." The thought of his own father flashed through his head, but he pushed it away instantly and thumbed the cap off his bottle of beer, changing the subject. "So how long?"

"How long what?" Luca replied.

"How long do we give Lord Fuddy-Duddy before we pay him another visit."

"We don't."

"Are you crazy? He's obviously our guy. Did you see how nervous he got?"

Luca nodded. "That's why we don't pay him another visit. We let him come to us."

"Like that's gonna happen!" Will scoffed. "The dude was petrified, you saw him. If he's got that book, he sure as hell ain't giving it to us." Will took a swig of his beer. "I tell ya, someone's got him spooked real good."

Luca leaned out of the shower and reached for Will's beer. Will handed it to him.

"Mark my words, there'll be a knock on our door before the day is out."

"Twenty bucks says you're wrong."

"Fifty says I'm right."

"Done." Will watched as Luca stood naked in the shower drinking from his beer bottle. His brown body glistened as the water slid down his every muscle, splashing against his large chest, running down his rigid stomach, caressing the length of his long uncut cock.

Luca felt Will's eyes on him. He looked sideways, pulled his lips away from the beer bottle and shook his head. "Na-uh. Not like last time."

Will grinned. "What?"

"I know that look. Remember Paris?"

Will's grin grew even bigger, his white teeth shining, his boyish good looks spreading from ear to ear. "Of course I remember Paris. So does the bulge in my jeans!"

Will indicated his own crotch, then peeled off his shirt.

"No," Luca said firmly.

"But I owe you. You saved my life today. That bus would have been the end of me. The least I can do is—"

"The least you can do is forget it. It's not happening."

"Tell that to your cock."

Luca didn't have to look down. He could feel his cock swelling fast. He felt the head slide out from beneath the long foreskin. He felt his shaft form a limb of its own, defying gravity, rising in an arc perpendicular to his body.

He turned off the shower and the water drew the last of its glistening patterns down his chest and stomach. He stepped out and reached for a towel, but Will got to it first.

He moved toward Luca with the towel in both hands and began to dry him with it, using long, slow, tender strokes. Like a painter, Luca thought. Indeed, despite his age, Will Hunter was quite the artist when it came to seduction.

Luca stood in silent surrender to Will's advance. He let Will take his left arm in his hands and towel it dry. He took his right arm in his hands and did the same. He ran the towel down Luca's large brown chest, drying the sparse trimmed hair, over the mounds of his abdomen, and down to his cock, so hard now it bobbed and pulsated. He wrapped it in the towel and gently squeezed.

Luca's eyes closed for a brief moment, his mouth falling open, just a fraction. A small gasp could be heard.

Will smiled at him and descended to his knees.

He took the towel and dried Luca's giant left thigh, followed by his muscled calf. He did the same to his right leg. Then he put the towel down by Luca's feet, knelt upright, and came eye to eye with Luca's throbbing cock. The sheath of Luca's foreskin had peeled back completely, his cock too long and its swollen head too large now to be concealed.

Will took the base of Luca's shaft in one hand and swallowed the engorged head, massaging it with his tongue inside his watering mouth. He slid his other hand down his own rigid stomach, stopping to unbuckle his belt, unzip his jeans and unleash his own stiff cock. He began stroking it, gently at first, then harder and harder as he built momentum.

Luca moaned a loud deep sound.

Will didn't want the fun to end too soon.

He slipped Luca's cock out of his mouth, then ran his tongue down the length of the thick-veined shaft till it reached Luca's balls. He took one ball, then both, into his mouth, and with his tongue, he juggled them slowly, tauntingly, from one cheek to the other.

He stopped stroking his own cock and ran both hands up and down Luca's massive thighs, feeling the muscles twitch with the jolts of pleasure that were shooting through his body. As he sucked and teased the balls in his mouth, he felt the heat of Luca's cock against his cheek, his eye, his forehead.

Luca's balls clicked together in Will's mouth.

Luca took in a short, sharp breath.

Will smiled and let the balls slip from his mouth like huge warm plums.

He followed the shaft back up to the head and enveloped Luca's cock with his lips again. The thickness of Luca's cock filled his mouth, all the way. He felt its huge head touch the back of his throat. He pulled back quickly, letting the cock slide from his lips.

It was a tease, a trick, and Luca fell for it. Hungry for more, he pushed himself back inside Will's mouth.

Will began sucking on his cock with increasingly deeper, swifter thrusts, listening to Luca's breath as it grew shorter and sharper, faster and faster.

Luca's hands seized Will by his tousled blond hair, guiding him, making certain his cock didn't slip from the embrace of Will's lips again.

With open eyes, Will watched Luca's dark pubic hair, his muscled lower abs, slide toward his face then pull back again.

In and out.

Faster again.

Faster still.

With one hand Will began to jerk himself off. With his other hand he grabbed Luca's balls. They were heavy and still wet with Will's saliva. He thumbed them, rubbed them, squeezed them in the cradle of his palm and felt them rise and fall like puppets in his hand, until soon they drew upward.

Further upward.

Preparing to release their load.

Luca groaned and the word "fuck!" slipped out between breaths, again and again.

Will quickened the stroke of his own cock—hot and hard and tall and thick—until his fist was slapping up and down its shaft. He felt himself on the brink of coming and tried to groan, but his mouth was full of Luca's cock, and his throat gulped down the sound at precisely the same moment that Luca let out a cry.

Once.

Twice.

Then suddenly, Will's mouth flooded with Luca's cum. It shot across his tongue, hot and sweet, and hit the back of his throat.

The taste of it, the sensation of it, launched a load of Will's cum up the shaft of his cock, spurting up into the air in a hot tendril, streaming and slapping across Will's stomach and chest.

At the same time, he swallowed hard on Luca's cock, feeling the cum slide down his throat into his fiery belly.

Luca cried out once more with the pressure of Will's suction on his cock.

Then slowly, almost precariously—when his balls were empty and his dick swollen, spent and tender—he pried Will off his cock.

Will gasped for air, a wide satisfied grin on his face.

Luca scooped him up, lifting the young American to his feet. They stood panting, leaning into each other, chests heaving. Then Luca kissed Will and could taste his own cum inside Will's mouth.

He pulled out of the kiss with a smile. "This won't happen again," he warned.

Will shook his head. "Of course not," he panted. "Never again," he whispered, as he planted another kiss on Luca's lips.

*

Luca showered again then wrapped a clean towel around his waist and fetched a fresh beer from the mini-bar while Will showered.

Luca took the cap off the bottle and drank his first mouthful, then came a knock at the door.

He glanced into the bathroom with a knowing grin.

Will had heard it, too, and poked his head around the shower screen. "You gotta be shittin' me!"

"Fifty bucks, remember?"

Luca opened the door and sure enough, Elliott Ebus stood before him wearing his tweed jacket, bowtie and spectacles. Clutched tightly in both hands was a small brown paper package tied with string.

"Oh," he said with surprise, eyes wide at the sight of Luca in his towel.

Behind Luca, Will suddenly appeared, also draped in a towel.

"Oh!" Elliott said louder, even more surprised, before his mind jumped to the logical conclusion. "Perhaps I should come back later."

"No, come in."

Elliott reacted to the invitation timidly, not moving or saying a word.

"It's alright, dude," Will smiled. "There's nothing to be scared of. No hidden surprises here." At that moment his towel lost its grip on his waist. It slipped off. He managed to catch it just in time.

Elliott Ebus looked away, embarrassed. He turned to leave, but Luca swooped out the door and collected him, wrapping his strong arm around the little man's shoulders. "It's alright, really. We know you have important things on your mind."

Luca gestured to the package in Elliott's hands.

"Yes," Elliott said.

"Come in."

With Luca guiding him, and taking one cautious step after another, Elliott entered the room. Luca closed the door behind him and locked it.

Elliott seated himself down on a sofa beside the balcony door. Still in his towel, Luca sat in a chair opposite him. Still in his towel, Will fetched three more beers. Elliott declined, then changed his mind and took the beer. "I don't normally drink. But I'm rather nervous."

"Is that the book?" Luca asked directly.

Elliott nodded. "Yes. Videlle's name is here, inside the back cover. I told you I'd never heard of the book. But that was a lie. I've known about it for a long time now. I've been its guardian. Its keeper. And it's been my curse."

"How did you come across it?"

"Five years ago, a man came into my store and said he'd sell me the book on one condition—that I never sell it to anyone else. That I never give it away, or even acknowledge its existence. He offered to sell me the book for a single euro, and in return he gave me ten thousand euros to keep the book a secret. It was an irresistible transaction."

"Have you read it?" Will asked.

Elliott shook his head, then nodded guiltily. "It's some sort of cipher. Half of it's written in Italian, the other half is all symbols and shapes. Almost like hieroglyphs, but not quite. It's a language I've never seen before."

Luca sat forward. "The man, have you seen him again?"

"Not since that first day. To be honest, I'd be happy if I never saw him again. As well as this book." With that, Elliott put the package on the coffee table in front him. "I may not know what it is or what it stands for, but after all these years I've decided that a secret worth that much money, is a secret I don't want to keep anymore. That's why I came. To pass it on. To let it go. You asked for the book, and now it's yours. I want it gone from my life, forever."

Suddenly Elliott let out a huge sigh of relief, as though years and years of stress and drama had suddenly been lifted from his shoulders. "Oh my," he smiled. "That does feel good. At last it's over."

But the sudden *CRACK* at the door told all three of them that the drama was only just beginning.

Crack! CRACK!

The hinges of the door buckled, the lock strained, the wood splintered. Somebody was trying to kick the door down.

Elliott gasped in horror, but Will and Luca were already on the move. Luca seized the book, shoved it between his towel and his waist, then swung about in time to catch the revolver that Will had snatched out from under the bed and thrown to him.

Will swiftly locked a cartridge into a pistol of his own.

Luca backed up behind the door.

Will leapt over the coffee table, grabbed Elliott Ebus by the collar of his tweed jacket and pulled him down behind the sofa.

CRACK!

Just then, the lock gave way and the door flew open.

The first black-robed man took a bullet right between the eyes, courtesy of Luca's steady revolver. The dead man's body jolted and stumbled backward into the six other black-robed men behind him, all of whom opened fire immediately.

Bullets took huge chunks off the walls inside the room, punctured the glass panes of the windows and sent feathers billowing into the air from the pillows on the bed.

Elliott Ebus squealed as bullets plucked stuffing out of the sofa he and Will were using as a shield. "I don't want to die!"

"Keep your head down!" Will snapped, shoving Elliott as low to the floor as possible.

Will fired off several bullets, taking out another of the black-robed assailants before they could get through the door.

Luca, too, continued his fire, killing a third intruder then kicking the door shut again.

As he did so, Will leapt over the sofa and kicked the coffee table along the floor toward the door. It skidded to a halt at Luca's feet. Luca snatched it up and slammed it against the door, wedging one end against the door handle and one end into the floor. A precarious doorstop indeed, but enough to buy some time.

"The balcony!" Luca yelled. "Go now!"

Will kicked the balcony doors open and broken shards of glass fell away.

Behind them, their attackers shot several more bullets into the door and rammed themselves against it. The coffee table held strong for a moment or two, then began to give way.

Will seized Elliott off the floor and shoved the blubbering little man out onto the balcony.

"Let me go! I don't want to die!" he sobbed.

"Do what I say, and you'll be okay," Will said sternly.

He steered him out onto the balcony, and Luca followed them out, his revolver still firing shots at the barricaded door.

The moment the three of them made it onto the balcony, the coffee table slid across the floor and the door burst open.

The sound of gunfire filled the air.

Will grabbed Elliott and pushed him out of the line of fire, to the left of the balcony door, forcing him over the balcony railing and onto a precarious ledge, two stories above the street. Elliott shrieked as he looked down at the busy Piccadilly traffic passing below. He began to lose his balance, but Will had him by the jacket.

"Steady there, big guy!"

Will glanced back and saw that Luca had dived right, now scaling the opposite balcony railing, climbing away from them.

"You got the book?" Will shouted over the traffic and gunfire.

"Yeah. You got him?"

Will nodded and rolled his eyes, not overly happy about his end of the bargain.

"Vienna," Luca said.

Will nodded again. "See you there."

The men in black robes would come charging through the bullet-tattered curtains that billowed onto the balcony any second.

Will shook Elliott. "When I say jump, you jump."

"Jump!" Elliott gasped. "Are you crazy! I'm not going to—"

"Jump!"

Elliott glanced down in horror. A double-decker tourist bus was about to pass underneath them, its top deck open and filled with American and Japanese tourists taking happy holiday snaps.

"Now!" Will shouted.

Elliott hesitated, but Will didn't.

With Elliott's collar clenched firmly in his fist, and his towel fastened firmly around his waist, Will jumped off the ledge, taking Elliott with him.

The two flew through the air to the wail of Elliott's squeals.

With a thud, they landed in the aisle of the upper deck of the bus, much to the shock and surprise of the tourists on board. Precious Japanese newlyweds jumped up in their seats and screamed as though a mouse had just skittered under their feet. Overweight Americans gasped, clutching at their chests as though protecting their hearts from a coronary. Then in unison, as Will pulled Elliott to his feet, every camera on board the bus began firing away.

Will, with his gun tucked deep into his towel and out of sight, quickly pulled Elliott away. "Come on, downstairs. We gotta get outta here." He towed the dazed Elliott toward the stairs of the bus as quickly as he could.

Behind him, a large middle-aged American woman patted her chubby husband excitedly on the chest. "Herb, look, I told you we'd see someone in a kilt!" She snapped a photo, just as a gust of wind lifted the towel and revealed a glimpse of Will's butt cheek. The woman grinned excitedly. "That photo is a keeper!"

As the bus continued on its way, the black-robed assailants poured out onto the balcony of the Piccadilly Hotel.

Luca checked the book was securely tucked into his towel, then jumped from the ledge, landing with a thunk onto the roof of a black London cab. He tucked his revolver into the back of his towel and threw one last glance back and saw the men in black robes leaning over the balcony railing, firing random shots into the traffic. Cars veered, horns blared. Luca rolled off the roof of the cab and flipped himself in through the open window of the back passenger door.

He landed recklessly on the backseat of the cab, his towel up around his stomach, the book sliding onto the floor.

Quickly he snatched it up. Then, almost as an afterthought, he pulled down the towel to cover himself, glanced up and saw the smile of the fifty-year-old woman in the back of the cab with him. Her hair was pink, her lipstick bright red, and her fake eyelashes fluttered frantically.

"Please keep driving," Luca told the confused cabbie, "as fast as you can. To the airport."

Luca looked at the woman in the back with him. "I'm sorry to take you out of your way. It's something of an emergency. I hope you don't mind."

The woman put both palms to her flushed cheeks and said, "I don't mind at all." Then whispered so that the cabbie couldn't hear, "So long as you lose the towel."

She gave Luca a big fake-eyelashed wink.

He gave a nervous gulp.

IX

ANKARA, TURKEY

The streets of Ankara were loud and dusty and filled with cheap rusted cars tearing along at speeds that seemed impossible for their age. Eden and Shane found the Ankara Museum of National Treasures on a busy corner in the northern end of the city. The curator, a man named Ahmed Musa, was expecting them. He quickly led them through room after room filled with the ruins of statues and altars and pillars and tombs and into his office where he locked the door behind them. The office itself was like a miniature version of the museum. Ancient vases and small statues lined dozens of shelves; old rusted jewelry and wooden utensils, each with a tag attached, filled several glass cabinets; and in the corner behind the door, standing upright and looking very imposing, was an enormous black sarcophagus with its lid closed.

Shane took off his cowboy hat and stepped curiously over to the sarcophagus. He touched its smooth cold surface.

"Don't touch that!" Mr. Musa shouted.

"My apologies." Shane pulled his hand away.

"It's very old," the curator snapped.

"Mr. Musa, are you alright?" Eden asked.

The curator paused nervously a moment. "I'm afraid I've broken the law," he announced skittishly, speaking in a soft, hurried voice. "But

I had to. Otherwise there would be no hope of finding Doctor Hadley's killers. The law enforcement agencies here can be easily bought."

"Slow down," Eden said calmly. "Tell us what you know."

Mr. Musa tried to pour himself a glass of water, but his hands were trembling. Shane took the pitcher and glass and poured it for him. The curator gulped it down.

"As soon as I found out about Doctor Hadley's death I got to the dig site as fast as I could. I arrived minutes before the authorities. I found the pit where Doctor Hadley was killed. You could still smell it. His flesh. I shone a flashlight into the well and there he was—or at least, that's where the body was—charred and smoldering. It was the most horrific thing I've ever seen in my life. He was my friend, my colleague."

Mr. Musa guzzled the rest of his water, panting after it was gone. For a moment, he looked as if he might cry, but then he took several deep breaths and opened a drawer to his desk.

"At first I didn't see it. All I could see were the burned remains. But then, through the smoke, I saw something glinting in the beam of my flashlight. Doctor Hadley was clutching something in his charred fist. Before anyone could stop me—before I could stop myself—I slid a ladder into the pit, climbed down and took the object from poor Doctor Hadley's dead hand."

Mr. Musa then pulled something out of the drawer. It was a tightly folded handkerchief. He unwrapped it to reveal a blackened silver chain.

"I managed to climb out of the pit just as the police arrived and rounded everybody up for questioning, at least those who were still left. Those who hadn't fled or been driven away. I didn't tell the police what I'd found. I know I'm tampering with evidence, but it would have ended up around the neck of some corrupt official's wife, a mere trinket. I couldn't let that happen. I knew it would be safe with Professor Fathom. I knew it would be safe with you."

Eden lifted the chain gently off the unfolded handkerchief and held it up. The chain itself was snapped, as if it had been ripped from someone's neck. At the end of it hung a small metal ring of thorns, dark red in color.

"The Crimson Crown," Shane said.

"You've heard of them?" Mr. Musa asked.

Eden nodded. "It appears they're on the same trail we are."

"The only question is," Shane added, "who'll reach the end of the trail first?"

"Do you mind if we take this with us?" Eden asked.

"Not at all. In fact, I'd be relieved." At that point, Mr. Musa leaned in and said in a hushed tone, "This is about The Cross of Sins, isn't it. I've heard the stories, but I never once believed any of them were true."

"At this stage, Mr. Musa, the less you know, the better," Eden advised the curator. "Tell nobody about the chain, and tell no one we were here—for your own safety."

With that, Eden and Shane bid Ahmed Musa farewell.

As soon as they were gone, Mr. Musa became more anxious and nervous than ever. He poured himself another glass of water and turned his back to the door. He took one frantic gulp, then froze as he heard the ominous creak of something opening.

It wasn't the door.

Slowly he turned around, eyes wide with dread, to see the lid of the black sarcophagus swinging slowly open, revealing a hooded figure in a black robe and a white sash standing inside the ancient coffin.

The figure stepped out of the sarcophagus and stopped, staring at Mr. Musa.

"You should have left it for the police to find," the figure said in a stern voice. He had a distinctly American accent. "Now that mere trinket is going to cost you dearly."

Mr. Musa's voice trembled. "But I did what you wanted. I did what you told me to do."

"Yes," the black-robed figure whispered. "And now your job is done."

From beneath his robe, the figure pulled out a revolver with a silencer on the end. The curator gasped. He dropped his glass out of sheer terror. Water splashed and glass smashed across the floor.

He staggered backwards clumsily.

He heard a short, sharp muffled sound, like something just snipped at the air. It was the last sound he ever heard.

Ahmed Musa was dead before his body even hit the floor.

*

"There's just something about it that doesn't seem right," Shane said to Eden. They had walked three of the four blocks from the museum to their hotel, and were now pushing past shouting fruit merchants, feuding butchers and haggling shoppers in the middle of a large colorful bazaar.

"I agree," Eden said loudly over the noise all around them.

"So where to now? The dig site?"

"Yes, but I'm going alone."

Shane pulled Eden up. "What do you mean, you're going alone?"

"If I take you with me, the authorities will never let us on the scene. I'm a scientist, a doctor and an expert in forensics. With a little persuasion I can convince the Turkish police I have reason to be there. You have —"

Shane propped his hands on his hips. "I have what!"

"You have a cowboy hat. That's not going to get you anywhere."

"So what do you suggest I do? Sit by the pool and write postcards?"

Eden shrugged.

Shane threw his hat on the ground in frustration and stamped a boot heel into the dirt. "Goddammit, Eden!"

*

The sun was high and scorching hot. Shane lay on a sun lounge by the hotel's glistening aqua rooftop pool, high above the chaos and commotion of the city below. He wore only his cowboy hat tipped back on his head, Ray-bans and a pair of black Speedos. His brown body was beaded with sweat.

In his hands was a pack of cheap postcards. The photos on the front looked as though they had been taken back in the sixties, but with a city like Ankara it was hard to tell.

There was not a soul in sight, which, given his mood, was probably a good thing. Shane was pissed. Eden was on his way to the dig site to try to uncover more clues, Will and Luca were in London looking for the book, and here he was, sitting by a hotel pool staring at a bunch of old postcards.

He started flipping them into the pool, one by one.

They melted into the water and floated just below the surface, turning soft and soggy.

"Not a good look," said a voice from behind Shane.

The Texan dropped the remainder of the postcards, sat bolt upright in the lounge and glanced behind him.

A young man in his early twenties stood there smiling, with a small backpack draped over one shoulder, a towel draped over the other, sunglasses on and a red Speedo. The young man's swimwear was very tightly packed, which didn't go unnoticed by Shane.

He gestured to the postcards in the pool and said to Shane, "That limp, flaccid look is never very encouraging."

"Trust me, they weren't much to look at before they went for a swim either." Shane had noticed the accent. "You're American."

"Eric Landon. From Arizona." The young man took off his sunglasses and shook Shane's hand. His eyes were a rich soothing brown, the same color as his short spiky hair. He had smooth tan skin, a strong body, muscular for his age, and a young handsome face with blinding white teeth. "Pleased to meet someone who's not shouting abuse or driving like a maniac."

Shane smiled back. "Shane Houston. Texas. Likewise."

"I see we have the place all to ourselves. Not a bad pad."

"You're staying here at the hotel?"

"Hell no, I'm backpacking. College students can't afford places like this. We just cruise around looking for pools with no hotel attendants on duty." He looked around and also noticed there was nobody behind the small bar in the corner of the rooftop terrace.

Eric's smile spread further across his handsome face. "Even better, nobody manning the bar!"

He rushed excitedly over, jumped the bar and helped himself to the bar's refrigerator. "You want a beer?"

Shane shrugged. "Hell, why not. It's not like I've got anything better to do. Just leave a note with my room number on it. It's—"

"Hell with that," Eric said with a grin. He uncapped two bottles behind the bar, then jumped it again and pulled up the sun lounge next to Shane. He handed him his beer and they chinked bottles.

"I guess I'll let them know when I check out."

"Whatever." Eric took a good long drink, then said, "So, what brings a big handsome Texan like you to a dustbowl like Ankara?"

Shane took a sip and smiled at Eric's comment. He didn't look down, but he could feel the bulge in his Speedo start to grow. "I'm gonna avoid that question by pointing out, where you and I come from, there's plenty of dustbowls. Hell, they're a specialty of the house."

"Yeah but our dustbowls come complete with diners and drive-in movies and hot half-naked mechanics in sweaty auto-shops on lost lonely highways. Don't you agree?"

Shane felt his cock swell even more, beginning to point vertically into the air. "I do," he said before taking another confident gulp of beer.

Eric glanced happily at Shane's ever-stiffening cock and put his own beer bottle to his lips once again. Then he stood, proudly revealing his own bulging crotch, the outline of his cock's bulbous head so clear it was pointless for him even to wear his Speedo. It was enough to send Shane rock-hard, the head of his own dick straining against his Speedo and pushing itself toward the vast blue sky.

Eric raised one eyebrow. "You need a hand, cowboy?" he asked. Then he turned away and walked to the edge of the pool. There he glanced back, winked and added teasingly, "A hand to clean these postcards out of the pool, I mean."

With that he dove into the sparkling aqua water.

Shane quickly drained the last of his beer then got up, unashamed of his owning throbbing bulge. He stood at the edge of the water as Eric skimmed along the bottom of the pool from one end to the other, the refracting light dancing across his body, a trail of tiny air bubbles fluttering behind him.

Eric broke the surface at the other end and smoothed back his short hair. Without the slightest inhibition, he slipped his Speedo off and tossed it onto the edge of the pool, then climbed up the pool's ladder and strode completely naked past Shane.

His cock stood up hard and thick.

He touched his fingers to his grinning lips as he walked by. "Don't know about you, but I'm thirstier than ever."

Eric strutted his way to the bar and jumped over it again, this time his stiff cock swinging and his perfectly round balls bouncing in motion. He fetched another two beers, opened them and again hurdled the bar.

Shane drank.

Eric watched him, then guzzled his own beer and dove back into the pool. When he surfaced, he looked at Shane and shouted, "So cowboy, you getting naked with me or what?"

Shane drained his beer completely. He peeled off his Speedo and, like a tightly wound coil being released, his large hard cowboy's cock sprang free, swinging straight up and slapping him against the stomach.

He dove into the pool and surfaced in front of Eric, whose fingers plunged straight into Shane's short wet honey-blond hair and pulled him into a hard, deep kiss.

Shane wrapped one hand around the back of Eric's head while his other hand seized a nipple and twisted it firmly between his forefinger and thumb. He enjoyed the force of Eric's tongue pushing its way around the inside of his mouth. He felt Eric's cock, its head large and bulbous, jabbing him in the stomach in the water below. The beer and the sun and the thrill of the moment began to make him light-headed. He pulled away from Eric for a moment.

Eric simply grinned, then took a deep breath and slid beneath the water.

Down below, Shane felt Eric's lips wrap themselves around his throbbing cock.

Shane groaned and let his head roll back, face up to the sun. He closed his eyes, feeling more and more giddy with every passing second, but he was too caught up with pleasure to care.

Beneath the water, Eric took the entire length of Shane's cock in his mouth. Shane could feel the tip of Eric's tongue dance along the base of his shaft. He felt Eric's hands take hold of each ass cheek, then slowly, Eric began to slide his mouth up and down the length of Shane's cock. Small choppy waves formed on the surface of the pool as Eric created currents underneath, moving faster and faster every time he took Shane's cock inside his throat, increasing suction and pressure until Shane groaned again, louder this time.

Suddenly from behind him, he heard a rather startled, "Disgusting!"

Quickly he half-turned, his cock still in Eric's mouth.

Through his now swirling vision, he saw standing on the edge of the pool two plump middle-aged women in one-piece swimsuits, sarongs, and large-brimmed hats. Both stood watching with their mouths agape in horror and contempt, though it didn't stop them from slowly lowering their sunglasses for a better look.

Shane quickly reached down and pulled Eric off his cock.

Eric surfaced, saw the women and started to laugh. "Don't mind us, ladies. I was just demonstrating to Shane how to use a snorkel. The trick is to blow into the mouthpiece nice and hard." He looked at Shane. "It's a shame, really. It would have been fun to go out with a bang." Eric leaned forward and kissed him on the lips, then smiled and said, "How's that beer going down?"

Shane tried to blink away his double vision. His brow suddenly creased, suspicion taking hold. "What did you say?"

Eric didn't answer. He simply grinned, swam to the side of the pool and climbed out. Stark naked, his cock still hard, Eric strolled confidently past the two women, who couldn't take their eyes off him. "Ladies," he winked. Then he scooped up his backpack, wrapped his towel around his waist and swiftly left through the terrace doors.

Shane suddenly held his spinning head. "This ain't good," he mumbled to himself, trying desperately to get himself to the edge of the pool. The water felt like quicksand, his legs struggling to push him through it, his feet slipping on the bottom. One hand finally gripped the edge of the pool. With great effort, he somehow managed to pull himself out of the water, every muscle straining. He rolled naked onto the edge of the pool and clambered to his unsteady feet.

"Look how drunk he is!" one of the women uttered with contempt. "I'm calling the hotel manager!"

"Poison," Shane slurred to himself. "He poisoned the beers." He glanced at the empty beer bottles by the pool, his head rolling wildly on his neck. His weight shifted suddenly to the left, he teetered dangerously close to the side of the pool, then hurriedly he stumbled to the edge of the terrace.

He hit the railing too fast and had to stop himself from toppling over the edge of the building. The city of Ankara in all its chaos and commotion bustled below. It was a mad blur. Shane stopped a second, steadied himself, and tried to focus.

Suddenly on the footpath below he saw Eric emerge from the hotel, now wearing jeans and a white t-shirt and stuffing his towel into his backpack. He stepped up to the curb just as a black BMW pulled up. Eric opened the passenger door, got inside and the car sped off into the busy traffic.

"Shit," Shane mumbled.

He spun around and reeling manically from left to right, he weaved his way quickly across the terrace. The two ladies gasped and he nearly ran straight into them. "Sorry ladies," he mumbled, ever the Texan gentleman, even as the poison turned his head into a washing machine. "My apologies."

But the women squawked and fumbled frantically to get away from him. One of them side-stepped in a panic, lost her footing on the edge of the pool and screamed as she plunged into the water. "Esther!" the other woman wailed. Then, pointing to Shane, she shouted at the top of her lungs, "Help! Somebody stop him. He tried to attack us! Somebody do something!"

But Shane was already gone.

He found the stairwell and stumbled his way down the stairs as fast as he could.

He tried to read the floor numbers at each turn.

He tried to remember which floor his and Eden's room was on.

He found the right door.

He ricocheted off the walls of the corridor.

He found the room.

He reached for a key in his pocket and realized he was still naked. He had nothing. The key was still up by the pool.

His chest tightened. He was having trouble breathing. He gasped for air, stepped away from the door and with all his might he kicked the door in. It burst open. Shane practically fell inside the room.

He dragged himself into the bathroom, looking desperately for something that wasn't there. He staggered out into the bedroom. He dropped to his knees and looked under the bed. He snapped open the closet door and found it empty. "Goddammit Eden, where is it!"

Shane winced as the poison squeezed his lungs and knotted his heart. He could barely see at all now, his vision was so blurred. He felt his consciousness slipping away. Desperately he crawled to Eden's suitcase and threw open the lid. He tossed clothes aside, he rummaged through blindly, and then he found it.

The medi-kit.

He unfastened the clasp.

He emptied the contents on the floor.

Bandages and vials spilled everywhere.

Shane's hands snatched up the largest syringe he could find. He ripped open the cellophane packaging, bit the cap off with his teeth and spat it up. He snatched up vial after vial, squinting as hard as he could to read the labels.

Morphine, cortisone, procraine, benzathine, lignocaine, xylocaine.

Adrenaline.

He stabbed the needle into the vial and drew the clear fluid down into the syringe.

Suddenly his throat tightened and sealed off all oxygen to his lungs. He tried to gasp but was unable to breathe at all. His face turned red, bright red. His throat thickened. His chest felt as though it were about to explode. Tremors shook his entire body. He collapsed onto his back, tiny glass vials breaking beneath his weight, their contents and Shane's blood seeping into the carpet together.

He didn't notice.

He couldn't feel anything anymore.

His eyes began to roll back into his head.

He had one, maybe two seconds of life left to cling to.

He held the syringe high above him, pointed it down toward his chest, and with all the strength he had left in him, he plunged it directly into his own heart and forced every last drop of the adrenaline into his body as fast as he could.

It were as though a million volts of electricity suddenly ran through him, blasting the poison out of his bloodstream, opening up his air passage, freeing his lungs, pulling him back from the brink of death at the last possible moment. His heart pounded in his chest, beating frantically, grabbing at life. With one enormous intake of breath, he sucked in as much oxygen as his lungs could hold.

Then suddenly he sat bolt upright, coughing and gasping and blinking crazily.

He could see again, and the first thing he saw was the syringe still protruding from his chest.

He plucked it out, threw it to the floor. Grabbing a pair of jeans randomly from Eden's bag, he pulled them on, snatched the gun from under his pillow then raced out the door.

Out on the street, car horns blasted and angry Turkish motorists swore and abused each other.

Shane looked down the road in the direction the black BMW had gone. There was no sign of it. He shoved the gun into the back of his jeans, then charged around the corner and down a lane at the end of which was a small market. Women were selling scarves, a small boy was selling nuts and figs, and a man had three lazy-looking camels he was trying to get rid of.

Shane burst out of the lane and quickly looked left and right. At the end of the next block, he saw a traffic jam. Horns were blaring, drivers were screaming at each other, and there in the middle of the gridlock was the black BMW.

Shane glanced around, his mind racing.

He saw the camels.

He grabbed the reins on one and the man selling them immediately began to abuse him in Turkish.

"I'll bring him back, I promise. I just need to borrow him for ten minutes, that's all."

Before the man could stop him, Shane had jumped onto the camel's back, hanging onto its hump with one hand and the reins with the other. "It's gotta be just like ridin' a horse, right?" he muttered to himself.

He snapped the reins.

The camel broke into a wild sprint, almost throwing Shane off.

He held on as tight as he could and tried to steer the beast in the direction of the traffic ahead. At that moment, the cars began moving. The gridlock unlocked itself. The black BMW pulled away, sliding across several lanes of traffic as it picked up speed.

Shane dug his bare heels into the camel. "Yiddy-up!" he ordered the animal in a commanding voice. It was his childhood interpretation of his father's always stern giddy-up! Despite the many times he'd tried to impress his father, to prove he could be the man his father always wanted him to be, yiddy-up was the one thing he'd never managed to outgrow.

Somehow though, it always worked.

The camel picked up speed, a lot of speed.

Shane grabbed the hump with both hands, almost losing his grip on the reins. Somehow he managed to juggle the ropes precariously in his fingers and keep from sliding straight off the back of the hump at the same time. Below him the lanky legs of the camel threw themselves far and wide, churning up the dusty road beneath its hooves.

From his rocky point of view, Shane glanced ahead and saw the black Beemer pull off into a side street on the right, just as Shane and his camel careened into the bustling traffic. They were greeted with not surprise, but anger and a crazed cacophony of car horns. None of it seemed to perturb the camel; he maintained stride and speed, while Shane maintained his efforts to hang on for dear life.

He pulled the reins right.

He aimed the camel at the side street where the BMW had

disappeared.

Just then, a woman in a beat-up old car to his left screamed abuse and spat at him and his camel as they galloped alongside her.

"Do you mind!" Shane shouted, but the camel had already managed a reply of its own by regurgitated up a wad of God-knows-what and projecting it straight through the woman's open window. Yellow sludge slapped against the woman's face, tangling through her hair and sliding down her cheek. She squealed in horror, veered sharply to her left and smashed into the car traveling alongside her.

Not even the sound of metal crumpling and glass smashing distracted the camel. Nor the sound of more horns, and more smashing glass and grinding metal as they left a mounting pile-up in their wake.

Shane glanced back. Drivers and passengers were already leaping out of their broken cars to abuse and scream at one another, including the woman with camel sick on her face. Shane couldn't help but grin. He decided he kind of liked camels.

With that, he got into the swing of the animal's long-legged stride, and rider and beast picked up a rhythm.

Shane got a firm grip on the hump and a firm grip on the reins, and together they turned confidently into the side street, saw the black Beemer ahead, and picked up the pace.

The BMW reached the end of the block and turned left.

Shane kicked his heels into the camel, and it responded, taking the speed of its gallop up yet another notch. They hit the end of the block, and Shane turned the animal left then pulled it up to a halt.

"Whoa there buddy." Up ahead he saw the BMW was about to turn right onto a busy expressway. There was no way he could catch them now, not a camel.

He glanced to his right, quickly sizing up the location. Up ahead he saw a bridge spanning over the expressway. He snapped the reins in that direction.

"Yiddy-up!"

His camel obediently spun right and raced for the bridge.

"Come on, pal," Shane whispered. "We can make this... I think we can make this."

They hit the incline of the bridge and charged upward. Shane glanced left over his shoulder. In the speeding traffic on the expressway below he saw the BMW, weaving between lanes, soon to vanish under the bridge.

Shane snapped his heels again.

The camel pushed itself to the top of the bridge.

Shane caught one last glimpse of the Beemer in the second lane of the expressway, just before it disappeared somewhere beneath him.

"I can do this. I can do this."

He checked the gun was still jammed in the back of his jeans, then steered the camel along the edge of the bridge railing, pulled his feet up onto its hump, and, with one mighty push, let go of the reins and launched himself into the air, diving over the edge of the bridge.

Shane Houston had done stupider things in his life.

When he was six, he thought it would be fun to try to catch a rattlesnake. Luckily the local doctor was only five minutes from his parents' ranch and had spare anti-venom on hand. When he was nine, he thought it would be cool to learn to drive his uncle's Jeep... blindfolded. Luckily, the point of the ravine where he crashed wasn't too deep, and the Jeep had taken the brunt of the fall. And when he was sixteen, he thought having a crush on Mike Hanson, his father's head ranch-hand, was enough reason to try to kiss him. Not so.

As Shane felt himself fly over the railing and saw the speeding cars rushing below him, he wondered whether this was another one of those truly stupid things he sometimes did.

The answer was yes.

Shane shut his eyes.

Then suddenly he felt the clang and buckle of a car roof beneath him.

His hands grabbed desperately, locking onto the sides of the roof. His eyes shot open. And all he could see was red—metallic red.

He had landed on the roof of the wrong car.

It was a tiny red thing, and with the impact of his surprise landing, it suddenly started to veer crazily. He could hear screams from within. He pulled himself forward and peered over the edge of the windscreen. Two old women, upside-down in his vision, screamed hysterically at the sight of him. The car veered even more out of control. Shane held onto the roof as tightly as he could, his legs swiveling left, then right, then left again.

Other cars zoomed past, their drivers and passengers staring at him in amazement.

Then in the lane to his right, the black BMW sped up alongside him.

The passenger window slid down, and Eric looked at Shane with a grin.

He pulled out a gun.

The first bullet ricocheted off the roof of the red car with a sharp clink, a mere inch from Shane's right shoulder. It was followed by the howls and shrieks of the women inside the car. They tilted the wheel left, then right, in utter panic.

Shane could feel the gun still jammed in the back of his jeans, pressing hard against his butt, but he couldn't reach for it. There was no letting go of the roof now.

Chink!

Flakes of red paint flew off the roof of the car, right in front of his nose, as Eric fired a second shot.

Other cars on the expressway veered to get out of the way now. But for some reason, the two old women kept driving, careening uncontrollably from left to right.

"Brake!" Shane shouted. "Stop the car!"

All he could hear below him was a clatter of hysterical Turkish. But there was no stopping.

Eric fired again.

This time the bullet missed the car altogether.

The old women somehow managed to hold the car steady, just for a second.

Long enough for Shane to reach behind him and grab the gun from his jeans.

He held it out over the passenger's window of the car, aiming at the black Beemer, and for a second, he had Eric in his sights.

Then suddenly, an old woman's handbag appeared from the compartment beneath him, swinging violently at his hand.

He heard a deluge of abuse from below, and the handbag pounded his wrist several times until he lost his grip on the gun.

It clattered along the speeding expressway and was gone.

"Holy shit," Shane breathed, watching the gun spin and tumble under the wheels of a truck. "I'm tryin' to save us here!" he screamed through the roof of the car. "You wannna get us all killed?"

As if to answer that question for them, Eric fired another bullet, this time skimming the flesh on Shane's forearm, spraying blood into the air. A fifth bullet slammed into the top of the windscreen, shattering it into a million pieces.

The women squealed again as a million tiny cubes of glass rained over them.

Shane knew if he didn't do something now, the two old women were going to end up dead, not to mention himself!

He grabbed the chance to pull himself forward and swing himself through the shattered windscreen, landing very uncomfortably on the emergency brake, wedged between the two old women.

They screamed again.

Shane glanced right and saw Eric about to fire another shot.

He grabbed the old woman on his right and forced her head down, just as a bullet shattered her window and punctured the headrest inches behind her head.

Before Eric could fire another shot, Shane grabbed the steering wheel and turned it a hard left. Tires squealed on the expressway. Horns blared. Somehow he managed to steer the tiny red car out of the way of the truck that had pulverized his gun, across another two lanes of traffic, and into a side street that miraculously appeared before him.

The little red car with no windscreen careened into the dusty exit, Shane yelling at the top of his voice, "Brake! Brake! Brake!"

The old woman driving the car finally got the message and slammed her foot on the brakes. The car skidded to a halt, and a cloud of dust flooded the compartment.

The old women began spluttering at once, while Shane leapt out through the windscreen, slid across the bonnet and charged back up the side street toward the expressway.

His eyes scanned the fast-moving traffic, but the BMW was long gone. And so was Eric.

"Dammit!" he grunted through clenched teeth.

Behind him he could hear the cluck and howl of the two old women, scrambling out of their shot-up, beat-up, smashed-up car. It wasn't his wounded forearm that made Shane wince right now. It was the sight of two old ladies, storming toward him, fists shaking.

He glanced back to the bridge and saw the camel staring blankly about before the realization of its new-found freedom seemed to dawn on its big-lipped, dopey-eyed face. And with that, it trotted happily out of sight.

"Dammit, dammit!" Shane cursed.

*

A small group of Turkish policemen stood around the entrance to a large tent, smoking and laughing at a shared joke. They had looked sternly, authoritatively at Eden when he first approached, if only to assert some power of him. Once he showed them his credentials, however, they lost interest and more or less shooed him away in the direction of the crime scene.

Work had resumed on the dig site to a certain extent. Small sections of the site were still being excavated, buckets of sand and rubble were being hauled away, small instruments were being used by Turkish archeology students to brush away centuries of secrets.

But one section of the site was completely deserted, sealed off with barricades and police tape.

Eden climbed over the barricades.

He slipped under the tape.

Nobody batted an eyelid; if he had gotten this far, then he must have had clearance to be here.

The sun was high, and he wiped the sweat from his brow as he stepped up to the edge of a deep pit. He peered down inside. The sun shone directly in, illuminating the charred base of what looked like an ancient well. At the bottom of it, white spray paint had been used to outline the position of Doctor Hadley's long since removed body.

At that moment, Eden heard a small sniff somewhere off to his right.

He turned quickly and saw a young boy standing beyond the barricades, watching him.

"Hey kid," Eden said, smiling at the boy. "You okay?"

The boy looked upset.

"Do you speak English?" Eden asked.

The boy did not respond. Eden took a step toward him. The boy took a frightened step back. Eden stopped and held a hand up in some sort of gesture he hoped would stop the boy from running away. "It's alright, I'm not going to hurt you."

The boy's chin crumpled and tears began to well in his eyes. "They hurt Doctor Hadley..." he said in broken English. "They hurt him, and it's my fault."

"What do you mean it's your fault? Do you know the men who—"

But before Eden could finish his words, the boy turned and ran away.

Eden was about to follow him when his cell phone rang. It was Shane. Eden snapped it open. "I gotta call you back. There's a kid here. I think he knows something—"

"Eden, shut up. We gotta go. Right now! They know we're here."

"Are you alright?"

"Let's just say I've had my adrenaline rush for the day. Now get your ass back here. Now!"

X

THE CHALET, THE AUSTRIAN ALPS

The fire crackled back to life as Elsa threw another small log onto the glowing embers. It was late. She had been checking on Jake for most of the night, making sure he was comfortable in his morphine-induced slumber. Now, she sat back in her chair in the living room with her dressing gown wrapped tightly around her and watched the flames dance.

"You're a doting mother hen. Have I ever told you that?"

Elsa jumped in her seat and turned to see Professor Fathom standing in a doorway behind her. "*Mein Himmel*, Professor! You frightened the life out of me! I might've screamed. I could've woken Mr. Stone."

"I'm afraid it's too late for that," the Professor said, gesturing to a doorway that led down a hallway on the opposite side of the room.

Elsa turned and saw Jake emerging from the hallway, the sheet wrapped once more around his waist. He stepped slowly, cautiously, groggily.

Elsa rushed to aid him, supporting him by slipping an arm around his waist.

"You should be in bed," she said firmly, yet with a great deal of concern in her voice.

"Where are my clothes?"

"I said to bed with you."

"No. I wanna get outta here."

He pushed his way out of Elsa's grasp, but once in the living room, he had to steady himself by holding onto the back of a chair.

"Jake," said the Professor, "you need to give yourself time to recover."

"Enough with the bedside manner. What the hell am I doing here?"

The Professor paused a moment, but he knew there was no point beating around the bush. Jake was going to need a little convincing sooner or later. It might as well be now. "I need your assistance."

"If you think I'm gonna help you find whoever it was who killed your friend, I don't do that kind of work. I'm sorry for your loss, but this doesn't involve me."

"I think it does. You just don't realize it yet." Professor Fathom guided himself to one of the chairs in front of the fire and sat down. "This isn't just about the death of a friend," he said. "This is a complex matter. We need to find a treasure that has been lost for centuries. They call it The Naked Christ. Some call it The Cross of Sins. We need to risk everything right now, as did Dr. Hadley, not for money, not for glory, but for the sake of freedom. To keep alive the right to say and do and be whoever we are. It's a right most of us are fortunate enough to be born with. But sometimes that right is taken away. In some places, in some circumstances, who you are is considered criminal. But denying someone the right to be who they are is, in my opinion, one of the greatest crimes of all. I was hoping this wasn't something you would do for yourself, Jake, but rather for the greater good of what it represents."

Jake paused, then said, almost reluctantly, "I'm afraid you hoped wrong, Professor."

The reflection of the flames seemed to dim a little in the Professor's blind eyes. "As a gay man yourself, I'm sorry to hear that. I think the rewards might have been greater than you imagined."

"Hey, my sex life is none of your business. It's my life."

"A life you might not be living right now if Eden hadn't found you in the South Pacific and given you the medical assistance you required."

"You can't tell me you don't have an agenda, old man. You did what suits your needs."

"Those needs are not mine alone."

"Listen, I get paid good money, sometimes by bad people, and I'm fine with that. You wanna save the world, go ahead. You do what makes you feel good about yourself. But if you're asking me to pull out my soft and tender side, sorry. There's no getting that genie out of the lamp, pal."

"What about Sam?"

"What about him?" Jake snapped.

"You keep mentioning his name. You love him like a son, don't you?"

"Leave him out of this. He's just a no-good street kid who knows he's got a roof over his head when he needs it. That's all."

Elsa began to scurry toward the kitchen, suggesting quietly, "Why don't I make us all tea?"

"Don't bother," Jake said. "I'm leaving."

The Professor stood to face the dying embers. "I had hoped for more from you, Jake."

"A lot of people do."

The Professor knew there was no point arguing. "Elsa, please fetch Mr. Stone the keys to Will's motorcycle."

Elsa did as she was asked, disappearing down the hallway to Will's room.

"Don't bother," Jake said. "I'd rather walk."

"It's 40 miles to the nearest town."

Elsa returned with the keys. Jake shook his head. "I'll walk. I wouldn't wanna feel obliged in any way. Like you said, you saved my life. Thanks. Maybe someday I'll return the favor. Till then, let's you and me call it a day."

"Very well," the Professor said. "Eden has a spare set of clothes in his room. He won't mind. Elsa?"

Elsa put the bike keys in her pocket and hurried off to fetch the clothes.

"The road only goes in one direction down the mountain. I wish you well, Mr. Stone. Please... take care of yourself."

Jake nodded, "I will. It's what I do best."

*

The moon had set early, and the night was cold and dark. Jake pulled Eden's thick parka around him and zipped it up tightly. He was walking along the middle of the road that led down the mountain from the Chalet. Crickets chirped, and the odd unseen forest creature scurried through the trees on either side of the road, but apart from that it was silent. Dark and silent. Nothing but the insects and the sound of Eden's boots—which were a little too snug for Jake's large feet—clomping along the road.

But then another sound caught his attention.

It sounded like the distant drone of a car engine.

Jake looked down the road ahead of him. He could see nothing.

He glanced behind him, thinking perhaps Elsa was coming back to retrieve him. But there was nothing there either, nothing but a few dim lights still on up at the chalet. Elsa was probably still awake, no doubt worrying about the Professor. They seemed like good people, Jake thought to himself, there was no denying it. But Jake was a loner. He always had been, always would be.

He turned his attention back to the road in front of him.

That sound, that drone, it was still there. And it was louder now.

Jake squinted at the darkness ahead of him. There were no headlights that he could see. No lights at all.

And yet that sound was unmistakable. It was definitely a car engine. No wait, it was the sound of two engines.

The noise grew louder quickly, still with no visible sign.

Jake decided to get off the road.

He moved swiftly into the forest at the side of the road and crouched low behind a tree, watching.

Suddenly the sound took shape as Jake watched two sinister black cars speed by him, heading up the road, one behind the other, neither of them with their headlights switched on.

The moment they were gone, Jake hurried back out onto the road watching the cars journey up the mountain.

He knew the road led up to the chalet and nowhere else.

He knew immediately that Elsa and the Professor were in danger.

Jake started sprinting as fast as he could, back up the mountain road.

*

Elsa had already decided that with the troubles the Professor was going through there would be no getting to sleep tonight. She was sitting by the fire when she thought she heard a noise outside. It sounded like a branch snap. The Professor had only just retired, and he desperately needed his sleep, and the last thing Elsa wanted to do was disturb him with stories of suspicious noises. Besides, it was probably just a falling branch. It happened a lot out here.

Nevertheless, Elsa got out of her chair, tied her gown tightly around her thick waist and warily approached the window. She peered into the darkness but saw nothing.

That's when she heard a different noise, something much more alarming—the sound of somebody trying to break the lock on the door downstairs.

Elsa was in the Professor's bedroom within seconds, shaking him awake.

"Professor!" she whispered urgently. "Someone's trying to break into the—"

At that moment she heard the pang and smash of a window breaking somewhere in the house.

The Professor sat bolt upright.

Elsa was already rummaging desperately through the drawers of his bedside table. "Where's your gun?" she asked frantically.

"You know I don't believe in keeping guns in the house!"

"When someone's trying to break in and kill us, I do! And thank goodness, so do the boys!"

She grabbed the Professor's hand and yanked him out of bed.

Together, they hurried silently down the hallway and into Shane's room where Elsa closed the door behind them. She hauled open the drawers of his dresser and instantly found a pistol wrapped up in a pair of jeans.

At that moment, they both heard footsteps in the hallway.

Elsa grabbed the Professor's hand, glanced around, then quickly and quietly packed them both into Shane's closet, pressing hard up against his jeans, jackets and cowboy shirts.

She shut the closet doors soundlessly and pointed the gun at the closed closet doors in anticipation, both of them holding their breath.

In the next few moments, the Professor counted not one, not two, but three pairs of feet treading as quietly as possible around Shane's room.

A fourth person entered the room.

Elsa and the Professor heard a hushed voice. "He's not in his room."

"Shhhh!" came the harsh reply, frighteningly close to the other side of the closet door.

Elsa's eyes bugged in terror.

She held the gun tightly in both hands, her finger pushing as hard against the trigger as she could manage without squeezing it.

Slowly, the door handle to the closet began to turn.

Elsa raised the gun higher.

The door handle turned as far as it would go.

Elsa shut her eyes tight.

The latch on the door clicked open.

Elsa pulled the trigger.

There was a loud clack!

But no gunshot.

No bullets.

Just the hollow clack of a trigger being pulled on an unloaded gun.

Elsa opened her eyes in horror.

At the same time, the doors flew open.

Four men in black robes stood facing them, all with guns. The man directly in front of them had a merciless, toothless grin and only one arm.

He laughed.

Elsa screamed, and before any thoughts of consequences had time to cross her mind, she raised her knee as hard and as fast as she possibly could and launched the one-armed man's balls straight up into his chest.

The man's laughter slid quickly up into a shrill squeal. He dropped to his knees, clutching his groin, at which point Elsa threw her empty gun at him as hard as she could. It conked him on the head and knocked him clean unconscious.

Elsa pulled the closet doors shut, grabbed the Professor and pulled him down to the floor of the closet just as the other three black-robed men opened fire.

Bullets shredded the closet doors above their heads as Elsa rummaged frantically for something—anything—on the floor of the closet that might protect them.

There were boots.

Stirrups.

Hats.

A belt.

A holster on the belt.

A gun in the holster.

Bullets in the gun!

As shards of splintered wood rained down upon them, Elsa opened fire, shooting bullets randomly through the closed doors until there were no more bullets left in the gun, and the sound of gunfire ceased completely, both from within the closet —and the room outside.

In the sudden silence, Elsa and the Professor both took a deep breath—the first in what seemed like minutes—and slowly, Elsa pushed open the doors.

To her utter astonishment, the three remaining assailants lay on the ground, dead, blood oozing from beneath their robes.

"Oh Elsa," whispered the Professor sensing the carnage. "What have you done?"

"Oh pssh-pssh! No time for lectures, Professor. We have to get out of here now!"

"Not without the stone tablet," he said.

Elsa clambered out of the closet then helped the Professor out.

Stepping carefully over the unconscious one-armed man and rushing from the room, Elsa and the Professor raced into the living room where Elsa grabbed the stone tablet, wrapped it in its cloth and slid it snugly inside her dressing gown pocket.

Then she took the Professor by the hand, turned for the door and gasped.

There in the doorway, leaning to one side with obvious pain and angry determination on his face, was the one-armed man.

Elsa fired at him in vain, forgetting her gun was empty.

The one-armed man spluttered out a pained laugh and raised his own pistol.

Elsa and the Professor took a fearful step back with nowhere to go.

The one-armed man began to squeeze the trigger, when suddenly there came from behind him—

"Hey! Why don't you pick on someone your own size?"

With a sudden scowl on his face, the one-armed man spun around, just in time for Jake's boot to collect him across the face.

There was a grunt and the man staggered backward, dazed.

He blinked fiercely, tasting blood, then managed to raise his gun again.

Jake threw another high kick, this time snapping the gun clean out of the one-armed man's hand.

The weapon flew across the room and landed directly in the fireplace. Like a swarm of hungry ants, the scorching red embers lapped the pistol up instantly, turning the edges of the metal a luminous yellow before the gun literally exploded, sending bullets, sparks and tiny ember fireballs across the room.

Elsa screamed, and she and the Professor ducked just as a fireball shot over their heads and slammed against the curtain.

Flames engulfed the curtain with a ferocious appetite, then spread rapidly up to the ceiling.

Jake looked up and saw the flames. "No, no, no," he whispered to himself, shaking his head as the ceiling fully ignited. Just then, the one-armed man's fist smashed into Jake's jaw.

He reeled backward a step or two, regained his balance then retaliated with an upper-cut straight to his opponent's chin.

"Elsa, get the Professor outta here now!"

"We're not leaving without you," the Professor shouted over the roar and crackle of the flames, which were now climbing down all four walls from the burning ceiling.

"If you don't go now, none of us will be leaving here at all. Now do as I—"

Jake took another blow to the jaw before he could finish his sentence. He stumbled and fell into a chair.

Fiery chunks of ceiling began to fall and set fire to the floor. With a loud groan, a beam crashed to the ground, narrowly missing the Professor, whom Elsa pulled out of the way.

"Go!" Jake shouted at them.

Elsa didn't need to be told again. She seized the Professor's hand, and guiding him through the spot fires that had started all over the living room, she hurriedly led him down the stairs.

Another burning beam fell from the ceiling and shattered. The one-armed man seized the shaft of broken wood, burning at one end and suddenly charged at Jake in the chair.

Jake sprang from the seat just as the burning shaft rammed into the chair, at the same time swinging another punch at his opponent's face, then a kick to his stomach. But the one-armed man responded by pounding Jake in the chest with the flaming beam.

The force of the blow knocked Jake flat on his back.

He heard a loud crack and looked up from the floor.

Directly above him, a huge part of the burning ceiling was about to give way.

Jake looked at the one-armed man. He was so focused on finishing Jake off that he hadn't noticed the ceiling about to collapse on them both. Instead, he loomed over Jake, laughing and raising his flaming beam high above his head.

Jake pulled himself up onto his elbows, poised, ready spring at precisely the right moment.

He watched the one-armed man's beam rise even higher over his head.

He watched the glowing cracks in the ceiling splinter and spread, cutting a jagged line like a crack in an iceberg that made its way almost all the way around the ceiling.

The one-armed man chuckled, still oblivious to the roof about to fall and announced to Jake in a thick cockney accent, "Time to die."

"You took the words right out of my mouth."

The one-armed man looked at him, suddenly puzzled.

Above them, the slab of ceiling gave a loud groan and a shudder, and tiny droplets of fire showered down upon them.

The one-armed man gasped and shook off the sizzling cinders before glancing up in alarm.

Jake seized his moment and sprang clear, landing on his feet and leaping for the stairs.

Before the one-armed could do so much as move an inch, the ceiling gave way and smashed down upon him in a fiery blaze.

The force of the crash threw Jake down the stairs. He rolled and tumbled and spilled onto the floor, bruised and charred but otherwise intact. He collected himself quickly, bolted for the door and raced out into the cold night to the sound of a motorcycle engine roaring to life.

He glanced over his shoulder and saw Elsa at the handlebars of Will's Ducati. The Professor sat behind her, holding on tight. She twisted the throttle, then proceeded to jerk and jolt forward before braking fiercely beside Jake. "Get on!"

"Are you crazy?" Jake asked.

"Apparently so," the Professor said.

Elsa glared at both of them and said, "All the other keys are in there. Do you two have any better ideas?"

"Then let me drive," Jake said hurriedly.

Elsa shook her head and gestured over his shoulder. "No time!"

Jake turned and saw, to his shock and amazement, the one-armed man staggering from the door of the burning chalet toward one of the black cars now parked near the dark of the woods. He was badly burned and his robe was torn and smoldering, yet he still managed to open the car door and grab for a spare gun. He aimed it straight at Jake and let slip that evil, spluttering laugh.

Elsa revved the bike.

The one-armed man fired.

The bullet missed Jake by a fraction and ricocheted off a nearby tree.

"Get on!" Elsa screamed.

Without hesitation, Jake jumped on the back of the bike behind the Professor, and Elsa twisted the throttle and let go of the brakes.

The front wheel left the ground, and all three of them nearly slid straight off, but Jake clung to the Professor, and the Professor clung to Elsa, and Elsa clung to the handlebars as tight as she could. As the front wheel bounced back onto the ground, Elsa veered and swerved recklessly down the road, haphazardly trying to avoid the spray of bullets that clipped the back license plate and fractured both side mirrors.

Jake stole a glance behind them to see the one-armed man climb behind the wheel of the car. Fire up the engine. Turn the headlights to high beam.

"Jesus," Jake muttered to himself, "This guy just won't give up!"

He turned back and shouted to Elsa, "We got company!"

Elsa glanced in one of the broken side mirrors and saw the bright headlights of a car behind them, approaching fast.

"What do I do?" Elsa asked, panicked.

Jake called back over the roar of the engine. "Open out the throttle, all the way!"

"I'll kill us all!"

She was right, and Jake knew it. The Ducati was a powerful beast. It wasn't the kind of bike for a novice, let alone a novice with two other passengers on the back and a crazed gunman on their heels.

Jake glanced back again.

The car was gaining on them—fast.

They had only one option.

"Go into the forest!" he shouted,

"The forest?" Elsa shrieked.

"Trust me!"

Elsa did.

With a deep breath, she turned the handlebars and steered the bike straight into the woods. The Ducati plunged into the darkness, its headlight bouncing wildly off the oncoming trees.

Elsa turned left, right, left again.

The bike bounced and rocked. It charged up a small embankment, became airborne for several seconds, then hit the ground again.

"Elsa! Keep it steady!"

"Steady!?!" Elsa screamed back to Jake. "This thing has a mind of its own! It's steering itself!"

If that were indeed true, it was entirely the fault of the Ducati that it steered itself straight into a giant mossy log.

The headlight smashed, the front wheel buckled, and the whole bike instantly crumpled, throwing Elsa, the Professor and Jake clear over the log and crashing into a thicket of ferns and shrubs.

Jake was up on his feet almost the second he landed.

"Professor! Elsa! You okay?"

He scrambled through the darkness, found the Professor and helped him sit up.

"Are you hurt?"

"No, I think I'm okay. Where's Elsa?"

"Elsa!" Jake called.

Somewhere deep in the thicket, Jake and the Professor heard a long, pained groan.

"Elsa!" Jake hurried in the direction of the sound and found Elsa staggering out of a prickly nest of twisted branches.

"I think I've broken my hinterteile!"

"I don't even know what that is."

"You don't want to know."

"Can you walk?" Jake asked, concerned.

"Yes," she said. "I think so."

Jake looked through the trees, and in the distance he half-glimpsed the headlights of the one-armed man's car pulling up on the side of the mountain road. "Good," he said, "because we gotta keep movin'. Now."

He gathered up Elsa and the Professor, and together, the three of them limped and scurried into the pitch-black forest.

*

The sun rose over the mountain and broke through the trees. At some point during the night, Jake felt confident that the one-armed man had given up his search through the dark woods. With daylight, came the reassurance that their assailant was nowhere to be seen.

At the foot of the mountain the trees gave way to a clearing and beyond that a beautiful field.

The Professor picked up a scent. "I smell eggs. And coffee."

"There's a farmhouse," Jake said.

They walked through the long grass, and Elsa looked back up the mountain. She saw a tendril of smoke rising from the top of the distant trees and realized the chalet was gone.

"We've lost it all," she whispered.

The Professor heard her, and held out his hand. "We can rebuild it."

"It won't be the same," she shook her head.

The Professor smiled. "Of course not. Every day is different. Every day is a new adventure."

When they arrived at the farmhouse, Elsa knocked on the door. A little old man with a gray beard beamed at her with surprise and gave her a hug. They spoke to each other in German. The little man looked stunned and saddened when Elsa pointed to the smoke at the top of the mountain.

"Do you know him?" Jake asked the Professor.

"He's a neighbor," the Professor said with a nod. "Some years ago, his donkey fell very ill. I called Eden and he saved the donkey's life. You do these things because you want to, not because you expect a favor in return."

"You think he'll do us a favor now?"

"No," the Professor smiled. "He'll do what he wants to do."

Elsa mentioned Vienna and then the word auto.

The little man grinned and nodded emphatically and quickly led her, the Professor and Jake to a dilapidated barn. He pulled open the doors and disappeared inside.

Elsa, Jake and the Professor jumped when they heard a sound like a gunshot from inside the barn. It was followed by the rattle and splutter of an old engine. The three of them stood back as a tiny, ancient Fiat chugged out of the barn with the little old man grinning behind the steering wheel.

He got out and said something to Elsa, who turned to Jake and the Professor. "He wants us to have it with his blessing."

"We're gonna need more than a blessing to get us to Vienna in that," Jake muttered.

The Professor smiled graciously to the little old man. "*Vielen dank fur die freundlichkeit.*"

The little old man smiled and said in a thick German accent, "Anything for my neighbors."

The Professor turned to Jake. "So does this mean you're coming to Vienna with us, Mr. Stone? Or would you still rather walk to the nearest town?"

Jake sighed reluctantly. "I'll come to Vienna, but that's as far as I go. After that, you're on your own."

"We'll never be on our own," the Professor smiled. "But if that's what you wish for yourself, then I'll just have to respect that."

XI

VIENNA, AUSTRIA

The journey from London to Vienna was a long and trying one for Will Hunter, not just because Elliott Ebus had a fear of flying and refused to board a plane, but because Elliott Ebus was afraid of just about everything.

When the two of them had been thrown off the tour bus—for no particular reason other than the fact that Will was wearing nothing but a bath towel—Elliott worriedly muttered, "My goodness, what ever will those people think of us!"

When Will dragged him quickly through Liberty's department store in search of clothes, through the scarf hall where dozens of female shoppers blushed and gawked and gasped, Elliott stammered, "Good Lord, d-d-do you think they'll have us a-a-a-arrested?"

When they reached Victoria Station and booked two Eurostar train tickets to Vienna via Paris and Munich, Elliott said rather urgently, "I'm afraid I need to find a lavatory. All this stress makes me rather —"

"I don't need to hear it," Will said, scanning the station for potential assailants. He saw a sign pointing to the restrooms. "Come on, let's go."

He pulled Elliott towards the toilets, but Elliott resisted. "You're not coming with me, are you?"

"You bet."

"But you're... I mean, back in the hotel room... With the other gentleman... You both looked like..."

Will could not deny a hint of amusement buried somewhere beneath his frustration. "Luca and I looked like what? Like we just had our way with each other? That's pretty perceptive, Lord Fuddy-Duddy. Now do you need to take a piss or not?"

"Yes, but I'd rather go alone, thank you very much."

"If you think because I'm gay I'm gonna make a pass at you in the toilet, tempting as it sounds, you're really not my type."

"All the same, I'd feel more comfortable if—"

"Listen," Will said, grabbing Elliott's jacket collar with one fist and pulling him near. "I don't know anything about you. I don't know why you had that book. I don't know what's in it. And I sure as hell don't know where your friends in the black robes are right now. But what I do know is, between here and Vienna, you're not leaving my sight for one second. Do you get that?"

A stunned Elliott Ebus stared up into Will's face, unable to talk. Suddenly a woman walking by noticed the frightened look on Elliott's face and asked him with concern, "Is this man hurting you?"

Will glanced at her, then back at Elliott's intimidated face, then quickly planted a big passionate kiss on him.

Whether he was still stunned, or whether he harbored deeper secrets, Elliott didn't struggle.

Will pulled out of the kiss and with a smile turned to the woman and said, "Lover's tiff. We're fine."

Embarrassed, the woman apologized and scurried away.

Will turned back to an even more stunned Elliott and couldn't help but grin. "Admit it, you loved it."

Elliott Ebus didn't say another word until they pulled into Westbahnhof Station in Vienna.

The Royal Hotel was located between the Danube and Stephensdom, Vienna's thirteenth century Gothic cathedral. At the front desk of the hotel, Will asked for Dr. Ivan Jastrow. No matter where in the world he stayed, the Professor always used the name Ivan Jastrow.

Within minutes, the elevator doors in the hotel lobby opened and Luca poured out. He saw Will and Elliott and gave Will a hug so hard it almost knocked the air out of him.

"It's good to see you," Luca said, kissing him hard on both cheeks.

"You, too," Will said. He stepped back and sized up Luca's clothes with a smirk on his face. The young Italian was wearing an oversized Hawaiian shirt and bright purple pants. "Nice threads."

"I stole a suitcase off a baggage cart at Heathrow. I didn't get very far in the towel."

Will raised his eyebrows, amused and intrigued.

Luca shook his head. "It's a long story. I'll tell you about it some other time." Luca's face took on a serious expression. "Will, the chalet's been destroyed. Burned to the ground."

"The Professor? Elsa?"

"They're fine. Luckily Jake was there to help out. Come on." Luca gestured to the elevator. "Everyone's here waiting for you."

The large suite was dark, and Elliott Ebus was almost too scared to enter. Will and Luca guided him inside, using more than a gentle shove.

"It's alright, Mr. Ebus." The Professor's calm and collected voice came out of the darkness before he did. When he appeared, he smiled and held his hand out. "Forgive the drawn curtains, but I'm sure you understand."

Elliott shook the Professor's hand in a rather limp fashion. "Who are you people?" he asked both suspiciously and fearfully. As his eyes adjusted to the darkness, he saw they were in a large drawing room, and there were several people here: Will and Luca were behind him; Eden was standing behind the Professor; Shane was standing behind Eden; Elsa was sitting on a sofa; and Jake was standing beside a closed curtain, occasionally opening it a quarter of an inch to check for any sign of trouble or concern outside. "I could call the police, you know," Elliott said, his feeble threat sounding more like a complaint. "I could tell them I've been kidnapped."

"You can if you like, but I don't think you'll be doing yourself any favors. My name is Professor Fathom. This is Eden Santiago, Shane Houston, Jake Stone, and my housekeeper Elsa. I believe you've already met Luca and Will."

"I want to know what I'm doing here! I already gave you the book. What else do you want with me?"

"Nothing," the Professor said. "But the same can't be said for the people who followed you to Will and Luca's hotel room. Do you have any idea who they might have been?"

Elliott shook his head unconvincingly.

"Have you read the book, Mr. Ebus?"

"No. Yes. But I didn't understand any of it."

"Do you know its history?"

Elliott shook his head. "I was offered a lot of money to keep it a secret, by a man I didn't know. I've never seen him since. I don't want to. That's all I know."

"Then I suggest we keep it that way," the Professor said. "You're safest not knowing anything else, and you're safest here with us. It's my recommendation, Mr. Ebus, that you remain with us until all of this is over. Would you agree?"

Elliott didn't look happy about it, nor did he protest.

The Professor took his silence as consent.

"Very good. Perhaps you'd like a rest, you seem tired. Elsa, would you please show Mr. Ebus to one of the rooms, while the boys and I adjourn to the sitting room?"

Elsa nodded and began to guide Elliott down the short hallway of the suite. The Professor touched her arm as she passed. "Please let me know if he has trouble sleeping."

"*Ja*, Professor."

Once Elliott was safely tucked away, the Professor opened the doors to the sitting room and led the boys inside. It was like entering a mini-makeshift version of a NASA control room. Computers were set up everywhere, their screens filled with satellite maps and digital data, all busily blipping and bleeping and rendering information.

"Where the hell did you get all this?" Will asked. "I thought the chalet—"

"This is home now," the Professor said before Will could finish. "At least for the time being. Fortunately, I have friends here in Vienna."

"Evidently they're very well-connected friends," Will said, inspecting the computer screens more closely.

"Don't touch anything, Will. Do you know how long it takes a blind man to set up a global scanning system and government file decoder in his hotel room?"

"I guess that means the cable TV reception's pretty good in these parts."

"Not anymore," the Professor said, taking a seat in front of the computers. His fingers began to glide over the Braille keyboard. "Now pay attention, all of you." Instinctively he added, "Will, that includes you."

Will was already toying with things, namely a small metal device that looked a lot like a tiepin. "What is this, anyway?"

The Professor took it off him to ascertain what it was, then placed it on the desk out of Will's reach. "It's a tracking device. And if you play with it, you'll end up breaking it."

"What's it for?"

"In case we need it. Although rest assured I won't be giving it to you; if ever I need to find you all I have to do is look for trouble. Now listen up. The book is a code. Each symbol in it has a meaning. Since Luca arrived with the book, we've tried to transcribe all the symbols and their corresponding meanings, but so far the message on the first half of the stone doesn't make complete sense."

"All we can make out are the words home, fire, damnation, seek, and cave," said Eden. "We're hoping that once we join the two halves of the stone together, the symbols will make more sense."

"What about the Crimson Crown?" asked Shane. "What if they've already got the second tablet?"

"They don't," replied the Professor.

"But we don't even know who they are," said Will.

"We know a little more now," replied the Professor. His fingers felt their way to another Braille keyboard, and he began logging into files and databases. "I've managed to piece together as much information as I can on the Crimson Crown, and from what I've learned, there are three leaders: the Holy Father, the Holy Son and the Holy Ghost. I can't find any information at all on the Holy Father. He's something of an enigma, I'm afraid. But we now know the identities of the other two."

He entered a password into the computer, and a police profile of Eric Landon appeared on a screen to his left.

"This is Eric Landon, otherwise known as the Holy Son..."

Shane shook his head. "Son-of-a-bitch. I wish I had've known that two days ago."

"So you've already made his acquaintance?" the Professor asked.

"That's one way to put it," Shane answered.

"He comes from a fanatically religious family in Arizona and discovered a small faction of the Crimson Crown operating within his college campus. It wasn't long before he dedicated himself to the cause and quickly rose through the ranks."

"He quickly rose for me, too," Shane said. "He didn't seem like the religious type to me, Professor."

"Trust me, these men will do anything. Religion is a powerful thing."

"So is denial," Shane added. "Unfortunately, he's still out there."

"As is this person," the Professor said, entering in a second password. A police file appeared on a screen to his right and a mug shot of the one-armed man appeared. "Meet Dominic Dixon, otherwise known as the Holy Ghost. He discovered the Crimson Crown on the internet while serving ten years in a London prison for armed robbery, assault with a deadly weapon and raping three women. He lost his arm after it was crushed in machinery at the prison workshop. One of the guards maintained it wasn't an accident, that Dixon did it to himself on purpose, to cleanse his soul. Nevertheless, Dominic Dixon was granted early parole on medical grounds. With only one arm and his newfound faith, the board believed he was no longer a threat to society. Elsa and I would argue otherwise. We had a close encounter of our own up at the chalet. Thankfully, Jake was there to lend us a helping hand."

"Not for much longer," Jake added from behind them all. "Now that you're all one big happy family again, I'm outta here."

Jake turned for the door.

"Don't you want to find the second half of the stone?" the Professor asked. "Aren't you in the least bit curious?"

"Like you said to the other guy, the less I know, the better. I got enough people tryin' to kill me on a day-to-day basis."

"What if I told you I know the exact whereabouts of the second tablet? It's in the safest place on earth—under the nose of a man who has no idea what it is."

"I'm still not interested," Jake said, reaching for the door handle. "There's already too many stupid people on the planet. If one of them has the stone tablet and doesn't know it, I don't care."

The Professor smiled. "What if this particular stupid person was a collector by the name of Pierre Perron."

Jake froze.

The Professor informed the rest of the room, "Mr. Stone and Monsieur Perron share, shall we say, a rather unique history."

"The bastard tried to kill me." Jake turned, his hand not leaving the door handle, his eyes narrowing with suspicion. "So that's why I'm here. To get to Perron."

The Professor nodded then turned to Jake. "You once accused me of having an agenda, and you were right. I'd be lying if I hadn't already taken your relationship with Monsieur Perron into account. And so yes, we saved your life for what I believed to be a very good reason. But now you've saved ours in return. If you believe that makes us even, if you believe you no longer have any reason to stay, then go."

Jake hesitated a moment, the door handle still in his grip. He didn't let it go, not just yet, but asked the Professor, "How long have you known about the second half of the stone being in Perron's possession?"

"Over seven years. But there was never any point revealing its whereabouts until the first piece of the puzzle was uncovered. By keeping it a secret, I've managed to keep it hidden from the Crimson Crown. It's what keeps us one step ahead—for now."

"But if he's a collector, how can he not know?" Luca asked.

"Because he's an arrogant, fat, egotistical, pompous, rich idiot!" Jake answered in no uncertain terms. "He collects priceless relics and ancient artifacts for no reason other than he can. He's wealthy, and he's obsessed with his money and with his ability to accumulate irreplaceable treasures. But he has no idea of their history or importance. His motivation is simple—if somebody else might want it, then he must have it. No matter what." Jake let go of the door handle and lifted his shirt, showing them all the slowly healing wound in his side. "He doesn't care who gets in the way."

"How do you know him?" Will asked.

"Jake has been contracted by Monsieur Perron several times in the past," explained the Professor.

"For money, not love," Jake assured them all. "And I know what you're all thinking. If he's got the addiction, I'm supplying the goods. But some of us didn't grow up as rich idiots. We just grew up idiots. Well, for what it's worth, the contract between me and Perron is now well and truly terminated."

The Professor smiled. "Not quite yet—unless of course, you're still certain about walking out that door."

Jake glanced back at the door handle, then to Eden, Will, Luca, Shane, and finally the Professor. He couldn't help himself. "Where is it?" he asked reluctantly.

"In his mansion in Venice, on the Grand Canal. The Palazzo di Perron. It's his own personal museum."

"That place is like a fortress," Jake said. "How the hell am I supposed to get inside that?"

The Professor continued to smile and shook his head. "Jake, when you're with us, you're not an I. You're part of a we. And you're not the only one with a foot inside Perron's door. As it turns out, Eden knows Perron's nephew—quite well."

"I do?" Eden asked, just as surprised as everyone else in the room.

"Yes," the Professor told them all. "Jacques Dumas."

"How the hell do you know a family like that?" Jake asked Eden.

"Jacques is a marine biologist. We spent three months together in the Galapagos studying the eco-structure of the islands. Jacques never spoke to me of an uncle. And I can assure you, he's not arrogant or fat or egotistical or pompous or rich. And he's certainly not an idiot. We became very—close."

Will grinned and slapped Eden on the back. "Sounds like your idea of work is my idea of fun. Way to go, Doc!"

The Professor smirked, reached into a drawer, and pulled out five first-class train tickets to Venice. "Speaking of fun," he said, "it appears the five of you are about to have an absolute ball."

XII

VENICE, ITALY

The Palazzo of Monsieur Pierre Perron was situated along the Grand Canal of Venice, between the famed Palazzo Grassi and the Ponte del' Academia. It was an impressive structure, three stories high with no fewer than twenty-four rooms, including a ballroom and its own gallery wing. It went without saying that Perron's Annual Masquerade Ball was one of the great social events of the Venetian calendar. Monsieur Perron spared no expense in showcasing his priceless treasures and his glittering mansion on the banks of the canal. His 900 guests, dressed in the gowns and garments of Italy's very best designers—and each wearing a mask of gold, diamonds or silk—enjoyed Europe's finest champagne, Russia's most succulent caviar, France's sweetest black truffles, Canada's most delicate smoked salmon, and Tahiti's juiciest mango slices. There were rock stars and royalty, models and media moguls, pop divas and pop artists. Everyone and anyone with any amount of wealth or celebrity was invited. Guests arrived by speedboats or gondolas shrouded with satin veils and lit with traditional Venetian lanterns. They docked at the palazzo's canal landing one-by-one and ascended the stone steps—dressed in exotic gowns and long flowing capes, their faces concealed behind masks of every color and description—to the grand palazzo entrance where they milled about, guessing who was who behind those beautiful, amusing, and sometimes grotesque masks.

"This goddamn shirt is choking me to death!" Jake growled through clenched teeth, twisting a finger between his neck and the collar of his shirt. He started to attack his bowtie, but Eden and Will both wrestled his hands away. They were all in a Riviera Classic RC speedboat with Luca driving, steering the boat wide of the many Saturday night gondolas meandering down the Grand Canal.

All of them wore black tuxedoes.

Shane had on a white horse mask.

Eden had on a silver crescent-moon mask.

Jake wore the face of a golden lion.

Luca had on a burning blood-red sun.

Will wore the mask of a mischievous monkey.

"Take it easy!" Will chuckled now, pulling Jake's meddlesome fingers from his shirt collar. "For a tough New Yorker, it doesn't take much to get you unstuck, does it?"

"Don't push me, kid!"

"You won't be wearing it for long," Eden assured him. "We get in, get the stone tablet, and get out."

"You're making it sound very easy," Jake warned.

"The plan's all set," Eden reminded him. "You distract Perron. I track down Jacques and find out which room the tablet is in. Shane and Will take care of security, while Luca stays near the boat, just in case."

"In case this shirt strangles me to death!"

"No, in case we need a fast getaway," Eden replied.

"Which I assure you we will," Jake answered back. "Perron's that kinda guy. The kind you wanna get away from real fast, as soon as you can, when things go wrong."

"There it is." Luca veered the Riviera toward a massive stone mansion lit with torches, with dozens of boats, large and small, docking at its canal entrance and unloading party guests adorned in satin gowns, dinner suits and masks.

Luca pulled the boat up to the entrance and secured it to a pontoon before the five of them stepped off the Riviera and walked up the steps of the canal landing. The palatial stone residence had been transformed into a medieval Italian fortress for the party. The vestibule landing was an open air courtyard looking over the canal, interspersed with thick Doric columns and lit by a multitude of low hanging cast iron chandeliers, each burning brightly with the glow of three dozen candles melting slowly into ornate drip trays directly beneath them. The courtyard itself was filled with music and people and food and drink.

A waiter appeared and offered the five of them champagne in tall thin flutes.

Will, Luca and Shane each took a glass. Eden took two and handed one to Jake. "How's your shirt?"

"It's tryin' to kill me, but I'll survive."

Eden smiled. "You're an intriguing man, Jake Stone."

"What the hell does that mean?"

"You can venture into a volcano about to erupt, but you can't handle a simple button. You're quite a complex creature."

"On the contrary, I'm as simple as they get."

Eden shook his head. "I don't think so. In the meantime, I need to try to find Jacques."

"I'll track down Perron," said Jake.

"Come on," Shane said, tugging at Will's jacket. "You and I are on security duty." He glanced up at the walls of the Palazzo. "Cameras everywhere. The security room should be this way."

Will turned to Luca. "You okay here?"

Luca nodded and asked Eden, "You have the stone?"

Eden patted his jacket, indicating the stone was tucked safely in the inside pocket. "And you have the book?" he asked Luca.

Luca patted his own jacket. "Safe and sound," he said.

Although the boys had argued that the stone and the book stay in the Professor's possession in Vienna, the Professor himself had insisted that the items go with the boys. If they found the second stone, they could decipher the code quicker if they had all the pieces in the one place.

Luca winked at the others now. "I'll have the motor running as soon as you guys have outstayed your welcome."

With that, Eden, Jake, Will and Shane disappeared among the party guests.

Eden meandered past women dripping with jewels and men

dressed in the finest Mediterranean haute couture. He walked slowly, looking not for a face because everyone's face was concealed behind a mask. No, Eden was looking for more telling features—features he once knew very, very well: the shape of a young man who would've now been twenty-six, if Eden remembered his birthday correctly; he looked for shoulders that were broad from swimming and diving; an ass that was solid and strong, able to kick his legs and propel him through the water, sometimes with ease, sometimes to escape a predator twice his size; and hands that were strong and tough, the hands of a man who had spent most of his life in the water, unafraid of sharp coral reefs and tropical fish with razor-sharp fins.

But apparently, Eden's own features were just as identifiable.

"Eden?" he heard a voice from behind him. "Eden Santiago?"

He turned, and there behind a sapphire-blue dolphin mask, was a man he could not mistake anywhere. "Jacques Dumas," Eden smiled.

The two men rushed forward and hugged each other warmly, firmly. "God, I've missed you!" Jacques breathed in his melodic French accent. "What the hell are you doing here?"

Eden tried to speak, but the words stalled in his mouth. He had a lie all worked out—that he was here with an old biology professor who was on a lecture tour through Europe—but even with the mask on, when it came to telling Jacques a lie, Eden couldn't do it. In the time they had spent together on the Galapagos Islands, not a single false word or emotion had passed between them. Eden suddenly decided he wasn't about to ruin that now.

"Circumstances," he offered vaguely.

"Do you know my uncle?" Jacques asked.

"No." Eden finished his glass of champagne in one gulp. "You never even told me you had an uncle."

"That's because he's not really worth talking about," Jacques said. "My God, how long has it been? It's been too long. I wrote you, you know. Did you get my letters?"

Eden nodded. "Every one of them."

"But you never replied. You're busy, I know. We've got a lot to catch up on. What do you say we start right now? I spent summers here as a kid. I know a quiet corner of this mansion that nobody knows about."

At that moment, a waiter swung by, and Jacques not only took two glasses of French champagne, he grabbed a whole bottle as well. "Come on, what do you say I steal you away and you and I catch up. I want to know what you've been doing. I want to hear it all. God, I've missed you so much!"

Jacques' passion, his beautiful smile, the genuine joy that radiated from him, made Eden remember why he had fallen so in love with this man in the first place, all those years ago. He wondered why he had let such a love slip away. Was it work? Was it complacency? Or was it—circumstances?

*

Jake ventured inside the palazzo where hundreds more party guests mingled, drank and spoke in dozens of different languages. He sidestepped into a group of beautiful women laughing at a joke someone just told.

"Excuse me," Jake said, awkwardly stamping out their laughter. The women didn't mind. They could tell immediately from his New York accent, from the shape of his jaw, from the tussled black hair, that behind the lion's mask was a handsome American. They smiled.

"Ciao," purred a girl in a Cleopatra mask.

"Hi there. I'm looking for Monsieur Perron. Have you seen him?"

The girls giggled, then Cleopatra said, "Non parlo Inglese."

Jake knew what this meant, and, concentrating as hard as he could, managed to say, "Sto cercando il Signor Perron."

To this, the girls laughed even louder.

"Your accent is terrible," Cleopatra smiled. "But you're very cute. Perhaps after you see Pierre, you'll come back and join us for a drink?"

"Perhaps," Jake lied.

Cleopatra ran a long slender finger down his jaw line. "Pierre's in his study. Upstairs. I think he's working on a new project. If he is, tell him he's being very boring and rude, missing out on all the fun. Tell him that from Giselle."

"I will," Jake said, pulling away.

Cleopatra, now known as Giselle, grabbed him by the arm. "Promise you'll come back?"

"I promise," Jake lied again.

Giselle let him go, and the girls all giggled again.

Jake found a wide marble staircase and jumped the steps three at a time to arrive at the upper level of the Palazzo. There were fewer guests up here, only four or five, seeking solitude or an intimate romantic moment. Jake slipped past them all, heading down the hall and turning a corner to see a door guarded by two large men.

"Goons," he said to himself. "This must be the place."

He walked up to the door and, as he expected, was stopped by the two large men, one of whom pressed his big palm against Jake's chest to stop him in his stride.

Jake lowered his lion's mask. "I'm here to see Monsieur Perron."

"Do you have an appointment?" asked the man with his palm on Jake's chest, his English relatively good.

"No," Jake said. "But I know he'll want to see me. Tell him Jake Stone is here."

The goon frisked Jake and found no weapons, then spoke softly into a wrist microphone.

Ten seconds later, the doors to Perron's study burst open and Pierre Perron himself stood puffing on a cigar, a grin from ear to ear.

"I don't believe it! I thought I killed you," he muttered in astonishment, then suddenly he burst into laughter. "My God, you're even more stubborn than I thought. Are you here to kill me? Because if you are, I'll tell my friends here to break your neck right now."

"No," Jake said calmly, "I'm not here to kill you."

"Good! Then come in! Come in!"

He invited Jake into his large ornate study, ordering the two goons to wait outside, shutting the doors behind them. There was a beautiful antique mahogany desk at the far end of the room, huge leather chairs everywhere, one wall filled with volumes of books, journals and maps that Jake was sure Perron had never read, and a vast balcony overlooking the lights of the Grand Canal.

Perron pointed out the surveillance cameras in the room. "Just in case you do have plans for me, it would be unfair of me not to let you know we're being watched by a roomful of my security guards. After all, the last time I saw you—"

"—you tried to kill me." Jake finished for him.

"Technically it wasn't me who fired the spear," Perron chuckled with a shrug. "I simply gave the order. Cigar?"

He offered an open box of cigars to Jake.

"I'd be insulted if you didn't take one," Perron insisted. "Look at the label."

Jake picked out a cigar and saw Stone Cigars written on the label.

"Are you trying to flatter me?"

"I'm always trying to flatter you. That is, when I'm not trying to kill you. That's what I love about our relationship, Mr. Stone. It's complex. So many layers. So many textures. Like a good cigar, wouldn't you say?" Perron tossed Jake his silver lighter. "Tell me what you think."

Jake flipped open the lighter and lit the cigar. He took a puff and coughed a little. "It's strong," he said.

"Well noted," Perron laughed.

Jake slipped the lighter into his pocket without thinking. Perron was so distracted by Jake's presence, he didn't even notice.

"So," the fat Frenchman said, sitting back in the large armchair behind his desk, "if you're not here to kill me then what are you doing here? I don't recall seeing your name on the guest list."

"That's because it wasn't."

"Such audacity. I suppose that's what I pay you for to fetch me my treasures. To dig holes. To find those long buried bones. Just like a dog." Perron smirked patronizingly. "Tell me, Mr. Stone, what kind of dog are you exactly?"

"Not yours," Jake said, his face serious.

Perron laughed. "You could have fooled me. Tell me, have you already spent the hundred thousand I gave you? Is that why you're here, to ask for more?"

Jake stepped forward and stubbed his cigar into an ashtray on Perron's desk. "Let's cut the bullshit, Pierre. I'm not here to kill you. I'm not here on anyone else's agenda. Either I walk out of this place with the money you owe me, or I walk out of here with the Devil of Kahna Toga."

Perron's eyes narrowed, a little suspicious. "Someone else's agenda?" he asked. "Why would you say that?"

"No games," Jake warned. "I got a two-inch hole in my side where my patience used to be. Now tell me where the Devil is or pull your checkbook out of your drawer now. It's one or the other."

*

According to the blueprints the Professor had shown them in Vienna, the palazzo's security room was located on the ground level, in the south wing of the mansion.

Will and Shane made their way swiftly but discreetly through the milling crowds, past women in witch's masks and men dressed as demons. They found a long lonely corridor stretching off the main vestibule that led to a closed door. There, a man in a black suit guarded the door. Will and Shane walked purposefully toward him.

"Arresto," the guard said firmly.

Shane looked at Will without breaking his stride. "Did you understand what he just said?"

Will shook his head. "No idea."

They walked faster and faster toward the guard, who quickly panicked and reached for a pistol stashed in the back of his trousers. But before his fingers had a chance to touch the hilt of his weapon, Will and Shane rushed him, both men ramming their shoulders into the guard's chest and slamming him hard against the wall, instantly winding him.

The guard collapsed, gasping for air.

Before he could get his breath back, Shane laid a swift punch straight into his jaw, knocking him out cold.

"Nice work," Will observed before kicking the door to the security room open.

The two guards inside the room instantly jumped up from a console of monitors and radio equipment. Will and Shane rushed inside, slamming the door shut behind them. Shane took on the taller of the two guards, Will handled the other.

Will threw a high kick and the toe of his shoe connected sharply with the guard's chin, knocking him backward.

Shane dealt a blow straight to the taller guard's face, collecting him in the cheek. The guard reeled back before responding with a fist in Shane's eye. Blood splattered over the collar of Shane's shirt.

"Hey!" Shane blurted angrily. "This tux is brand new!"

And with that, he slammed his hardest punch yet straight into the guard's nose.

The guard's head jolted, he staggered backward, then collapsed unconscious against the bank of monitors.

At the same time, Will threw a right hook, then a left hook, into the second guard's face, nailing him against the wall and knocking him out cold with one last upper cut.

The guard slid down the wall and came to rest on the floor.

"The last guy I did that to ended up giving me a blowjob in the shower after the game," he said, stretching his now bruised knuckles.

"No time for that sort of thing tonight," Shane said.

Will glanced at the bank of monitors, and one in particular caught his eye. "Try telling that to Romeo," he said, nodding at one of the screens.

Shane looked at the monitor to see Eden in his silver crescent-moon mask stroll into a small and intimate stone courtyard with a man he could only hope was Jacques Dumas.

*

The small, intimate stone courtyard was something of a secret, hidden beyond several walls and walkways within the palazzo.

"I used to come here as a kid and hide whenever my family came here to visit. Nobody ever comes here. Nobody but me."

"It's beautiful," Eden whispered.

Indeed it was. The stone walls were draped in deep green ivy and glistening moss. There was a fountain in the middle of the courtyard, and at one end, several stone steps led down into a man-made grotto where the blue waters from the Venice canal lapped and played. Light reflecting off the water danced in graceful shifting shapes on the walls and ceiling of the grotto.

Jacques pulled off his mask, kicked off his shoes and socks, rolled up the legs of his suit pants and stepped down into the waters up to his knees. "I used to dive in here as a kid, you know. I went in search of lost coins and trinkets and anything else I could find."

"Did it make you rich?" Eden asked, taking off his own mask, shoes and socks before walking down the steps into the water with Jacques. They both sat down on the cool stone steps with their feet submersed.

"I fell in love with the water, it made me who I am today," Jacques replied. "So I guess the answer is yes, it did make me rich. Do you ever miss our days on the Galapagos?"

"Yes," Eden said without having to think. "You haven't changed, you know."

"You have."

"How?"

Jacques shrugged. "I don't know. You seem so—secretive. You still haven't told me what you're doing here."

Eden paused for a moment. It was impossible for him to tell a lie to this man; this man whose bed, whose love, whose trust he had once shared. And so, without any fear of blowing the entire operation, Eden said quite simply: "I'm here with four other men to steal a stone tablet from your uncle."

Jacques stared at Eden, a little stunned at the response, and didn't say a word for several moments.

"Have I shocked you?" Eden asked eventually.

Jacques paused another second, then smiled and shook his head. "No. If I learned one thing on the Galapagos, it's that I know you well enough to trust you, but not enough to predict what you're ever going to do next. You loved me without question. Yet you left me without saying goodbye. You keep me guessing, Eden Santiago. And I love that about you."

The words almost melted Eden's heart. He looked into Jacques' eyes, and for a second, he was almost willing to give up everything for that beautiful, honest face.

Almost.

But what about the Professor?

What about Luca and Shane and Will?

And Jake?

"What about your uncle?" was the question that finally came from Eden's mouth.

Jacques laughed. "Pierre? Whatever you're looking for, I'll help you find it. My uncle deserves whatever's coming to him. He used to beat me as a child if I used the wrong fork at the dinner table or hiccupped in front of guests. He's an asshole. All he does is steal, lie, cheat and throw his money around to impress people. That's the only thing he's good for. Right or wrong, the only reason I'm here tonight is to ask him to help fund my research with the pink Amazonian river dolphins in Brazil. My government grant has expired, the money's all but dried up. If he thinks it'll get him an invite to an ambassador's ball somewhere in South America, Pierre will open his checkbook. At least that's what I'm hoping."

*

Pierre reached into his drawer and opened his checkbook, with Jake's eager eyes watching his every move. But even with the sharpest eyes, what Jake couldn't see from where he stood was Perron's index finger press firmly against a silent alarm button fixed to the inside of his drawer, then slide an automatic pistol to the front of the drawer, within easy reach, before leaving the drawer slightly open and pulling out his checkbook.

"One hundred thousand U.S." Perron muttered airily. "If memory serves me correct."

"I'd be happy to take the Devil off your hands if you have any issues with the money," Jake said. "It's here somewhere, isn't it? You just don't know what to do with it. You're scared of it. You don't know anything about it, other than it's worth a fortune. So you've buried it, probably in a room full of things you've plundered from different cultures, different countries. Things you don't know anything about. Am I right?"

"Perhaps." Perron was beginning to blink nervously for two reasons. Firstly, Jake was closer to the truth than he cared to admit. Secondly, the alarm should have notified the guards in the security room by now, who in turn should have notified the guards at the door.

But there was no sign of movement from beyond the door whatsoever. Which meant one of two things.

Either the guards outside the door had vanished—or Jake's intrusion was an orchestrated attack, and someone had broken into the security room in the south wing.

*

A buzzer began to ring and a small light flashed next to a monitor with a birds-eye view into Perron's office.

"Will, take a look at this," Shane said, pointing Will's attention away from Eden and Jacques in the grotto and over to the monitor with the small flashing light.

They could see Jake standing in front of Perron's desk, and Perron himself sitting down behind the desk. There was a checkbook in front of him. Perron began writing in it, but then his pen appeared to run out of ink. He shook it about, then shrugged at Jake and reached into his drawer as if to pull out a second pen.

Instead, he pulled out a gun and pointed it straight at Jake.

"That doesn't look good," Will said. "Hold the fort."

Before Shane could stop him, Will was out the door.

*

"We're looking for a small stone tablet," Eden said. "About so big, with markings on it like ancient symbols."

Jacques shook his head. "I don't recall seeing anything like that, but that doesn't mean we can't find it. My uncle keeps half his treasures stashed away in a secret room, until he can be bothered to call in an expert to explain what they are. He takes for the sake of taking, but doesn't display anything until he can brag about it."

"Will you take me to it?" Eden asked. "The secret room?"

Jacques smiled and nodded. They put their socks, shoes and masks back on and Jacques led Eden out of the grotto and through the gathering of guests in the main courtyard. Past party-goers in costumes both dazzling and freakish: a woman with a beak and a face of feathers and a man with a decorative elephant's head pushing down on his shoulders; a bright copper flower and a grinning goat's head and an angry tin centurion from a legion of the Roman army; a woman wearing a crown of live, slithering snakes.

They made their way across the vestibule overlooking the canal, then away from the party again, into the palazzo's vast antechamber, to a flight of marble stairs that veered down into a deserted basement, then along a corridor so slender the two men had to turn their shoulders sideways to walk through to the other end of it.

To a wide wooden door.

Into a cold stone room.

Its walls were adorned with dozens of antique weapons, ranging from guns and rifles to foils and axes that were hundreds if not thousands of years old.

"A morbid collection," Jacques commented. "My uncle is so proud of it. I think it's ghastly. But this isn't the room we want."

He pointed Eden's attention to a large, ancient cast-iron furnace built into the far wall.

There was a detailed depiction of seventeenth century Venice painted on its cracked, glazed surface. Dozens of merchants and menace-makers, countrymen and clergymen, peasants and noblemen, grocers and gondoliers all thronged the busy streets or peered from open windows or floated down the intricate network of canals.

Jacques laid his blue dolphin mask aside and unhooked a large latch in the center of the furnace.

Eden hadn't noticed it before, amidst all the detail and color of the portrait of Venice. Nor did he notice the thin crevice that ran all the way down the middle of the enormous boiler. But now, as Jacques pulled on the latch and stepped back, it all became clear. And much more impressive.

The furnace was fake.

As Jacques pulled, the furnace split in two and opened outward, forming a secret entrance leading into a black chasm even further inside the depths of the palazzo.

Eden's eyes drank in the inky darkness that opened before him, his mind swimming with intrigue.

As the heavy cast iron doors of the furnace opened fully, Jacques stepped inside and flicked a switch. Four small gas lanterns inside the pitch dark chasm spontaneously ignited, casting a luminous glow over a large low chamber.

There were five short steps leading into the chamber, which was filled with thousands of relics, some large, some small, stacked high and low in no discernable order whatsoever. Some objects were covered in sheets or wrapped in plastic, others looked as if they had just been tossed to one side or placed carelessly in a spare corner, out of the way and out of sight.

"He calls it his vault," Jacques said.

"So many treasures," Eden whispered, astonished. He stepped into the chamber and walked among the stacks of disorganized relics as if he were walking through a jumble sale. "What a waste. All just sitting here, rotting away."

"Not rotting," Jacques said. "It's too cold in here for that."

He walked up behind Eden and led him to the far wall of the chamber. Gently he took Eden's hand in his and laid them both against the rock surface of the wall. "It's freezing," Eden said.

"That's because the Grand Canal is on the other side of the wall. It keeps the temperature down in here. Until Pierre finds out what he's got stashed down here, he doesn't want any of his trinkets depreciating in value as a result of light or heat."

Eden felt the cool of the wall against the flat of his palm and the warmth of Jacques' hand on the back of his.

Jacques suddenly stole the moment, leaning in and kissing Eden on the lips.

*

"Enough fooling around," Perron grinned at Jake, suddenly pulling the gun on him and snapping off the safety. Perron stood from behind his desk, not taking the gun off Jake.

"How many times do you want to try and kill me?" Jake asked.

"That depends how many lives you think you have left to spare. It'd be a shame really. In a strange way I'll miss you once you're dead, not to mention the treasures you find for me. But it's all just part of the journey. There're more thrill-seekers where you came from."

At that moment, something very hard and very heavy pounded against the closed doors of Perron's study.

Perron and Jake both looked.

A moment later there was another thump from the other side of the doors, even louder than the first.

Perron looked very concerned. A drop of sweat ran down his fat forehead and dribbled its way between his beady eyes. Suddenly the doors exploded open and Will burst into the room, packing the security guards' pistols, one in each hand.

Panic-stricken, Perron fired a reckless shot at Will, but missed him completely.

Will responded with a shot directly to Perron's right hand, knocking the weapon out of his chubby fist and taking off the top of his index finger.

Blood spurted.

Perron squealed and clutched his severed hand, horrified.

Jake smiled. "You were saying something about there being more thrill-seekers where I came from—?"

"You shot me!" Perron screamed. "You shot my fucking finger off!"

"And now we're gonna tie you up," Will nodded matter-of-factly, throwing one of the guns to Jake and ripping the cord out of the phone on Perron's desk.

"And after that," Jake said, "you're gonna tell us where you keep all your precious cargo. Unless, of course, you think you've got a few more lives left to spare."

*

When Jacques led Eden past the man with the grinning goat's mask and the angry Roman centurion in the main courtyard, there were two things Eden didn't notice that Shane, watching on one of the security monitors, did.

First of all, the grinning goat only had one arm.

Secondly, as Jacques and Eden past, the centurion pulled off his mask for a fleeting moment, seemingly to get a better look at Eden.

"Holy shit!" Shane whispered, jumping to his feet. "Eric Landon."

The grinning goat and the centurion immediately began to trail Eden and Jacques through the crowd.

Shane was out of the security room in a flash. He raced down the corridor then, in order to avoid suspicion, slowed his pace to a brisk walk as he rushed into the main courtyard. Over the heads of hundreds of party-goers, he saw the horns of the goat and the helmet of the centurion move determinedly into a vast antechamber at the far end of the courtyard.

They picked up their pace.

So did Shane, but in doing so, he ploughed straight into a middle-aged woman in a fox mask, whose champagne went all the way down her fox fur coat.

"You idiot!" she exclaimed.

"I'm sorry," Shane apologized, ever the gentleman. He tried to wipe the spill away with his jacket sleeve, but the woman slapped at his arm. "Get your hands off me! You're ruining my coat!"

Shane suddenly backed up angrily and shouted, "I'm sorry to tell you lady, but that coat wasn't yours to begin with!"

The woman gasped and indignantly muttered something about damn nuisance animal rights activists under her breath, but before she could make any more of a scene, Shane had vanished into the crowd.

He emerged at the far end of the main courtyard, ran through the deserted antechamber and slid to a halt at the top of the marble staircase leading down.

The goat and the centurion were already halfway down the stairs when Shane slid the white horse mask off his face and called, "Hey Eric! You and I got some unfinished business."

The Roman centurion stopped, turned, and slowly Eric removed his helmet to reveal his handsome smiling face. "Hey there, cowboy. Nearly didn't recognize you with clothes on." He quickly turned to the one-armed grinning goat and said, "You go on. I'll take care of this."

The goat disappeared down the narrow corridor at the foot of the stairs.

As Shane charged down the marble staircase, Eric charged up it, meeting Shane halfway and slamming into him, sending them both toppling and sliding down the stairs.

*

As Jacques leaned in and stole his kiss, Eden reacted instantly, unleashing a passion that had been bursting inside him since he had first laid eyes on Jacques that night. He cupped his lips around Jacques', holding onto the kiss, enjoying the sweet taste of Jacques' champagne still lingering on his tongue.

Jacques' fingers swept over Eden's shoulders. His firm hands found Eden's throat and caressed the muscles in the back of his neck before pulling on his bowtie like a string. It unraveled and floated to the floor.

Without breaking the kiss, Jacques peeled the jacket and shirt off Eden's shoulders and lowered them gently to the floor. He unbuckled his belt and unzipped him, letting the rim of his pants sag loosely about his hips. Jacques tore away from their kiss momentarily and eyed the torso of rich brown skin and muscle that stretched from Eden's chest down to the top of a dark pubic patch sprouting from the band of his briefs. Below it, his pants were caught by a stiff protrusion, trying to lift its way out from under the clothing.

Jacques wanted more, but Eden caught his hands and lowered Jacques to the stone floor. The handsome young Frenchman co-operated and lay out on his back. Eden untied Jacques' bowtie and unbuttoned his shirt, revealing his wide swimmer's chest and a strong, rigid stomach. Eden ran his fingers over Jacques's smooth tan skin. The canvas of his flesh broke out in goose bumps at Eden's tender touch.

"You're trembling," Eden said.

"I've waited for you to come back for so long," Jacques whispered. "There were times I thought I'd never see you again."

"I'm here now," Eden smiled, although reality told him it wasn't for long. "Let's make the most of it."

Nimbly, he maneuvered himself over the top of Jacques, positioning himself a slight inch or two above him. They were both breathing harder now, as though lust was trying to steal the air from them. As their bellies heaved in and out, the peaks of their muscled stomachs touched, ever so slightly.

Eden held himself up with one hand, while his other pushed his own pants down a short way, past his pulsing penis, setting it free. The rounded helmet of his long hard Latino cock slapped against Jacques's stomach before Eden pressed himself flat against his lover.

Sprawled on his back, Jacques let the heat of Eden's body seep through him. He closed his eyes.

Eden leaned in and kissed Jacques' neck, feeling the grooves of their bodies gently rubbing against one another. He felt his own aching shaft wedged between their stomachs, burning against his skin. He felt the soft bristle of stubble against his wandering tongue. He felt Jacques' cock pressing hard against the constraints of his own pants, desperate to be freed, longing to rest against Eden's flesh once more.

The Brazilian reached down and unzipped Jacques' trousers. He wasn't wearing any underwear; Eden remembered he never did. In fact, the young marine biologist hated clothes altogether, and when he and Eden were alone on Jacques' research yacht, Jacques would often dive into the oceans as naked as the day he was born.

Now, with no underwear holding it back, Jacques' thick hard cock sprang from its hiding place.

Eden looked down at it, smiling at the thought of all the pleasures that cock had given him. But suddenly, without warning, his joyful eyes grew wide and his lips stopped caressing Jacques' neck.

"Are you okay?" Jacques breathed, suddenly concerned.

Half naked, Eden pulled himself off Jacques and crawled across the floor, his eyes fixed on something he had caught a glimpse of, beyond Jacques, tucked beside on old stone Grecian bust and a badly rolled tapestry.

On hands and knees, his cock still hard and pressing against his belly, Eden reached for the object.

"What is it?" Jacques asked, pulling himself off the floor and crouching next to Eden.

"The stone," Eden breathed, holding the object up. Without taking his eyes off the tablet, his hand grabbed at his jacket on the floor and pulled the original stone tablet from the inside pocket. He held the two stone tablets side by side, closing the centuries old split. The two stones fit together perfectly, and the name "Z E F F E R I N O" was finally complete along the top.

"It's the stone. It's complete. For the first time in almost four hundred years, Zefferino's stone is back together again."

Suddenly, a gruff voice bellowed from behind them. "Sorry to interrupt such an intimate moment, but I'll be takin' vem off yer hands, fanks very much."

Eden recognized the accent as cockney and without even turning around, he knew it was the one-armed man.

Jacques leapt to his feet and spun around, startled but asserting himself. "Who are you?" he demanded, pulling up his pants and staring down the man in the grinning goat's mask.

The man laughed, and with his only hand, he peeled off his goat's head, revealing his burnt face and toothless grin. Calmly, he reached for the gun inside his jacket and pointed it straight at Jacques.

Eden shoved the two stone tablets behind the Grecian bust, jumped to his feet and pulled Jacques back as soon as he saw the gun.

Dominic Dixon, the one-armed man, looked down at Eden who was still exposed and laughed. "You ain't too good at hidin' fings, are you!"

Eden wasn't embarrassed or intimidated at all; he had no reason to be. Nonetheless, he put himself away and zipped up his pants. If he was about to take on Dominic Dixon, he wasn't going to get very far with his pants around his thighs.

"Who the hell are you?" Jacques demanded again.

"I assure you," Eden said, pulling Jacques behind him. "He's not on the guest list. He's not one of your uncle's associates. He's not even one of his enemies. He's one of mine."

"You know him?"

"His name's Dominic Dixon."

"Ovverwise known as da Holy Ghost of da Crimson Crown," the one-armed man grinned proudly. "And I'm here for da stones."

"If you're going to shoot us, then shoot us," Eden said, his hand reaching behind him now, feeling for something—anything—he could use as a weapon. "But even if you do find the stones, you still don't have the book. So like I said," Eden bluffed. "Go ahead and shoot."

Dominic smirked. "Shoot you?" he asked. "I don't fink I will." He placed the gun down beside him, on top of an ancient urn, then reached for something hidden behind the urn. "No, I found somefink in the next room that'd be a lot more fun."

With that, he produced a gigantic two-headed medieval battle-axe, each blade broader than Eden's shoulders.

"Jesus," Jacques whispered.

Eden swallowed hard, and his fingers fumbled behind him desperately now. He felt some sort of handle. It was long. Like a scepter—which is exactly what it was. He gripped it firmly and whipped it out from behind him, as though brandishing a sword. It was silver and gold with the large crystal orb at the head. It seemed little match for the heavy battle-axe in Dominic Dixon's hand, but it was better than nothing.

The one-armed man looked at it and laughed, then said, "En guard."

*

Shane pulled up near the bottom of the stairs, clambered to his feet and quickly swung his head around to look for Eric. In the same split second—thwack!

A boot collected Shane in the jaw.

He toppled backwards onto the steps, stunned.

Eric threw a punch, but Shane saw it coming and rolled out of the way. Eric's fist slammed into the marble stair where Shane's face was. Several of his knuckles cracked—the bones breaking—and Eric screamed in pain.

Shane took the opportunity to return the favor of planting his boot in Eric's grimacing face. Blood splashed across the steps. Shane leapt to his feet. Eric grabbed groggily onto the stairs, trying to maintain his balance.

"What's the matter?" Shane asked. "Feeling a little light-headed? Funny—that's exactly how I felt last time we met."

Eric wiped the blood from his lip and half-smirked, half-snarled. "I dropped enough poison into that beer to kill a bull in its prime.

How the hell did you survive that, anyway?"

Shane smiled. "Something else got to my heart before you did."

"I'm not aiming for your heart this time," Eric said, slipping a set of brass knuckle dusters out of his inside jacket pocket and sliding them onto his right fist. "This time, I'm aiming for that handsome cowboy face of yours."

Suddenly, Eric leapt up.

Shane stopped him with a right hook, straight to his chin.

Eric reeled backward, but only momentarily. He threw a left punch at Shane. It was a decoy—and Shane fell for it.

He blocked the blow but didn't see the right hook coming.

Each brass knuckle had a small stud inserted in it, sharp and pointed and designed to leave a permanent scar.

Eric's right fist impacted with Shane's jaw with such force, that it knocked the cowboy clean off his feet and into the air. Shane came crashing down on the marble staircase, three steps up.

He lifted his head and his eyes blinked frantically, trying to stay focused and conscious. But blackness swam across his vision, his eyes slid up inside his skull, and his head rolled back on his neck, coming to rest with a heavy thud on the marble step.

Eric knew it would have been easy to finish Shane off there and then. Laying there on the steps, unconscious, made the cowboy a sitting duck for a few massive blows to the face.

But easy is one thing, messy is another.

And then there was the tantalizing option of a hostage. The mere thought of tying Shane up, of slipping a lasso knot around his hands and feet and turning this cowboy into his captive, was enough to turn Eric on. He felt himself harden at the thought almost immediately.

Yes, it was indulgent, but he was, after all, the heir to the leadership of the Crimson Crown. He had every right to take whatever he wanted, and deal with the consequences later.

Eric wasted no time pulling one of Shane's arms over his shoulders and hoisting him to his feet. He was heavy, but Eric was strong; strong enough to drag Shane up the stairs and, somewhat audaciously, into the midst of the party where he would simply tell people that his friend had

had a little too much to drink.

He placed the white horse mask back on Shane's face to cover the blood and bruises.

*

Eden and Jacques inched backward as Dominic Dixon stood in place, swinging the battle-axe back and forth, getting a feel for the immense weight of the weapon. All the while, he laughed his gruesome laugh.

Eden looked around at the ceiling. There were no security cameras here.

"Get the stones," he told Jacques in a low voice, who bent instantly and snatched the stone tablets from beside the Grecian bust. "Take them and get help. Find a security camera. Wave at it, and someone will come and find you."

"I'm not leaving you here," Jacques told him.

Dominic nodded. "He's right about vat."

At that moment, the one-armed man put down the axe, and grabbed his pistol off the top of the urn. Before Jacques could so much as move, Dominic Dixon fired a single bullet straight into Jacques' bare stomach.

Jacques gasped and stumbled backward against the wall of the chamber, before sliding to the floor, blood spouting from the wound.

"No!" Eden roared.

He dropped the scepter, fell to his knees beside Jacques and grabbed his shirt, still lying on the floor. He pressed it hard against Jacques' wound and looked intensely into his stunned eyes.

"Listen to me! Look at me! You've been shot. You have to hold this, hold this firmly against the wound. I'll get you out of here."

Jacques nodded, half in shock, half in pain. The stone tablets slipped from his hands, and he pressed the shirt hard against the wound as he was told. Just then his eyes widened in horror. "Behind you!"

Eden spun around fast and saw Dominic Dixon behind him with his battle-axe raised high, ready to take them both out. But with one sharp kick to Dixon's shin, Eden sent their assailant staggering backward.

Eden jumped to his feet.

Dominic regained his balance and came at him with a savage cry.

Eden moved away from Jacques and used himself as a decoy, making his way along the canal wall. He grabbed a large ceramic vase and threw it at Dixon.

It hit the one-armed man square on the head and shattered into a million pieces, but barely slowed him.

Eden snatched up a small metal statue of Mercury, grabbing it by the head. As Dixon approached, he swung it at the one-armed man, aiming high. With a terrible thud, one of Mercury's winged heels dug into the flesh of Dixon's neck.

But the one-armed man didn't seem to feel a thing.

He simply plucked the Roman god out of his throat, ignoring the trickle of blood that came with it, and slammed his boot straight into the middle of Eden's chest, knocking him against the wall.

Eden's skull hit the stone wall hard.

His eyes clamped shut with the pain.

As his head swirled, he felt a rush of air beside his ear, a swooping noise, then a sharp clang.

His eyes shot open, sparks filled his vision, and he saw the head of an ancient battle-axe smash into the stone wall next to him, missing his head by an inch.

Dominic chuckled, genuinely amused, then pulled back the axe and came in for another swing.

Eden dropped to the ground and kicked his leg out again, this time in a sweeping arc. The move knocked Dominic Dixon off his feet altogether, giving Eden enough time to somersault further along the wall. His aim—to get Dominic as far away from Jacques as possible.

But as Eden rolled out of his somersault and back onto his feet, Dixon was already up and wheeling toward him, spinning the axe dramatically and spiraling across the chamber like a tornado with a blade. Eden turned away swiftly, but Dixon cut off his escape with another strike that narrowly missed his face and pierced the wall between two stones with an ear-splitting crack. Chips of rock blasted into the air as the massive battle-axe buried itself into the wall.

Dixon tried to pull the axe free, but the weapon was wedged deep and fast, and all he managed to pull away were more chunks of wall.

Eden seized the moment, charging Dominic Dixon with the full 200 pounds of his weight, wrapping his arms around him and crash-tackling him with all his might.

The one-armed man lost his grip on the axe, and the two of them slammed against the floor—and suddenly Eden realized the two of them had just skidded facedown in a small puddle of water.

Quickly he looked back at the wall.

The axe was still protruding from it.

And a thin but forceful jet of water was spurting into the chamber from around the axe.

"Oh my God," he whispered, the gravity of the situation setting in fast. The Grand Canal was on the other side of that wall—

—But wouldn't be for much longer.

Eden shot a glance over at Jacques who was struggling now, trying to maintain the pressure on his wound. But his hands were slipping away. He was losing consciousness fast.

There was another sound now, the hiss of pressure and the trickle of more rocks falling.

Eden glanced back at the wall.

It was beginning to splinter like a fractured damn wall, cracks were spreading outward from the axe, and a much larger jet of water was now shooting halfway across the chamber.

He had to get Jacques out of there.

He had to get them both to safety.

But those were the last thoughts that crossed him mind before he glanced up and saw the Grecian bust—the same one he had hidden the stone tablets behind—come crashing down on him from the hands of Dominic Dixon.

Eden raised an arm to try to shield the blow.

The statue broke apart.

Broke his arm.

The bust shattered into a hundred marble shards, and Eden Santiago's world turned to darkness.

Dominic Dixon giggled, almost like a girl, at the destruction he had caused. He crossed the chamber to Jacques, who was now unconscious, and took the stone tablets lying beside him.

The water level was up to his ankles when he walked up to the battle-axe and, with all his might, yanked it clean out of the wall.

It was like pulling the cork out of a bottle; water began to flood into the chamber with unstoppable force.

Just for the hell of it, Dominic Dixon raised the axe and thrust it into the wall again, forming a second splice in the stone. He laughed again, then headed out of the chamber, out through the furnace doors.

That's when he heard two sets of footsteps rushing down the narrow corridor toward him.

Quickly, the one-armed man stepped into the darkness behind one of the furnace doors.

*

Will and Jake followed Perron's instructions to the letter: downstairs; through the courtyard; across the vast antechamber; down the marble staircase where, only two minutes earlier, Eric Landon had knocked Shane unconscious and carried him away; through the narrow corridor and into the antique weapons room where they would find a furnace that would open up to reveal the vault.

Only the furnace doors were already open.

And inside, Eden lay motionless, Jacques was bleeding and unconscious, and the chamber was flooding fast.

"Holy shit!" Will exclaimed before leaping through the furnace doors, down the steps and crashing into the water.

Jake wanted to stop him, but he knew this was no time for caution and bolted after him.

They reached Eden first, the water level already covering his face completely.

Will held his head up and rested it in his lap.

Jake felt for a pulse.

"He's not breathing!"

He looked around quickly, part of him scanning for trouble, part of him looking for somewhere drier to lay Eden. He saw an old stone altar. "We gotta lift him."

Will took Eden's shoulders, Jake took his feet, and together they hoisted him swiftly up onto the altar. Jake immediately tilted Eden's head back, pinched his nose and clasped his lips firmly over Eden's. He began pushing air into him, breathing hard into his mouth, filling his lungs.

He stopped and gripped his hands Eden's ribcage and began to pump, counting under his breath.

He gave him the kiss of life once more.

Breathing into him.

Holding his face in his hands.

Tasting his lips.

Feeling nothing back, until—

—Eden suddenly gasped and splashed up a lungful of water.

His eyes shot open, and the first thing he saw were Jake's piercing green eyes, staring down at him. Smiling down at him.

"Welcome back," Jake whispered to him, an unexpected tear of relief gathering in his eye.

Eden sucked in the air. "Jake," he breathed, startled and happy, then alarmed. "Jacques!"

"I got him," Will shouted, dropping to Jacques' side.

The Frenchman was still propped up against the wall, unconscious, the water rising quickly up his chest.

Jake went back into control mode. "Get him up," he told Will.

"He's been shot," Will shouted, lifting the soaked shirt off Jacques' stomach and sizing up the wound.

"I don't care," Jake replied. "We gotta get everyone outta here now before the water gets any higher."

"Where the hell's it coming from?" Will asked.

"My guess is the canal." Jake turned to Eden. "Can you walk?"

Eden nodded. "I think my arm is broken, but I'm okay. It's him I'm worried about." He was gesturing toward Jacques. "We've got to get him to a hospital now."

"We will," Jake said, easing Eden off the altar at the same time that Will put Jacques' arm around his shoulder and lifted him up.

That's when they all heard it—

Clang!

Jake, Eden and Will looked up at the same moment to see the cast-iron furnace doors slam shut. The next sound they heard was the latch on the outside locking.

Then, from the other side of the furnace doors came the distinct sound of Dominic Dixon's insidious laugh.

*

Luca was beginning to get anxious, very anxious, when he saw Shane's white horse mask bobbing through the crowd. He started to make his way hurriedly toward him when he realized that Shane was not walking on his own two feet: he had one arm around the shoulders of a man in a centurion's mask and was being carried along.

That could only mean one thing—trouble.

He snapped off his red sun mask, when suddenly he heard a gruff voice behind him.

"You're da one he wants."

Luca spun and saw a grinning goat's head facing him, but it was a sight he saw for only a second.

Before Luca could do so much as move, Dominic Dixon shoved a Cupid's mask in his face. The inside of the mask had been heavily doused in chloroform.

Luca went down like a stone wall collapsing.

Dominic caught him.

He found the keys to the Riviera in one of Luca's jacket

pockets—and the code book in the other. With one hand, Dominic managed to keep Luca propped up against him and slot the book into his own pocket, alongside the two stone tablets.

"Have you got everything?" Eric asked, coming up alongside Dominic with Shane in tow.

"We got it all!" the one-armed man nodded, then asked, "What are you doing wif him?"

"Treating myself to a little amusement," Eric smiled.

The Riviera was still docked at the pontoon. Dominic and Eric slumped Luca and Shane next to each other in the back seat, then Dominic untied the ropes, and Eric started the engine, steering the boat swiftly down the Grand Canal and into a dark side canal where they vanished from sight.

*

Will heard a heavy splash. He turned and saw a chunk of rock the size of a football tumble from the crumbling hole that the axe had made in the wall. The water began to gush like a fire hydrant now. "Ah, guys! Whatever we're plannin' on doing to get outta here, can we plan it faster?"

Will was standing with Jacques' arm hooked over his shoulders, holding the Frenchman up on his feet and pressing hard against his stomach wound to try to stop the bleeding.

Jake spun around from the furnace doors where he and Eden where trying to figure out a way to unhook the latch from the inside, but there were no latches or locks at this end. "We're workin' on it," he boomed over the increasing volume of the water rushing in.

At his feet, he watched the water level reach the first of the five steps, then quickly rise over it and reach the second step.

Within seconds, it splashed over the third step.

Jake said, "Eden, swap with Will. I need his shoulder to help me break down this door."

"You need all three of us for that," Eden argued.

"You've got a broken arm. You could have a concussion. I'm no doctor, but right now you're more valuable to me conscious than unconscious."

Eden nodded, then took Jacques in his arms while Will and Jake rammed their shoulders into the furnace doors.

With each blow, a heavy clang echoed through the flooding chamber—but the doors themselves wouldn't budge.

"It's no use," Will said, rubbing his pounded shoulder. "It's cast iron. There's no way we can break it down."

Jake looked around desperately for another way out.

The water level had reached the furnace doors some moments ago, and while a small amount trickled through the slit between the two doors, the majority of the flow was still contained within the chamber—which was filling up fast.

The water was already up to their knees.

Some of the light-weight treasures in the room began to bob and float and swim about, while the majority—made from iron and silver and gold and marble—took quietly to their watery new grave.

Jake knew if they didn't find a way out soon, it would become their grave as well.

"We gotta find something that can pry this door open."

"What about the axe?" Will said.

Jake shook his head. "We take that out, we'll only increase the flooding."

"A scepter!" Eden suddenly recalled. "I had a scepter. I dropped it, over here somewhere."

The water was up to their thighs now. Jake said, "Eden, stay with Jacques. Keep him up. Will, you search left. I'll go right."

Jake and Will both vanished beneath the surface of the water.

Sifting along the chamber floor, Will's hands came across the severed head of the Grecian bust, then the centuries old tapestry that had unraveled completely now and was hovering along the chamber floor like a stingray, and then—

Will broke the surface with the scepter in his fist. "I got it!"

Jake, on the other hand, was still under the water—and had

found something else altogether.

Through his blurred vision beneath the water, Jake saw the shimmer and glitter of the diamond Devil of Kahna Toga. It was wedged between a Roman statue and a Egyptian pot, and as the water levels rose, the thin sheeting in which it had been wrapped unfurled and floated away, revealing the mythical idol in all its glory.

Slowly, Jake began to reach for it, when suddenly a hand grabbed his shoulder and hauled him to the surface.

"What!" he roared.

"You okay?" Will asked, worried. "You were down there a long time. I found the scepter."

Jake saw the scepter in Will's hand, then saw the water was above their waists now. He knew the Devil of Kahna Toga was useless to a dead man.

Hurriedly, he and Will waded toward the furnace doors and tried to dig the narrow end of the scepter into the slit between the doors. But it was too big for the crevice. It slipped and slid out of the groove between the doors, unable to hook into anything, unable to give them any sort of leverage whatsoever.

Jake threw the scepter into the water, frustrated and angry.

"Guys!" Eden called.

Jake and Will looked up quickly and saw that Jacques was fading fast. "He's freezing," said Eden. "I don't know how much longer—"

"We'll get him out of here," Jake shouted determinedly. Then, under his breath, "I'll get us all out. You just might not like how I do it."

Jake pushed his way across the flooded floor, the water now at mid-chest, and with all his strength he hauled the battle-axe out of the wall. Nobody questioned him; they knew the consequences, but they also knew they had no choice.

He pulled the axe free in a cascade of rock and stone.

The water flooded into the chamber even faster.

Jake returned to the furnace doors, raised the gigantic axe over his shoulder and with all his strength plunged the head of the axe into one of the cast-iron doors.

The metal bent and a small crack formed.

Jake swung the axe into the door again, and the crack gave way a little more. He continued to hack away at it until he had made a hole big enough for his arm to reach through. Blindly he felt his way along the other side of the door to the latch.

But something sharp sliced his fingers. He winced and yanked his hand away, then warily his bloody fingers felt their way back to the latch.

They tapped against a metal object jammed in the latch.

The doors had been booby-trapped on the outside, wedged shut with what felt like a razor-sharp sword, its edges serrated with dozens of jagged spines.

The water splashed against the walls of the chamber, soaking around their chests now. Carefully Jake grasped the sword outside, tried to force it from its lodged state, but the hot trickle of blood filled his palm and no matter how hard he tried, he couldn't get a grip on the sword.

Soon he pulled his arm back, letting water flow out through the hole he'd made in the cast-iron door. But the water filled the chamber faster than it could drain.

Jake nursed his lacerated hand, looking desperately for another way out.

The water was up to their necks now. Jake's eyes scanned the room. Treasures bobbed and rocked on the surface of the water. He sized up each floating treasure and assessed its value to them in a situation like this—a Renaissance canvas with its colors running into the water; the wooden mask of a Mayan priest; a drum dating back to Neolithic times—all priceless, yet to the four of them trapped in the chamber now, all completely worthless.

He looked at the walls.

The ceiling.

The walls!

For the first time since racing into the chamber, he noticed there was a gas lantern on each wall.

At that moment, several more chunks of stone tumbled from the hole in the wall and the deluge that followed thundered into the chamber. Then the thunder stopped—but the water didn't.

The level of the water had risen above the crumbling hole.

Eden struggled to hold the unconscious Jacques above the waterline.

"We gotta do something," Will said to Jake desperately.

"I got an idea," Jake said to both Will and Eden. "You just gotta do what I say, when I tell you."

Will and Eden both nodded, pushing their chins upward to stay above the rising water.

Jake disappeared under the water and emerged seconds later with the scepter. He swam quickly over to the first lantern and used the scepter to smash the glass and expose the pipe blasting out gas into the remaining air trapped near the ceiling of the chamber.

Jake cut through the swirling water to the second lantern and hammered it off the wall. By the time he sledged away the third and fourth lanterns, they were all starting to cough and choke on the gas.

The water was brimming over their chins.

Eden held Jacques' face higher than his own and held his breath as the water rose above his own nose and mouth.

Will swam over to Jake.

"I'm not gonna ask you if you know what you're doing," he said, "but I think I like your style." Will smiled.

Jake nodded. "Thanks. I'll see you on the other side of that door."

Jake let go of the scepter and let it drop to the chamber floor, then reached into his pocket and pulled out Perron's silver lighter, the one he had thrown to him to light his cigar.

Will swam quickly back to Eden and Jacques.

Jake shook the water off the lighter, hoping it wasn't too waterlogged, hoping it would still work. There was no chance to test it—the lighter would either work or not.

Jake looked at Will and Eden, who knew exactly what he was about to do.

As Jake nodded his head at them, Will and Eden took a breath and submerged themselves, taking Jacques under the water with them, holding his nose and mouth closed.

The moment they were gone, Jake slid beneath the water as well.

All but the one hand with the lighter vanished beneath the surface.

Then his thumb triggered the lighter.

The lighter gave off a single spark before the entire gas-filled airspace impacted with a thunderous blow.

Jake pulled his hand down fast as the air above ignited. Flames rolled and cannoned outward, demolishing the furnace doors and shattering the wall standing between the chamber and the water beyond.

With an almighty force, the entire Grand Canal folded in on the chamber.

Jake started to swim like hell away from the flood, as did Will and Eden with an unconscious Jacques in tow. But all four were snatched up by the current like a leaves in a hurricane, sweeping them out through the shattered cast iron furnace doors.

As the canal completely flooded the chamber, it instantly extinguished the flames from the explosion. But the blast pummeled the walls and the countless dislodged stones and rocks.

Suddenly, the whole of Perron's palazzo began to quake on its foundations.

Tumbling head over heels through the torrent, Jake, Will, Eden and Jacques were ejected through the ruined furnace doors and swept into the armory room. They swirled and swiveled through the flood as dozens of deadly weapons—from hatchets to bayonets to daggers—cut and cleaved and sliced at them through the charging wall of water, missing them by inches. Rocks tumbled away from collapsing walls and rained down from the ceiling.

The water carried all four of them through the narrow corridor at lightning speed, banging their shoulders, limbs, heads against the tight walls before spitting them out at the foot of the marble staircase that was now flooding furiously.

Jake spilled across the floor and picked himself up. Will was already on his feet and the two of them scooped Jacques out of Eden's arms. Eden hauled himself to his feet nursing his broken arm, and the four of them staggered hurriedly up the marble staircase.

As they reached the top of the stairs and rushed through the unstable foundations of the palazzo. An enormous chunk of the ceiling suddenly gave way, and one of the antechamber's columns came crashing down a few feet behind them.

In the courtyard, party guests were already screaming and running for their lives. Columns were sinking into the floor all around them, crumbling like cracking icebergs. Iron chandeliers dropped from their chains and pulverized their ceramic drip trays, spitting fire and liquid wax everywhere.

Jake and Will helped Jacques while Eden dodged giant chunks of rubble and leapt over twisted traps of cast iron, looking desperately for Luca and Shane. He charged onto the boat landing and saw the Riviera was gone.

Police boats were already speeding down the Grand Canal, taking in dozens of panicked party guests.

"We need help here!" Eden shouted. "This man's hurt!"

Eden, Jake and Will helped Jacques onto one of the many emergency boats that arrived, sirens blaring and lights flashing, and watched the canal bubble and erupt beneath them as the bowels of the Perron's palazzo rumbled and rocked, transforming the mansion into its own ancient ruin.

A hand landed on Jake's shoulder. He turned and saw Eden, drenched to the bone. "Thank you," he said in a soft, low voice.

Jake nodded and said, "Is he gonna be okay?" He looked over to see Will with Jacques. The Frenchman had been laid out. Police had gathered with first aid kits. Bandages were unraveled. Injections were administered.

Eden said, "They're taking us straight to the hospital." He began to move back to Jacques, to be with him. Jake watched as Eden returned and nursed Jacques' head, keeping him safe as the police assisted.

There was another crash and boom from somewhere deep within Perron's mansion. Jake looked back into the blackness of the gushing water below the palazzo as they left it far behind, knowing with absolute certainty that the Devil of Kahna Toga was a hidden treasure once again.

He wondered what was more valuable in life—a diamond Devil, or an angel like Eden. He glanced back once more at the handsome

Brazilian.

And for the first time in his life the thought crossed his mind: If he wanted a life of adventure, maybe he didn't have to live it alone after all.

XIII

VIENNA, AUSTRIA

Elliot Ebus waited until Elsa and the Professor had both gone to sleep before creeping out the door of the hotel suite and down to the lobby. Elsa had warned the Professor he would try this. The Professor responded by saying there was no point caging Elliott like an animal. Nobody can influence the destiny of another if they choose to take that destiny into their own hands. They had all warned Elliott Ebus of the danger he was in, but Elliott thought otherwise.

He scurried down the street, hastening through the cold Vienna night, until he reached a phone booth on the corner. Through the glass panels of the booth, he could see the Royal Hotel. He watched closely to see if the Professor or Elsa might emerge, but nobody came for him.

Elliott pulled coins and a small, frayed piece of paper from his pocket. Dropping the coins in the slot, he looked at the number that was written on the paper in faded ink. Elliott had been holding onto that piece of paper for a long time, hoping he would never have to use it, hoping he would never again see the man who had sold him that cursed book. He had been told to call the number on the piece of paper if ever anything happened to the book.

Slowly, carefully, he dialed those dreaded digits.

A man on the other end of the line picked up. "Mr. Ebus. I've been expecting your call."

"Things have gone wrong. Terribly wrong." Elliott's voice was quivering with absolute terror. "It wasn't my fault."

"I understand. It's alright. The book is in safe hands now."

"You have it back?"

"My men do, yes."

Elliott breathed a sigh of relief. "Then it's all over. This whole wretched mess is finally over." He actually began to smile.

"That's right," said the man on the other end of the line. "There's just one small matter left to clean up—and that's you."

The smile quickly faded from Elliott's face. Panic returned to his voice. "No, you don't have to do that. I won't tell a soul, not a word! I don't know anything. I'll vanish. I'll disappear. You'll never see me again."

"I can see you right now."

Elliott Ebus gasped. He swiveled on his feet in the booth, his eyes frantically scanning the surrounding area until finally, they landed on a man standing in the shadows across the road, wearing a hooded crimson robe. The man pulled one hand out from under his hood to reveal a cell phone. His other hand emerged from inside his robe holding a pistol with a silencer on the end of it.

Elliott let out a tiny shriek.

He dropped the phone receiver.

He heard the splinter of glass cracking, then looked down to see a small bullet hole in the phone booth, in a direct line between him and the robed figure.

That's when the blood began to spread across his tweed jacket. It was the last thing he ever saw. His eyes rolled back into his head, and Elliott Ebus collapsed in a lifeless heap on the floor of the phone booth.

The man across the street slid his weapon back under his robe and turned his hood in the direction of the Royal Hotel.

*

The heavy knock on the door woke both Elsa and the Professor instantly. They both put on their dressing gowns and emerged from their rooms with a curious look on their faces before stepping up to the door.

The knock came once more, and they both jumped.

"Who is it?" Elsa asked.

A voice called through the door. "It's hotel staff. We have found your companion. He seemed quite lost. And to be perfectly honest, I think he may have been drinking."

Elsa looked through the peephole and saw the top of Elliott's head. Seemingly, he was looking down in shame, or perhaps even passed out. Another man to the side of Elliott was propping him up, but Elsa's view of him was somewhat obscured.

"I told you he couldn't be trusted," Elsa said to the Professor, but the Professor was already moving briskly to his makeshift workstation in the sitting room.

Elsa removed the latch, and suddenly the door exploded open.

She was unconscious before she hit the ground.

*

Will, Jake and Eden left San Giovanni Hospital in Venice shortly after Jacques regained consciousness. Doctors had removed the bullet and stabilized his condition.

"He'll have to stay here for a couple of weeks," one of the doctors told Eden while Will and Jake downplayed their reports of the incident to police. "But he's young and healthy. With the proper rest and care, he should make a full recovery."

Eden, his arm now in a sling, went in to see Jacques, who was still groggy from the anesthetic. "The doctor says you're going to be alright."

Jacques gave him a faint smile. "I can't remember a thing."

"You were very brave. Perhaps a little too brave."

"Wait. I remember a man—he only had one arm."

"He's still out there somewhere," Eden said. "And two of my

friends are missing. I'm going to come back, but first I need to find them."

"Are they in trouble?" Jacques' voice was full of concern.

"I don't know."

"You have to go help them. Do what you have to do."

"I won't be gone long. I'll come back. I promise," Eden said. He leaned in and gave Jacques not one soft, sweet kiss, but two, one on each eyelid.

"I believe you. I'll be waiting."

Eden, Will and Jake left Venice in a rented BMW driving as fast as they could over the mountains and into Austria. They tried the Professor's cell phone the entire way, but there was no answer. They did not call the hotel reception for fear of attracting any undue attention to the Professor.

At the Royal Hotel, in Dr. Ivan Jastrow's suite, they found no sign of the Professor or Elsa. Their luggage was all still there, undisturbed. Will opened one of the closets in the hall to find all their clothes still hanging and folded there.

Eden opened the next closet, and the lifeless, crumpled body of Elliott Ebus rolled out onto the floor.

Eden dropped to his knees, felt for a pulse and checked his skin for temperature and his limbs for signs of rigor mortis. "He's been dead for ten hours, perhaps twelve."

At the other end of the suite, Jake opened the doors to the sitting room and saw that the Professor's computer equipment had been more or less destroyed. The floor was littered with shattered glass and cracked Braille keyboards. All the monitor screens were punctured. "Hey guys," he called. Eden covered Elliott Ebus with a sheet, and he and Will joined Jake in the sitting room.

"Looks like Dominic Dixon isn't the only one who likes swinging an axe around," Eden said.

Jake examined one of the screens. "Actually, they're bullet holes. My guess is whoever did this used a silencer."

Eden tried to turn the monitors on, to see if the Professor had left any clues before his disappearance.

One of the monitors blew up with a surge of energy.

Another powered up, then sizzled and hissed and powered down forever.

But a third monitor, despite its splintered screen and the occasional spark, came to life, revealing a fractured image of Italy. There was a small red flashing dot on the screen, just above Sicily.

"That's no glitch," Eden said.

"What is it?" Jake asked.

They all crowded around the sparking monitor. Eden zoomed in. The red flashing dot appeared to be moving north off the shores of Sicily.

"The tiepin," Will breathed, realizing what they were looking at. "The Professor's got the tiepin."

Eden stood bolt upright and raced for the door. "Come on, we have to be on the next plane to Palermo."

"But he's not in Sicily," Will said. "He's heading north of it. We don't know where the hell he's going."

"Yes we do," Jake nodded, suddenly tapping into Eden's wavelength. "The words on the first stone. Home. Fire. They're heading to the home of fire. They figured out the clues."

"I don't get it," Will shrugged, frustrated.

"The Cross of Sins—" Eden answered. "It's on the island of Vulcano."

XIV

TYRRHENIAN SEA, NORTH OF SICILY

The storm came in the late afternoon, turning the sky black and sending twenty-foot waves crashing into the bow of the cruiser as it cut its way across the Tyrrhenian Sea, heading for the island of Vulcano.

The cruiser itself was a small ship, a 100 ft Azimut with three reconditioned suites. As lightning lashed at the savage peaks of the waves, the ship dipped and tilted wildly, smashing through the breaking crests. In silver writing on the stern of the boat, the name Salvation vanished beneath each wave then came up glistening in the reflection of the relentless electrical storm.

Inside the vessel, thunder drowned out the tortured cries that came from onboard.

"Uck you!"

The nine tails of the whip whistled through the air and cut into Luca's shoulders and back like knives. The sound that came from him was stifled by his clenched jaws, half the consonants lost, but the meaning still there, escaping in a gush of pain.

Dominic Dixon laughed as he pitched and lurched, trying to keep his balance in the storm. He may have only had one arm, but he knew how to use it; the whip in his hand was dripping with blood.

The two of them were the only ones in this particular suite, which had been transformed into something of an interrogation room. The lights had been dimmed almost to black. The bed had been removed, along with any fittings and luxuries. All that remained was a chair fastened to the floor in the middle of the room, on which Luca now sat, bleeding, his hands tied behind his back.

He had been conscious for an hour, but it was apparent Dominic Dixon had started the lashes long before that. Luca had woken to a body covered in cuts and lacerations. His shoulders, chest and stomach were shredded. He clenched his teeth and breathed in short tight bursts as if trying to keep the pain inside, trying to conquer it.

He was completely naked but for the ropes and the small silver crucifix around his neck.

"How dare you wear vat!" the one-armed man sneered, staring at Luca's cross. "You don't deserve to have Him hangin' 'round your neck. You ain't noffink but a dirty, little bugger."

"What do you want from us?" Luca snarled through gritted teeth. "We won't tell you anything. We've got nothing to say to you."

"I don't care," the one-armed man sneered. "I'm not doin' vis to get any information outta ya. I'm doin' it to get da Devil outta ya. Da Cross of Sins must be destroyed, along wif anyone who tries to stop us from destroyin' it." He cackled with wicked delight. "I'm just takin' my sweet time doin' it."

Thunder cracked outside, and the ship pitched wildly.

The one-armed man staggered backward a little, then raised his whip and came down with another strike of the cat o'nine tails, straight across Luca's bare bleeding chest. There were small studs at the end of each strand, and every time the whip came down, the studs embedded themselves deep into Luca's skin before Dominic Dixon ripped them out again.

Tiny gems of blood filled the air and splashed across the floor.

Luca stifled another roar.

"Do you know what vat pain is?" Dominic Dixon taunted. "It's da demons inside ya, tryin' to get out. People like you—your filfy type—you're full of demons. Da more you bleed, da more pure you become.

Like me."

"You call yourself pure?" Luca practically spat the words out. "What about those women you raped?"

Dominic shook his head. "You don't understand. God has forgiven me. I have atoned for my sins. It's time for you to do da same."

The one-armed man brought the whip down again, and Luca smothered yet another scream.

"Fink of it dis way. I'm doin' you a favor. I'm savin' your dirty soul before your wretched body goes to hell. That's where fire and brimstone await you, my litt'l darlin'!"

He brought the lash down again.

And again.

Across Luca's shoulders.

His chest.

His arms.

Until Luca's eyes eventually fluttered closed, and his head came to rest on his bleeding chest, and consciousness mercifully slid away.

*

The boat angled up over a foaming crest then dropped dramatically, slapping against the trough of the next wave with a boom. In a suite almost identical to the one holding Luca, Eric Landon maintained his balance and rolled up one bloody sleeve, then the other. In front of him sat Shane. Like Luca, he was naked and tied to a chair that was fastened to the middle of the floor. His nose was bleeding, his lips were cut and swollen, and there were several gashes around his eyes. It was evident that Eric didn't need a whip to torture his victim—his weapons of choice were his bare hands.

Shane's head suddenly twisted sharply with another crack to his cheekbone.

Eric smiled and shook his limp hand, which was red raw and swelling fast. He stretched his fingers and blew on his inflamed knuckles, trying to cool them down.

"Well," he said. "I have some good news and some bad news for you, cowboy. The good news is I'm having so much fun beating the crap out of you that I've decided to kill you last. I'll let you watch your friends die first, so you know what to expect."

"That's the good news?" Shane breathed heavily through his cut lips and bleeding nose. "What the hell's the bad news?"

"The bad news is you and I don't have much time left together."

Eric moved in swiftly, and Shane braced himself for another blow to the head, but instead of hitting him, Eric straddled Shane and lowered himself onto Shane's naked lap, facing him. He smiled and leaned in close, then slowly ran his tongue all the way up the side of Shane's face, licking his bleeding cheek and bruised eye.

Eric licked his lips then. "Your blood is so sweet. Tell me you're not enjoying this, even just a little." He ran a hand down Shane's chest and stomach and slid it between his naked legs before kneading and caressing Shane's balls and cock in his fingers. "You've been a bad cowboy, and bad cowboys deserve to be beaten within an inch of their life."

Eric looked down, then raised his eyebrows and smiled.

"Make that five inches. No, six. Eight! So you are enjoying it."

"Why don't you untie me, and I'll really show you a good time." Behind his back, Shane was pulling on the ropes, but they were too tight to wriggle loose.

"And let you try to take my power away? Let you escape unpunished? No, this is necessary. It's what He wants. Sooner or later, punishment always comes to your kind. The question is, do you resist the pain, or do you embrace your fate?"

"My kind?" Shane asked, incredulous. Suddenly, the Texan gentleman inside him left the building. "Are you delusional? You're the one with your hand on my cock. If you've got a problem with my kind, why don't you get the fuck off me, you fanatical religious head-case!"

Eric quickly stepped off Shane, suddenly furious, and threw a punch into the left side of Shane's face.

"Are you questioning my purity? I'm the Holy Son! The Holy Son of God! What I do, I do for Him! It's His will!

Shane stared, stunned, because despite his pain, he couldn't contain his astonishment. A smirk slid across his battered lips. "Holy Son? Right now I'm thinkin' you're just full of holy shit. I hate to be the one to break the news, given the fact that I'm tied up and you don't look too happy right now, but dude—you're gay!"

Another fist cut the air, this time slamming into the right side of Shane's face.

"Satan's words!" Eric screamed. "God created me! He created me pure and perfect!"

"God doesn't make anyone perfect. And He doesn't care that you're not! He doesn't give a shit if you're gay or cross-eyed or blind or if you've got three fuckin' heads! You're the one making a big deal of it! Trust me, it's okay! Just let it be okay!"

But the rage in Eric was so fierce he began to tremble. Tiny blood vessels burst in the whites of his eyes, and veins stood out like thick cables on his neck. He raised his arms, channeling all his fury into his hands, and one fist at a time, he began to lay punches into Shane like hammer blows.

First right.

Then left.

Then right.

Then left again.

All the while, he panted beneath his fuming breath, "He takes revenge on all who oppose Him and furiously destroys His enemies! His power is great, and He never lets the guilty go unpunished. He displays His power in the whirlwind and the storm. The billowing clouds are the dust beneath His feet. He sweeps away His enemies in an overwhelming flood. He pursues his enemies into the darkness of night—"

*

Lightning flared in jagged horizontal bolts, illuminating the dark night sky. It was like someone with a giant camera flash was taking photos just outside the porthole, second by second. Thunder struck, close by, and Elsa jumped with a fright.

Still in their pajamas and dressing gowns, Elsa and the Professor were locked inside a suite in the ship's starboard side. Unlike the interrogation suites, this room had been left unaltered. Elsa sat on the bed, the lines on her worried face lit by the glow of a bedside lamp.

The Professor stood near the cabin door.

"It's stopped," he said in a soft voice, listening as intently as he could to try to hear anything other than thunder and crashing waves.

"What has?"

"The pain."

Suddenly, he heard two sets of heavy footsteps outside. He took one step back.

Somebody unlocked the door and threw it wide open, and the bleeding body of Shane Houston, now dressed in the same tuxedo pants he'd worn to Perron's ball, was dumped on the floor inside the room.

Elsa and the Professor dropped to his side before the door slammed shut again.

"Oh *mein Gott*! Shane!" Elsa fussed, her hands shaking uncontrollably.

The Professor quickly found a pulse. "He's alive. Help me get him on the bed."

With great effort, the pair managed to lift him up and lay him on the bed.

Immediately, Shane began to stir.

Elsa wrapped the sheets and blankets around him to keep him warm.

"Shane?" the Professor said, leaning in close. "Can you hear me? Can you see me?"

Shane tried to open his eyes. The left opened fully, but his bruised and battered right eye could only open part of the way.

"Professor?" he croaked. "Elsa?" He saw her sitting on the bed beside him, too. "What are you doing here? Are you okay?"

"We had a visit from the Crimson Crown in Vienna. We're fine, but Elliott Ebus wasn't so lucky."

"Pssh-pssh, don't worry about us! Look at yourself! *Mein* dear poor boy!"

She couldn't help but swoop down and take his beaten face in her hands and plant motherly kisses all over him.

Shane winced in pain.

"Elsa," the Professor said, "He can probably do without that."

"It's okay," Shane tried to smile. "I prefer the company in this room to the other one."

"Can you sit up? I'm not sure how long they intend to keep us here."

"I think so."

With all his strength and help from Elsa and the Professor, Shane achingly managed to sit up on the bed.

"I'll get a cool towel," Elsa said, rushing to the ensuite.

"Was it Eric Landon?"

Shane nodded as Elsa returned and gently dabbed his swollen right eye. "I think he fancies me."

"I have a feeling all three of them are here."

"You mean the Father, Son and Holy Ghost," Shane said.

The Professor nodded. "As well as a small entourage of the Crimson Crown's disciples. I've counted nine sets of different footsteps so far. I think Luca may be onboard somewhere as well."

"How do you know?" Shane asked, concerned.

The Professor knew Luca's voice. It was the cries of pain, other than Shane's, echoing through the hull of the ship that made him certain the young Italian was somewhere in their midst. But he didn't tell Shane this. "Don't worry, I know everything will be alright. I have a feeling the others are already on our trail."

"How do you know?"

The Professor patted his stomach. "Let's just say it was something I ate. And let me tell you, I've swallowed more pleasant things in my time."

At that moment, there was a soft shudder as the ship's engines stopped.

Elsa raced to the porthole.

Outside, beyond the rolling white-peaked waves, three forks of lightning illuminated a mountainous island looming a short distance away.

"Professor, it's an island. There's no lights that I can see from here. No villages. Just a huge mountain rising up out of the ocean."

Something suddenly dawned on the Professor as he whispered under his breath, "Fire."

Shane asked, "Professor, what is it?"

"That's not a mountain. It's a volcano. They're about to uncover The Cross of Sins."

*

Thunder rolled, the ship shuddered to a halt and Luca's eyes opened slowly. His head was groggy, his vision blurred, but despite this, the first thing he realized was that he was now in a different room.

He was still onboard the ship.

He was still naked and bound to a chair.

But it was a different chair in a different suite.

It was bigger and brighter, and as his eyes continued to gradually pull focus, he saw something else.

Someone was in a chair opposite him, facing him.

It was a man.

Slowly he made out the man's features one by one—the deep brown eyes, the gentle lines that creased his forehead and the skin around his eyes, the mouth he knew so well—until Luca's eyes snapped wide open in fear and sheer panic.

"Marco! No!"

Luca saw that Marco's hands were behind his back, but at least he was conscious.

"Marco! Are you alright? Have they hurt you?"

Luca spun his head to see Dominic Dixon standing to Marco's left.

"You bastards! Don't you hurt him! Don't you lay a fucking finger on him or I swear to God—"

"God doesn't want to hear you swear," Dominic Dixon spat at Luca's feet.

"Let him go!" Luca roared. "He doesn't have anything to do with this. He doesn't know anything!"

"Actually," Marco said, speaking in a soft, calm voice. "I have everything to do with this. And I know—everything. I knew exactlly where the book could be found—"

"Marco, shut up!" Luca pleaded. "He's lying. He doesn't know what he's talking about. He's just trying to protect me, can't you see that?"

Suddenly Marco's hands appeared from behind his back—no sign of ropes or restraint whatsoever—and came to rest on the arms of his chair.

"Actually Luca, protecting you is the last thing on my mind. As I was saying, I knew exactly where the book was—because I'm the one who put it there in the first place."

Luca's eyes narrowed in confusion, shock, betrayal. "You what?"

The one-armed man chuckled, amused by Luca's stunned expression. He looked to Marco. "Anovver lashin', Holy Fadda? Just to help da news sink in?"

Marco maintained eye contact with the bewildered Luca, then calmly nodded.

Dominic Dixon brought his cat o'nine tails down on Luca's back and shoulders once again, but the young Italian barely felt it, barely flinched this time. He was already in a state of shock.

Disappointed by the lack of response, the one-armed man raised his whip again, but Marco held up his hand in an order to desist.

Dominic Dixon stopped the lashing in mid-air. "But he deserves it, Holy Fadda!"

"Enough!" Marco roared, his voice firm and dominant.
Snubbed and angry, Dominic Dixon put down his whip and grabbed the small silver crucifix around Luca's neck.

"At least let me take dis off him. He ain't worvy! Somefink dis precious shouldn't have to rest against his putrid skin."

Luca's whole body tightened. If not for the ropes, there was no telling what he might have done to the convicted rapist at that moment.

But he held as still as he could, dreading the noise it would make if the one-armed man should snap the chain from his neck at that moment; dreading the feeling of the broken chain sliding off his neck for the first time in his living memory.

"No!" Marco ordered. "It's too precious for your criminal claws. Now let it go and leave us."

"But—"

"I said leave!"

Luca let out a silent breath of relief as Dominic Dixon let go of the crucifix, then snatched his whip off the floor and stormed out of the room.

The door slammed behind him.

Marco stood from his chair and slowly paced the room.

"You're the Holy Father?" Luca finally found the words to speak, crushing back his astonishment, the betrayal, and the sudden hatred that was boiling inside him.

"You're shocked, I know. Understandably so. Things have changed since last I saw you."

"The last time you saw me was eight days ago! We fucked! Just like we used to! You told me you loved me!"

"I do," Marco said, not looking at Luca but at a table to one side of the room, upon which lay several objects that Luca could not make out from where he sat. "Let me rephrase my last sentence. Things have changed—" Marco spun aggressively to face Luca, "—since you left me five years ago!"

"Me leaving five years ago had nothing to do with you."

"It had everything to do with me!" Marco hissed. "It nearly destroyed me! Don't you understand? You were my muse! You gave me my gift! The ability to paint! The day you walked out the door, the paintbrushes turned to sticks, the colors dried up, the world was a different place. A lonely place. A place without any hope or comfort. Have you ever been there, Luca? It takes your soul. It changes who you are."

"But that day in Vita Sola, you hadn't changed at all. You were still the Marco I've always loved—"

"It was a mask!"

"Why didn't you tell me? If you felt so alone, why didn't you come and find me?"

Marco suddenly stormed up to Luca and snatched the crucifix around his neck. "Have you ever tried to find you, Luca da Roma? It's not easy, is it?" He let the cross drop against Luca's chest and returned to the table. "Besides, I was too angry with you. I loved you. And I hated you, too. Because the one thing I ever wanted to be was talented. And famous. Famous for my art. But you took that away!"

Luca shook his head, still not understanding anything he was hearing. "So you turned to a religious cult?"

"No," Marco laughed, almost pathetically, like he hadn't laughed for a long time. "Unlike the others, I don't give a damn about religion. But why should I tell them that. No, all I've ever cared about is art—and you. And fame. And everybody knows, if you can't be famous, be infamous, right? Or at least embark upon a quest to find the infamous. And in the entire history of art, there's nothing more infamous than The Cross of Sins."

Luca looked at him incredulously, as if he were looking at a stranger. "You killed Doctor Hadley, and God knows who else!"

"You're right, only God knows. God—and me."

"Marco, stop this. Listen to me, look at me. It's not too late to stop. It's not too late to change all this. I know you. I knew who you were. I can help you."

Marco laughed again. "But don't you see? I don't want help. I don't want to change any of it. I gave you the location of the book, so we could follow you, watch you hunt down the clues, do all the hard work, and eventually I knew you'd hand everything over on a silver platter. Like the head of John the Baptist." He laughed again. "Ask for it, and anything is yours. I can't tell you how many secret political associations and right-wing magnates are willing to throw money at you once you ascend to power of this kind. I've taken personal checks from the Vice President of the United States. The Pope has kissed my hand."

"So you keep the company of criminals and fanatics and powerful people just to satisfy your own agenda? You put on a hood for a mask, and you think anything is yours?"

"Yes," Marco said simply. "But the company I keep is irrelevant. I want to see it. I want to feel it in my hands. To find The Cross of Sins, to touch a work of art so renowned, so profound, so full of beliefs that the artist was willing to die for it—I can't imagine a greater gift from God."

"And when you find it?"

"I'll destroy it." There was no hesitation in Marco's voice. "I want to be the only one to touch it. I want to be the one person in all history—apart from the artist and his apprentice—to hold it."

Luca was nothing but astounded.

"I thought I knew you," he whispered, almost to himself. "I thought I loved you."

Marco said nothing. If there was shame or guilt or remorse anywhere inside him, he kept it buried deep and well concealed. Instead he walked over to Luca and untied the ropes that bound him.

"Can you stand?"

"What makes you think I won't try to escape? What makes you think I won't kill you, right here?"

Marco smiled. "I know you. I think you want to see The Cross as much as I do. If you really want to kill me, you'll wait. At least until after we find it. Now, can you stand? I want to show you something."

He hooked his hands underneath Luca's arm, but Luca shook him off and managed to find his own feet.

Marco lead him to the table on which sat the code book and Zefferino's stones, as well as a huge, ancient book with a brass latch.

The two stone tablets sat side by side now, with Zefferino's name joined across the top. All the inscriptions were lined up now.

Marco followed them with his finger as he transcribed: "The home of fire is the only place for those who seek The Naked Christ. But seek thine heart first, else eternal damnation awaits on the island of Vulcano."

Marco opened the large book then, the one with the brass latch, and flipped through its aged, frayed pages. It was an art book, filled with pictures of paintings and sculptures and sketches and notes. Soon he arrived at a painting of an ocean grotto. "It's one of Videlle's. A sea cave leading deep into the island of Vulcano, home of the Roman god of fire, the place where lightning was forged. This painting is the last piece in the puzzle. Videlle painted it in 1646. It's the only painting he ever did of Vulcano. According to locals, there is a rock shaped like a heart inside this cave, where the sea meets the lava." He turned to Luca, his eyes burning with passion, with determination. "Seek thine heart. That's where we'll find it. That's where Zefferino hid The Naked Christ, all those years ago, as though he had hidden it inside one of Videlle's own paintings. It's the only place it could be."

Marco reached out and touched Luca's shoulder, hot and bleeding from the lashes. "Now, my dear muse, it's time for you to get dressed. You're coming with me."

Marco ran his fingers down Luca's bare back, all the way down. Luca flinched, remembering a time when Marco's touch thrilled him. Now all it did was chill him to the bone. "What about the others?" Luca asked.

"They're staying here. I've given Eric instructions to take good care of them."

Luca couldn't look at Marco. He kept his eyes focused on the table. On the painting in the book. The painting with Videlle's trademark signature scribbled upside-down at the bottom of the canvas.

"How can you be so sure The Cross is where you think it is?" he asked.

"How can you doubt it? I have the book. I have the stones. There are no clues left."

He leaned in close, took Luca's face in his hands and whispered, "If I can't find it, who can?"

XV

THE ISLAND OF VULCANO, ITALY

The island loomed large against the backdrop of the electrical storm. The ocean waves rose up high, and the wind sliced the top off their crests before the waves rolled down and rose again. And through it all, Jake, Eden and Will shot across the swirling seas in a forty-four-foot Sea Ray Sundancer. It was normally used for diving expeditions off the coast of Sicily; now it was being used on a rescue mission, its long slender bow spearheading the waves as it streaked across the sea.

The three of them were drenched from the stinging spray and the driving rain, but they didn't care. All that mattered was getting to the island and finding the others before it was too late.

"Over there," Eden called. He was looking through a pair of binoculars and had spotted the lights of Salvation.

He passed the lenses over to Jake, who slowed the motors and handed the wheel over to Will.

"They've dropped anchor," Jake said. "Wait, there's a smaller craft. It's heading for the island."

Lightning flashed, illuminating the bigger picture for Jake.

"There's a large sea cave. They're heading for it."

"Who's on board?" Will asked.

"Six people, maybe eight." Suddenly he pulled the binoculars away and turned to Will and Eden. "They've got Luca."

"Will, take us to shore," Eden said, thinking fast. "Then stay with the boat and keep an eye on that ship. If it tries to leave, stop it."

"How?"

"You'll think of something."

"What about you guys?"

With his one good arm, Eden grabbed two flare guns out of the boat's emergency compartment, threw one to Jake and pocketed four flares. "We'll be fine. But if the Professor and Elsa and Shane are still on board that ship, we can't let it go anywhere."

"I'll take care of things," Will nodded, then turned the wheel and steered the boat swiftly toward the island.

Eden and Jake jumped ashore in waist-deep waters, fighting the turbulent waves as they mounted a slippery outcrop that twisted around the rock face and led to the cave opening.

Will reversed the boat out of danger, before the pounding waves pushed it onto the rocks. Then he turned the wheel and headed back toward the ship, keeping his distance from the larger vessel so as not to draw attention to himself.

*

The small craft maneuvered its way through the sea cave, its outboard motor echoing through the grotto and drowning out the crash and rumble of the sea and thunder outside.

The boat pulled up alongside a rocky ledge and one of the Crimson Crown disciples jumped out and tied it securely to a large rock.

Dressed in his crimson robe, Marco stepped onto the rocks first, his minion bowing and helping him ashore as though he were royalty.

Dominic Dixon followed, also in his robe. He dragged Luca out of the boat with him, now dressed in his tuxedo pants and blood-stained white shirt.

The other four disciples then stepped ashore. One carried

torches, one carried a thick wire cable and grappling hook coiled over his shoulder, one carried a pick and one a shovel.

Marco turned to Luca. "Are you ready to unravel history?"

Luca said nothing.

Marco simply smiled, then turned to his men. "Come."

He led the group along the rocky ledge. It climbed high above the waterline and through a small opening into the depths of the island.

As the group vanished inside, Jake and Eden appeared at the sea entrance of the grotto, negotiating the rock ledges with speed and skill as they made their way inside the ocean cavern.

They each held a flare gun in their hands.

Eden saw the last of the disciples disappear into the small opening. "Up there," he pointed.

*

Will pulled out the binoculars and wiped the rain from the lenses. He thought he saw movement at the stern of the ship, and the view through the binoculars confirmed it.

"Shit," he whispered to himself.

Elsa, the Professor and Shane emerged from inside the ship's cabin, their hands tied behind their backs. Shane was limping and looked as if he'd been beaten pretty badly. Elsa and the Professor looked unharmed, but certainly not out of harm's way. The three of them were being marched toward the back of the boat by Eric Landon and another disciple, both of whom carried pistols.

Will didn't waste any time.

He gunned the engines and took the Sea Ray up to full speed, launching it across the choppy waters like a rocket skimming the surface.

*

Marco led his mission deep into the island, past bottomless black tidal pools and naturally-formed sinkholes that gushed and sprayed with the force of the ocean that pushed and pulled its way under the island, unseen beneath them.

But it wasn't long before the spray of the sea turned into thick clouds of sulfur; before the chill of the ocean beneath them gave way to an unmistakable heat pressing toward them.

That's when Marco saw a passage ahead of them, glowing bright orange.

He grinned. "The home of fire," he whispered to himself.

"Eternal damnation," Luca whispered at the same time.

"Come!" Marco ordered.

He rushed forward and emerged onto a thin ledge overlooking a giant, slow-moving river of molten lava.

Marco's eyes widened with awe, glowing red in the reflection of the river below.

Luca appeared behind him, followed by Dominic Dixon and the other disciples.

"Blimey!" breathed the one-armed man, chuckling with wonder.

The ledge upon which they stood was narrow and ran the entire length of the bubbling, burning river, but that's not what grabbed everyone's attention; it was the two spectacular waterfalls of lava that cascaded from the wall opposite them into the river below—and in the middle of the waterfalls was a rocky ledge upon which sat an enormous, perfectly-formed, heart-shaped rock.

"This is the place," Marco smiled.

*

Onboard Salvation, Eric Landon smiled. "Check their ropes," he ordered his henchman, who forcefully spun Elsa, Shane and the Professor about, so they would face the back of the boat. The rain had stopped, but the black ocean still churned and lapped ferociously at the stern of the ship.

The disciple tugged on the ropes and tightened them even more. Elsa winced.

"Careful," Eric warned. "You don't want to cut off their circulation. You just want to make it impossible for them to swim."

With that, Eric stepped forward, placed one foot squarely in the middle of Elsa's back, then pushed her clear over the stern's railing.

"Elsa!" cried the Professor.

But it was too late. Elsa screamed as she plunged headfirst over the railing, landing in the hungry waves with a tremendous splash.

Shane instantly jumped up on the railing to dive in after her, but the disciple grabbed him by the rope behind his back and hauled him back to the floor of the deck.

Shane kicked at the robed man, striking him in the kneecap and breaking it with a sharp crack. The disciple screamed and fell to the deck in agony.

He dropped his gun.

Shane dived for it, but he couldn't grab it with his hands behind his back. All he could do was kick it away.

His opponent tried to stop him, but Shane got to it first, and the gun scuttled across the deck.

Suddenly Eric seized the Professor and pushed the snout of his pistol hard up into the Professor's chin.

Shane leapt to his feet, hands still tied.

"Hold it!" Eric shouted, his hostage firmly in hand.

Shane stopped, saw the Professor in danger, and for a moment everything fell silent.

Almost everything.

That's when they all heard the roar of a speedboat approaching fast.

Approaching too fast!

Eric and Shane quickly glanced to starboard.

All Shane could see was the speedboat coming at them at top speed. Then he saw a blur as someone leapt from the boat, into the water, setting the Sea Ray on a collision course for the ship.

"Will?" he whispered.

And then—

BOOM!!

The sound of the speedboat hitting the ship was like an explosion, all the more so because of the physical impact on Salvation. The speedboat pierced straight into the middle of the starboard side of the boat, lancing the hull and ramming half the length of its entire body in through the side of the larger vessel.

Salvation jolted and the starboard side lifted clear out of the water—with the speedboat lodged in its side—as though it might capsize.

The deck tilted sharply.

Shane and Eric, along with the loose pistol, slid down the deck and smashed into the portside railing.

The Professor, left blind and standing at the edge of the stern, was thrown from the boat and into the water.

The robed disciple with the broken kneecap rolled down the deck and over the edge as well.

The ship corrected itself and landed flat back on the ocean surface with an almighty slap!

That's when the sea began to pour in through the hole in the ship, between its own smashed hull and the slender, spearhead hull of the Sea Ray.

Shane tumbled back toward starboard, but with his hands still fastened behind his back, he was helpless to control his roll. The lunge sent him careening into the cabin and directly down a set of stairs into the lower deck of the ship.

Eric slid to a halt in the middle of the deck, his own gun in one hand as the disciple's gun skimmed along the deck and stopped directly in front of his face.

His grinning face.

*

When Will dove from the charging speedboat, the momentum of the Sea Ray catapulted him through the air and into the churning waves with incredible force, propelling him like a torpedo deep into the water, a split second before the speedboat plowed through the side of Salvation.

Once his momentum had stopped, the force of the waves wanted to push him back and forth like a tiny fish. The water, too, was almost pitch-dark, but the odd bolt of electricity still streaked across the sky, sporadically illuminating the vast black ocean.

In one flash, he saw the unmistakable sight of Elsa, sinking to the bottom of the ocean. Her legs were trying desperately to kick her up toward air, but her hands were tied behind her back, and her heavy, waterlogged dressing gown pulled her deeper and deeper down.

As the last bubbles escaped her lungs and ascended to the air above, Will used all his strength to push himself down toward her.

The ocean went black again.

Will kicked as hard as he could.

His arms pushed through the water, parting the current as if he were parting rocks.

And then, another flash of lightning.

And something else caught his eye.

Something on the surface, near the smashed hulls of the two conjoined boats.

It was the Professor, also with his hands tied behind his back.

Worse still, there was something else splashing in the water a few feet away from him. Will quickly realized the disciple in the black robe had toppled into the water as well.

Will stopped, his lungs burning, his eyes darting from Elsa—sweet, kind Elsa, sinking quickly to the seabed—then back to the Professor—the man who made everything happen, the man who had brought them all together, the man who strived for justice and equality—struggling on the surface.

In another flare of lightning, Will saw the disciple splashing awkwardly through the water before grabbing at the Professor, as if to keep himself afloat.

As if using the Professor as a buoy.
Dragging himself on top of the old blind man.
Kicking him down.
Sending him under.
Will had to think. He had to make a choice.
Save Elsa—
—or the Professor.

*

Marco himself seized the thick wire cable and grappling hook off his disciple on the ledge. He looped one end of the cable, and using it like a lasso, he hurled it wide across the river of lava.

It landed perfectly over the heart-shaped boulder, and Marco pulled it tight. He forced the grappling hook into a thin crevice in the wall behind him, and just for good measure took one of the shovels and pounded the hook into place.

He tested the strength of the cable to make sure it was taut enough, then said to Luca, "You go first."

As if to reinforce this instruction, Dominic Dixon pulled his gun on Luca. "You heard da Holy Fadda. Move!"

Luca took a deep breath for courage and stepped toward the cable, testing it himself. It seemed tight enough, but there was only one way to find out whether or not it would hold his weight.

With both hands on the cable, Luca lowered himself, head first, over the river of lava. The cabled bowed a little but held strong. Luca hooked his feet up over the cable, taking his weight off the ground completely, then, dangling like a cannibal's captive on a spit, he started to pull himself, hand-over-hand, over the lava and toward the rocky ledge on the other side.

He could feel the heat of the oozing magma, only fifteen feet below, scorching his lashed, bleeding back. He could hear the pop and spatter of bubbles exploding on the river's slow-moving surface. He shut his eyes and tried to push it all out of his head.

Hand-over-hand.

All he could focus on was one hand, then the other, slowly pulling him toward the rocky ledge on the other side,

"You're almost there," he heard Marco call.

Just then, a tremor rocked the entire cavern, as though Marco's words had sent a warning to the protective volcano.

Instantly, Marco and his men backed up against the wall behind them, holding fast. Rocks fell from the cavern's ceiling and turned to red liquid as they splashed into the river.

Luca held on as tight as he could, but the tremor sent a violent ripple all the way down the cable.

His feet slipped, and suddenly he was dangling by his hands over the glowing river.

He didn't know how long he could hold on in the one spot. Nor did he want to find out.

The rocky ledge was close.

Luca made a break for it, swinging quickly, recklessly, from one hand to the other, his legs swinging wildly beneath him, the cable quaking in his grip, until—

He let go.

He swung his legs toward the ledge—and landed on the very edge of it.

Small rocks trickled away under him. His heels slipped off the edge, but Luca managed to pull his weight forward and dropped safely to his knees on the ledge, facing the heart-shaped rock as if he were kneeling before an altar.

The tremor rumbled back inside the mountain, like thunder rolling away.

Luca turned back to Marco, who smiled, impressed. Perhaps even relieved.

"Well done," Marco said, not loud enough for Luca to hear him.

He turned to his disciples.

"I'll go next. Then the five of you." He turned to Dominic

Dixon. "You stay here. Mind the entrance."

The one-armed man looked at him, stunned and betrayed. "But—"

"Don't be a fool! There's no possible way you can make it across with only one arm."

Dominic Dixon gestured to his missing arm. "But I did dis for Him—for you, my Holy Fadda!"

"Then obey my order!"

The one-armed man bowed his head, reluctantly. "Yes, my Lord."

*

Shane crashed down the stairs into the cabin and slammed against the lower deck.

The first thought that crossed his mind was the water; the sea was gushing in through the crashed hull just ahead of him. The speedboat had completely smashed apart the suite where Elsa and the Professor had been kept and was now jutting across the corridor leading to the other suites at the bow of the ship.

The second thought that flashed through Shane's brain was: Where's Eric? This question was answered immediately.

The sound of a gunshot pierced the air, and the wooden panel an inch from Shane's head splintered into a million tiny shards.

Shane pulled himself frantically to his feet.

That's when the third thought entered his head. He needed his hands freed or he was a dead man.

Staggering wildly, he ran toward the incoming flood.

Behind him, he could hear the sound of Eric's footsteps crashing down the stairs before he splashed into the water.

All around Shane could hear the groan of metal and the snap of timber as Salvation began to sink and slowly break apart. He reached the hull of the speedboat and managed, against the rushing force of the flooding seawater, to squeeze under it, emerging in the corridor on the other side of the intruding Sea Ray.

He rushed through the first door he could find and kicked it shut behind him. He backed up against the door handle, and with his tied hands he managed to lock the door. Then he looked around desperately for a knife, anything sharp, that he might be able to use to cut the ropes.

But there was nothing in the room but two chairs, a rope on the flooding floor, and a table with several items on it.

These weren't just items though.

It was the code book, and the two stone tablets, and another large book that when Shane rushed over to the table, appeared to be an old book of art.

It was open to a page that had printed on it a work from Videlle. An ocean cave.

Shane glanced from the art book to the stones—and suddenly something dawned on him.

*

Will made his choice.

He swam upward.

He swam away from Elsa.

But he didn't swim toward the Professor either.

Instead he swam away from both of them, heading as fast as he could for the boats.

He reached the back of the sinking Sea Ray, protruding from the side of the ship, and pulled himself onto the dive platform at its stern, which was already half underwater. There was a compartment there, and he lifted to hatch, let the ocean rush in and rummaged through it as quickly as he could.

"Come on, come on, you gotta be here."

He found flippers, scuba masks, snorkels, and—an air tank.
He checked the gauge. It was almost empty, but there were a couple of minutes of oxygen left, which was all he needed.

He dug even deeper in the compartment, found a weights belt and strapped it on. Found a knife and slotted it inside the weights belt.

With the tank clenched in his fist he dove back into the swirling sea and swam as hard as he could, deeper and deeper, feeling the help of the weights belt pulling him down.

He glanced back once and saw the Professor, still struggling under the robed man. Will hated himself for leaving the Professor there.

But first—

There was another flash of lightning, and he glimpsed Elsa drifting further and further down into the black depths. She was no longer moving. Will kicked with all his might, descending with all the speed he could muster.

He gained on Elsa quickly, who floated peacefully downward.

He triggered the air on the tank.

Bubbles erupted from the mouthpiece.

Will held out his hand to grab Elsa and virtually crashed into her unconscious, drifting body. He snatched up the knife, unclipped the weights belt and watched it plummet like stone into the darkness below, and suddenly his descent instantly turned into an ascent. With another burst of bubbles he pushed the tank's mouthpiece into Elsa's mouth. He used the knife to cut the ropes.

There was no response.

At least not initially.

And then, with a sudden jolt, Elsa came to life. Eyes wide. Arms flailing.

Lightning lit up the water and she saw Will.

She tried to say something, but a gush of oxygen sent the words straight into her lungs.

Will wrapped one strong arm around her waist and with his other he began to swim upward, kicking frantically, pulling them both toward the surface.

Toward Professor Fathom before it was too late.

*

Marco jumped from the cable and joined Luca on the ledge, as did the first two disciples, one carrying the shovel strapped to his back, the other carrying the pick.

But when the second tremor hit, the other three followers of the Crimson Crown—still clinging to the cable—didn't stand a chance.

From the rocky ledge, Marco, Luca and the two disciples watched in horror as the men's hands and feet slipped from the shuddering cable, sending the three robed disciples screaming and flailing into the river of lava below.

They hit the surface of the magma one by one, their robes instantly exploding into flames before the men, still screaming and squealing, literally melted into lava.

On the narrow ledge by the entrance, Dominic Dixon couldn't help but giggle at the horrific vision before him. So distracted by the grisly sight was he, that he didn't even hear the two figures approaching in the passage behind him.

"Dominic Dixon," said a voice out of the darkness of the passage. "This is for Jacques Dumas."

The one-armed man swung about quickly, raising his gun, but before he could fire a single bullet, Eden pulled the trigger of his own weapon and a blinding flare shot through the passage like a comet and struck Dominic Dixon square in the stomach.

He screamed and staggered back a step, but before he stumbled over the edge, the one-armed man caught his balance.

With the flare sizzling like a tiny sun in his gut and his robe quickly catching fire, Dominic Dixon launched himself at Eden and Jake, firing madly.

On the rocky ledge opposite, Marco and Luca looked up at the sound of gunfire and saw Dixon aflame, charging away down the passage.

Marco snapped his fingers at his minions and pointed to the ground in front of the heart-shaped boulder. "Dig! Now!"

In the passage opposite, Jake and Eden dived for cover as Dominic Dixon, crazed and furious and burning alive, staggered recklessly through the passage. Flames devoured his robe and latched onto his hood, burning his eyes. He could barely see and was shooting at random now. Nonetheless, one shot collected Eden in the shoulder of his broken arm.

Jake returned fire, sending another flare across the passage and straight into Dominic Dixon's side.

He squealed again, then turned and began to stagger backward, away from the river of lava, out of the passage and back down into the darkness of the sea tunnel.

He was like a glowing beacon, burning and sizzling and smoking through the darkness, until eventually he fell backwards into one of nature's deep, gushing sinkholes.

The one-armed man screamed.

Then Eden and Jake heard a loud splash of water.

Then the burning light went out, and all they could hear from the well was the hiss of steam.

Dominic Dixon was gone.

*

Will kicked harder and harder, pulling Elsa up through the water alongside him. She, too, tried to kick as hard as she could. She could see Will's lungs were bursting and took the oxygen tank's mouthpiece out of her mouth and pressed it into his.

The air gave him an extra push, re-energizing him instantly. But it was short-lived. The oxygen thinned, and Will checked the gauge. Empty.

He looked at Elsa and a silent communication passed between them. She nodded she was okay, she could make it to the surface.

Will let the tank go.

It dropped into the darkness and the loss of its weight gave them even more speed as they ascended.

Above them, not far now, the Professor weakened in his struggle against the man in the robe. His movements were becoming more and more labored until soon he stopped moving altogether.

*

"Dig!" Marco ordered his disciples. "Faster!"

The shovel hit something hard, something that made a hollow thud.

Marco bent down to brush the dirt and rock away from what they had found.

At that moment, Luca smiled as he saw Jake and Eden appear on the narrow ledge on the other side of the river. They had reloaded their flare guns, each with one last flare each, then pointed them across the river.

Eden fired, and one of his flares hit the disciple with the shovel square in the head. The man's hood more or less combusted and he dropped to the ground dead, his body convulsing and his skull ablaze.

Luca grabbed the shovel. He smashed the flat end of the blade across the face of the other disciple, who reeled backwards, slipped on the edge of the ledge and plummeted screaming into the lava.

Marco reached inside his robe and pulled a gun.

Luca turned the shovel on him, but Marco pointed his gun straight at Luca's head. "Don't even think about it."

Luca froze.

Marco kept one eye on him and shouted back to Jake and Eden on the ledge opposite. "You shoot me, I shoot him. Now throw your guns into the lava."

At first neither Eden nor Jake moved a muscle.

Marco cocked the hammer on his pistol. "I said do it!"

Eden threw his weapon in first, which was already empty. Jake on the other hand still had one flare left.

"Throw it in," Eden whispered, nursing his wounded arm.

Jake swallowed hard. Giving in to an ultimatum like this was not the kind of thing he had ever done. He only ever had himself to look out for, and the risk always seemed worth it. But now—

"Jake, do as he says."

"But I can make the shot," Jake told Eden. "I can nail him."

"And if you don't?"

Jake swallowed hard.

"Jake," Eden whispered. "It's not worth it."

Jake glanced at Eden, who gently, subtly, shook his head. It was all he needed to do.

Jake pushed out a reluctant sigh and tossed the flare gun into the lava. The flare inside erupted in a blast of fireworks on impact.

Marco laughed.

"Good," he said, and then turned to Luca. "Now, you! Dig out my treasure!"

With the gun trained at his head, Luca pushed the shovel into the earth and dug around the edges of the treasure in the hole. Eventually, he dropped the shovel and knelt. He pushed the dirt and rocks aside with his bare hands and pulled from the earth an iron canister.

Marco's brow creased in confusion. Confusion that quickly turned to anger. He knew the stature was much bigger than this canister.

"What the fuck is that?"

There was a latch on the canister. Luca opened it and found a piece of parchment inside. He unraveled it. There was a message, written in Italian.

"What does it say!" Marco shouted. "Read it!"

"Welcome to eternal damnation," Luca said.

Marco stared at him in utter fury, then snatched the parchment off him and read it himself.

Suddenly Luca started laughing.

Suddenly the clues, the stones, the artworks of Videlle—everything—became clear to him.

"Don't you see? You read the clues wrong," Luca told Marco. "You were supposed to turn Zefferino's name upside-down. It's what Videlle always did. And it was Zefferino's final fuck-you to the world. The stones were the wrong way up. And so were the symbols."

*

Shane stepped back from the table containing the two books and the two stones and knew he was going to have to do something drastic to free his hands. He knew he couldn't slide his hands under his ass and legs and around to the front; his shoulders and chest were too broad and it was simply not physically possible with his hands bound behind his back.

But he knew he could do it—if he dislocated one of his shoulders.

Suddenly the door handle turned, then shook violently against the lock. There was a thud against the door. Eric was trying to get in but couldn't, unlike the water that was beginning to spray in streams and pressured jets around the rim of the door.

The ship lurched.

Shane didn't have much time.

He hurried to one wall, leaned to the left and aimed his shoulder into the wall, then with all his strength and speed he rammed himself at the wall.

There was a horrible klock!

It was the sound of his arm popping out of its shoulder socket.

Shane screamed, the pain rocking his entire body.

There were another two, three, four thuds against the door.

Shane fell to the floor, into the deepening pool of water, not because he couldn't deal with the agony, but to roll onto his back and lift his legs in the air while his right arm pulled his useless left arm down, sliding it under his ass and down the backs of his thighs. He bent his knees and pulled his arms around his heels and toes, bringing them up in front of him.

His eyes blinked back the pain as he staggered to his feet, and with his hands now bound in front of him, he took his left shoulder in his right hand, positioned his arm back into place, then leaned up against the wall and pushed with all his strength.

He roared with pain once more as his shoulder popped back into its socket.

With the next thud, the door actually bounced on its hinges. The lock held strong, but the hinges bent and buckled. They wouldn't hold for long.

Shane raced over to the table.

He had already figured out the same key to the puzzle as Luca.

The young Texan took Zefferino's stones in his hands now and turned them into an upside-down position.

He grabbed the code book, and flicked through the pages quickly to see if he could find the new, upside-down inscriptions.

They were there.

Sand.

Five.

Tree.

Sun.

Filfla.

His eyes scanned the message and pieced together as much as he could before—

—*Bam!*

With one more heavy thud and a tidal rush of water, Eric broke down the door and burst into the room.

*

Marco threw the parchment onto the ground and aimed his gun at Luca, but before he could fire Luca swung the iron canister at him, knocking the gun clean out of Marco's hand.

It flew through the air and skidded to a halt on the edge of the ledge.

Luca snatched up the shovel once more.

Marco grabbed the pick.

On the opposite ledge, Jake leapt onto the wire cable and started to climb across as fast as he could, hand over hand, to the other side.

"Jake!" Eden called.

"Stay there," Jake shouted back. "You're shot. Besides, I know what I'm doing." Then, under his breath, "I've done this volcano stuff before, trust me."

Marco swung his pick at Luca, who fended him off with a thud and a thwack of his shovel.

"You know you can't beat me at this," Marco warned. "I'm older than you. I'm wiser. And more powerful. I'm your creator, remember?"

Luca shook his head. "And I was your Muse. Was!"

He struck at Marco with his shovel, but this time it was Marco who deflected the move, retaliating with a blow directly to Luca's shoulder with the pick.

The pick-end plunged into Luca's muscle, and the young Italian reared backward.

Marco pulled the pick free and a small chunk of Luca's flesh came with it. Luca let out another roar then fell backward.

Jake watched from halfway along the cable and poured on the speed.

On the rocky ledge, Marco raised the pick high above his head, but before he could bring it down on Luca's skull, the young Italian stabbed the spade of his shovel directly into Marco's shin, slicing clean through flesh and bone.

Marco screamed.

He dropped the pick and staggered backward before giving in to the pain and falling on his hands and knees.

That's when he saw the gun, sitting on the brink of the ledge only a few feet in front of him.

Marco scrambled as fast as he could.

Luca saw him make a move for the gun. He dropped the shovel and lunged at Marco, but the momentum of his crash-tackle sent Marco, and the gun, crashing over the edge.

The gun toppled and spun and splashed into the lava.

Marco felt himself go over the edge and reached for anything his hands could grab onto.

Luca managed to stop himself at the edge, grabbing onto the

rocky surface with both hands, facing downward, but felt a sudden pull around his neck.

As he fell, Marco's fingers had hooked his chain, his silver crucifix.

Luca gasped.

The chain snapped and slipped from Luca's neck, clutched now in Marco's fist.

Luca's arm went wide and grabbed the other end of the broken chain.

Marco thudded against the small cliff-face, dangling over the lava, clinging to one end of Luca's chain.

At the end of it, Luca held on as tight as he could, himself hanging over the edge.

But the tiny silver necklace was slipping in his grip.

*

Eric Landon burst through the door, his expression an exhausted mix of anger, determination and pleasure. As he glared at Shane, there was no doubt he was going to enjoy this. He had two guns now, one in each hand, and he raised them both.

Shane looked around desperately. There were no portholes in the room, no weapons to grab, no escape except the door with Eric standing in the way, no furniture to use as cover except the table behind him, made of wood so thin a bullet would pass straight through it.

"There's nowhere left to run," Eric grinned. "No more narrow escapes, cowboy. Time for God to pass His judgment."

Eric aimed both guns straight at Shane's chest.

In the same second, Shane spun and with his bound hands he grabbed the first thing he could reach on the table.

He turned back, one of the stones of Zefferino in his hands, and raised the tablet in front of his chest like a shield, just as Eric pulled the trigger on both guns.

There were two ear-piercing cracks!

The stone tablet broke in two in Shane's hands then fell into the water.

He looked down quickly at his own bare chest.

Nothing. Not a scratch.

Then he looked up at Eric, whose stunned and confused eyes slowly looked down at his robe. He dropped both guns, and with his hands, he tore his robe open from the hood down, revealing his chest.

Blood began to pour from not one, but two small holes, one in each side of his chest. The bullets had ricocheted straight off Zefferino's stone, bouncing back into the man who had fired them.

Eric gasped and dropped to his knees, landing in water up to his waist.

Shane dropped down next to him, and with his hands still tied together he pressed his palms against the wounds in Eric's chest.

"You'll be okay. We'll get you to a hospital. You'll be fine."

But he couldn't stop the blood from pouring between his fingers.

Eric's bewildered face turned to Shane. "He made me—imperfect," Eric breathed, his voice suddenly straining. "I didn't want to believe it."

"He made us all imperfect," Shane whispered. "But He still loves us."

Eric smiled at that thought. Shane could actually see hope in his eyes. "Do you think so?"

Shane nodded. "Yeah. I do."

With that, Eric Landon's eyelids fluttered, and his head rolled back on his neck. His body shuddered ever so slightly, then fell limp into Shane's embrace.

At the same time, the ship groaned and suddenly the wood paneling along one wall began to buckle and snap.

Slowly, Shane lowered Eric's body down into the water. He knew there was nothing he could do for him now. But if he didn't get himself off the ship in the next minute or so, *Salvation* would become his final resting place as well.

Shane raced from the suite, through the door and back down the lower deck's corridor.

The water was well above his waist now, and the weight of the speedboat, still blocking the passageway, was putting pressure on both walls, pushing them inward. Salvation rocked, and Shane felt it drop another few feet into the sea. Water gushed in with even greater force and then rose quickly to his chest. All through the ship, he could hear steel bending, wood cracking and glass splintering under the crushing weight of the water.

There was no going over the speedboat in front of him. The only way through the passage was to go under it like before.

Shane took a deep breath and dived under the water.

He grabbed the hull of the Sea Ray and with his hands tied together pulled himself downward. He squeezed through the gap between the bottom of the speedboat's hull and the floor of the passageway and pulled himself through to the other side, but before he was completely clear, Salvation gave a massive shudder, as if in its final death throes, which caused the Sea Ray to groan and shift, dropping onto Shane's right foot before he could pull himself out of harm's way.

Still underwater, Shane grunted and precious air escaped his lungs as the speedboat crushed his foot. Trapping him.

He tried to pull himself free, tried to push the hull of the speedboat off his crushed ankle, but it was too heavy.

Air burst from his lungs.

*

Beneath the water, Will's hand reached up and wrapped itself around the Professor's ankle, pulling him down and away from the flailing robed man.

Mustering all the strength he had, Will swam with both the Professor and Elsa toward the sinking ship and the three of them broke the surface at last.

Elsa and Will gasped for air, but the Professor was unconscious.

"Professor! Professor can you hear me!" Will shouted.

As the three of them struggled on the surface, bobbing madly, it was Elsa who took the Professor's face in her hands and shook him hard. "Max! *Aufwachen!* I said, wake up!"

With one almighty slap across the face, the Professor's blind eyes burst open and his lungs sucked in all the air they could hold.

That's when two arms suddenly appeared behind him and latched onto his shoulders, dragging him under the water once more with a terrible gurgle.

It was the drowning disciple, his own face struggling to keep above the waves.

"Enough!" Will shouted.

As the Professor sank between him and the robed man, it gave Will a clear shot at him.

The young college student pulled back his fist and planted it squarely in the disciple's face. Once, twice, three times, shouting with each blow—

"Leave—"

"—the Professor—"

"—alone!"

On the third blow, the waves swallowed the Crimson Crown disciple, who drifted without a struggle into the black sea and was gone.

Will reached under the water, grabbed the Professor by the collar of his dressing gown and brought him back to the surface where he once again hauled in a lungful of air.

With an almighty groan behind them, Salvation dropped another few feet into the sea, jettisoning gusts of air from its compartments and cabins.

"I think Shane's still onboard," Elsa gasped.

"I'll get him."

Will swam directly for the sinking vessel, clambered on board and threw Elsa and the Professor a life-ring with the name Salvation printed around its rim.

Then he vanished from sight, racing down into the lower cabins.

Will charged down the steps to the lower deck and jumped into the water that lapped at his chest. He waded through it determinedly.

"Shane! Shane!"

Up ahead was the hull of the Sea Ray, like a wall blocking the passageway. Water flooded in all around it. Will rushed up to the hull of the speedboat and tried to shout over the top of it, assuming Shane may have been trapped on the other side.

Suddenly, something grabbed his foot and pulled him beneath the surface.

Under the water, Will's eyes bulged as he saw Shane thrashing his ankle, struggling for air, trying to free his foot which was trapped under the hull of the speedboat.

Will quickly resurfaced, took a huge lungful of air, then dived down to Shane, grabbed his face in both hands and kissed him hard, sealing their lips together. He breathed his air into Shane's lungs, then let go of him and began pulling on Shane's leg and pushing at the hull of the speedboat as hard as he could.

Nothing was budging.

Frantic, Will surfaced again, looking around quickly for something he could use as leverage. There was nothing. He raced back down the passageway, up the steps. He found a wooden oar, but knew it would only snap under the weight of the speedboat if he tried to use it as a lever.

He found shackles and a chain, but they were no use to him.

He found a rope. No good.

Then it occurred to him. "The engines," he said out loud.

Start the boat, gun the engines. The vibrations would destabilize everything onboard the sinking ship, and with any luck, shift the Sea Ray. The idea would either work for him, or against him, but it was worth a try.

Will raced as fast as he could to the cockpit, glancing into the water to make sure Elsa and the Professor were well clear. He spotted them clinging to the life-ring some distance away and knew they were safe.

He reached the ship's controls and switched over the ignition. A warning alarm sounded. "I know," Will shouted at the controls, "we're sinking. Now shut up!" He flicked an override switch on the alarm and felt the rumble of the propeller blades send a tremor throughout the entire vessel. He grabbed the throttle lever and pushed it forward as far as it would go.

That's when all hell started to break loose—and Salvation began to break apart altogether.

The windows in the cockpit cracked and shattered, but Will was already gone.

He jumped down to the stern deck, just as the entire deck itself began to split in two. The ship lurched, the stern completely reared out of the water, and two madly spinning propeller blades emerged from the ocean like angry shrieking sea monsters.

The bow of the ship nose-dived into the water then.

Will dived down below deck and heard an almighty *KARACK*!

The speedboat was sliding free. In fact, everything was sliding free.

In a cacophony of thuds and snaps, every door broke off its hinges, every wall splintered apart, every inch of flooring fractured into a million pieces.

Will swam beneath the water and found Shane, now unconscious and floating free amidst the chaos. The young college student seized Shane with one hand, and with the other, he managed to grab the bow of the speedboat as it slipped backward out through the massive hole it had made in the side of the sinking ship.

Will and Shane were swept out with Sea Ray, clear of Salvation, slipping into the depths of the black churning currents.

The speedboat was sinking, too, but not as fast as the ship as every last pocket of air gushed from its broken body, its propellers still spinning madly, sending it on a speedy descent to the bottom of the ocean.

There was a flash of lightning above, and Will caught one last glimpse of the silver letters SALVATION on the stern of the ship before the vessel disappeared forever.

At that moment, Will let go of the speedboat and watched the Sea Ray drift to the seabed as well, then with Shane in his grasp, he swam to back to the surface.

"Shane?" Elsa cried as Will towed him to the life-ring.

"Is he alive?" the Professor asked desperately.

As if to answer the question himself, Shane suddenly spluttered up water, took a lungful of air and opened his eyes.

"We're in the wrong place," he coughed. "I know where The Cross is."

*

The tiny silver cross glinted in the reflection of the gargantuan red river burning and bubbling below it. Luca felt the thin silver chain begin to slip through his sweaty grip. On the other end of it, Marco stared up, eyes horrified and pleading.

"Don't let go," Marco whispered.

But Luca was staring not at Marco, but the chain. "You have to let it go," Luca pleaded back.

That's when Marco noticed what he had snatched. Luca's precious silver crucifix—the only key to his past—hung precariously midway down the chain, between Marco and Luca's slippery grips, out of reach of both of them.

Marco laughed, his voice nervous and broken. "How ironic. There's nothing between us now but your own secret cross."

The chain slipped out of Luca's desperate hands by another few tiny links, and Luca pushed himself further down to try to tighten his grip, his entire waist now hanging on the edge.

"Let go of it," he said.

But Marco shook his head. "Pull me up. You can do it. Save me, and I'll tell you the secret behind your precious crucifix."

Luca's legs had nothing to cling to. He could feel them sliding closer and closer to the edge. "What are you talking about?"

"I told you before. I know everything. Do you remember a clown—named Valentino."

At that moment, another tremor rocked the cavern.

Luca's entire weight went over the edge.

Marco's eyes widened in horror.

Luca gasped, helpless to save himself.

Then suddenly, something—someone—grabbed his ankle.

"Hold on there, big fella," Jake grunted, snatching Luca's ankle in a one-handed grip as Jake himself was dragged toward the edge.

The tremor stopped abruptly, and with his free hand, Jake managed to grab a rock and cling to it. But if another tremor came, there would be no telling if that rock would hold.

Jake held onto Luca's ankle.

Luca held onto one end of the chain.

Marco held onto the other.

Through clenched teeth, Jake muttered, "Luca, let it go. I can't hold you both."

Luca shook his hand. "I can't. I let go of this chain, and I'll never know who I am."

Another tremor, the biggest of all, rocked the cavern without warning. Jake clung to the rock as hard as he could, but he could feel it dislodging.

"You already know who you are," Jake said, not having to yell over the roar of the quake. He knew Luca could hear him. Hear him loud and clear. "You're one of us."

Luca looked up, doubtful he had any idea.

Then he saw Jake's eyes.

This stranger.

This newcomer.

A new light who had arrived on Professor Fathom's doorstep. Jake smiled.

"It's okay. Let it go, Luca."

At that moment, Luca knew Jake was right.

He glanced back at Marco on the end of the slipping chain, and at the same time his fingers released the silver chain, Marco breathed:

"I know your real name."

Luca let out a short, sharp, shocked breath.

But the chain was gone.

And Marco was gone.

And with a scorching splash and an eruption of fire, both Marco and the silver cross were lost forever in the river of lava.

Luca stared at the fiery crimson stain Marco's body had left on the surface of the oozing blazing river, and suddenly he felt terrifyingly alone.

Then, with one almighty pull, Jake hauled him to the safety of the ledge and held him as tight as he could. "It's okay. You're one of us. One of us."

XVI

THE ISLAND OF FILFLA, MALTA

The sun shone down on the beautiful rocky beach as Professor Fathom's five boys made their way across the jagged rock and coarse sand to find the place they were looking for.

With two black eyes and a bruised jaw, Shane walked with the help of a crutch.

Luca's back was bandaged, and his arm in a sling from the pick wound to his shoulder. Eden's arm as also in a sling from the battering he received in Venice and the bullet wound to his shoulder. Will and Jake both carried shovels.

It was just after sunrise, and from a nearby hill, two wide branches—stretching upward from a tree so ancient it had petrified like stone—cast a V shape on the rocky shore.

Shane stopped and recited to the others, "The sun will rise, and the tree shall point thee to the five in the sand on the Island of Filfla. And The Cross of Sins, shall The Cross of Freedom be."

Will and Jake pushed their shovels into the V-shaped shadow on the shore and began digging away rock and sand.

Twenty minutes later, Jake struck something other than the island's rocky terrain. He and Will stopped digging and used their hands to push away the sand and stone.

Luca smiled when he saw it. He shut his eyes, and a single tear streaked down the side on his face.

In the crystal sunlight, Will and Jake heaved a wrapped object out of the ground. They unraveled the veil that covered it, revealing a five-foot tall figure of Christ on the cross, sculpted from marble. But it was Christ as nobody alive had ever seen him before.

Naked, but not vulnerable.

Beautiful, but not without his pain.

He was simply as his Father had intended him to be—a man.

XVII

VENICE, ITALY

All across Europe—all across the World—reporters stirred the controversy as *The Naked Christ* took its place in the Louvre. Religious leaders cried out in protest, conservatives demanded it be destroyed, free-thinkers rejoiced—and Eden rushed through San Giovanni hospital, one arm in a sling, the other carrying a bunches of flowers.

He pushed through the doors of Jacques' room and saw him sitting up in bed, the newspaper spread across his lap. Jacques looked up and saw Eden, and nothing could have wiped the smile off his face.

At first, neither of them spoke. Eden simply rushed to the bed and planted a long, soft kiss on Jacques' lips. "You're feeling better?" he asked eventually. "You look better."

Jacques nodded. "The doctors say I'll be out of here in a day or two."

"Then what?"

"You tell me," Jacques smiled. "I want you to tell me everything."

"There's nothing to tell," Eden baulked, not very well.

Jacques raised one eyebrow. "Eden, you crashed my uncle's party, tried to steal a stone treasure, and destroyed his palazzo. Not to mention the fact that I got shot by some axe wielding psycho!" He picked the paper up off his lap and showed Eden the front page story with a picture of protestors and supporters outside the Louvre. "And why is it I've got a funny feeling you had something to do with this?"

Eden simply smiled and held out the flowers. Lilies. "Your favorite, right?"

Jacques shook his head. "No. But if you don't disappear so soon this time, maybe you'll find out."

He pulled Eden in for another kiss, crushing the newspaper between them.

Jacques smiled mischievously, "Now where were we before that one-armed maniac so rudely interrupted?"

Eden closed and locked the door to Jacques' hospital room.

He lifted the sheet that covered Jacques. Apart from the bandage around his torso, he wore nothing but a pair of white cotton boxer shorts that left very little to the imagination, as Jacques' cock stood firm and upright, holding the fabric up like a tent pole.

Eden grinned and said, "Mr. Dumas, you seem to have developed a rather stiff condition. Fortunately, it's completely curable."

Eden's hands gently pulled down the waistband of the boxers until Jacques' beautiful hard cock flicked free. Jacques raised his eyebrows and put his hands behind his hand. "What treatment would you recommend, Dr. Santiago?"

"Well," Eden said, "with only one operable hand, you have a choice. I can either perform a single-handed operation, or I can administer oral treatment."

"Given the seriousness of my condition, I think oral treatment would work best."

"I concur." Eden winked as Jacques spread both legs wide, dropping his feet over the sides of the bed.

Eden took the base of Jacques' cock in his hand and bent low.

The head of the cock was perfect and smooth, its eye already gleaming with jewels of precum.

As the tip of Eden's tongue gently played with Jacques' slit, Eden tasted that first sweet taste and wanted more. His tongue danced around the swollen head, then his lips enveloped it, sucking on the edges of the helmet and forming a vacuum around the head.

For Jacques, the sensation was both tantalizing and taunting.

"Oh God," he breathed. The heart-rate monitor by his bed began to beep a little faster.

Then faster still.

Eden didn't want to tease him too long, not so much for Jacques' sake as for his own—Eden was hungry for the Frenchman's cock, he was thirsty for his cum.

With his lips open wide and his mouth wet with saliva, Eden swallowed Jacques' cock whole. His lips and tongue slid up and down the length of the shaft in time with the beeps on the heart-rate monitor, increasing with speed.

Jacques began to heave and moan with pleasure, louder and louder. "Yes," he breathed. "Yes, yes, yes."

The heart-rate monitor went into a beeping frenzy.

Suddenly, there came a knock at the door.

"Don't stop," Jacques said desperately. "Don't stop now."

Eden had no such plans. His head bobbed furiously as his mouth danced up and down the shaft of Jacques' cock, faster and faster, until Jacques' back arched, his face twisted as though in pain, and he cried out "Fuck, oh fuck!" before erupting inside Eden's mouth.

Eden's lips clamped around the head of Jacques' cock to maintain suction as he gulped hard on the hot surge, sucking Jacques' cum straight down, tasting the salty-sweet creaminess fleetingly on his tongue before it slid down his throat.

The heart-rate monitor sounded as though might explode.

The banging on the door became frantic. "Signor Dumas! Signor Dumas!"

Keys rattled in the lock.

Eden pulled back on the suction and let Jacques' cock slip from his lips. It smacked against his bandaged stomach.

Jacques uttered one last pained cry.

The door flew open.

Eden threw the sheet over Jacques, who was panting now, trying desperately to catch his breath.

A nurse came running in. "Signor Dumas! Are you alright?"

She checked cords and gauged readings as the beeps of the heart-rate monitor began to slow dramatically, returning to a normal, healthy rhythm.

"What happened?" she asked Eden, eyeing him suspiciously. "This patient needs rest. Did you say or do anything to excite him?"

She took Jacques' pulse and pressed the back of her hand against his sweaty forehead to check for fever, then noticed the bulge under the sheet. She looked quickly at Eden and noticed a similar bulge in his pants. She gasped with disapproval.

"It's alright. He's fine," Eden smiled reassuringly, quickly wiping dry the corner of his mouth. "He's just excited about the flowers."

Jacques chuckled like a naughty school boy.

He reached for Eden's hand and held it lovingly, knowing deep down that one day Eden would leave once again without saying goodbye. The beautiful Brazilian had too many secrets to stay in one place, to love just one man.

Perhaps it was one of the things that Jacques loved about him the most. The mystery.

In the meantime Jacques was just happy to have Eden around.

Just happy to hold his hand—

—at least while he still could.

XVIII

ANKARA, TURKEY

The camel merchant hated the English and the Americans. If they weren't self-righteous and ignorant, they were rude and obnoxious; if they weren't rude and obnoxious, they were stupid and fat; and if they weren't stupid and fat—they were thieves!

"Excuse me," he heard a man say in a Texan accent, somewhere behind him. He knew that voice. He spun around quickly and saw Shane standing there holding the reins of not just one, but three happy, healthy-looking camels.

The merchant immediately began cursing Shane in Turkish, his hands waving wildly and his mouth spitting all manor of abuse at him.

Shane nodded and took it all on the chin. "Whatever it is you're saying, I deserve it. I'm very sorry about stealing your camel and losing it. I'm sure he's quite happy wandering across the desert right about now, but I realize that doesn't help your livelihood—"

The man wasn't listening at all. He kept shouting abuse. In fact, to make matters worse, the camels themselves seemed to join in the game. One started slurping on Shane's hair, yanking at it; another starting sniffing his butt; and the third started chomping on his shoulder.

"Ow!"

But through it all, Shane remained the gentleman—or at least, tried.

"And so, by way of apology... hey!... I want to give to you... ouch!... these three... Stop it!... beautiful... Je-SUS!... camels!"

And with that, Shane shoved the reins into the waving hands of the crazed merchant and limped away as fast as he could!

The merchant kept abusing him as Shane scampered all the way to the end of the block. Then when Shane was out of sight, he stopped—and burst out laughing.

XIX

SAN DIEGO, CALIFORNIA

Slowly, being exhausted and jet-lagged, Will opened his eyes and saw the red blinking digits—10:11am.

"Oh shit!"

He jumped out of bed naked, his ample young cock swollen and semi-firm from a dream he could barely remember. He tucked his dick swiftly into a pair of jeans, frantically pulled on a t-shirt, grabbed a stack of messy ruffled papers off his desk and raced down to the garage, shouting to Felix in the kitchen on his way out the door.

"Assignment-due-gotta-go-home-for-dinner!"

The entire garbled sentence came out almost as a single word, but fortunately, Felix spoke fluent Will Hunter and knew exactly what he was trying to communicate. "Dinner at eight. Cordon bleu. Don't be late!"

A distant cry of "Awesome!" echoed through the house as the garage door opened.

Will grabbed the helmet off the back of his bike, swung one leg over the seat and the Ducati roared to life. A smooth, almost erotic vibration sent tremors up his crotch and through his torso. The back wheel spun out before finding its grip. Then with a hard twist of the throttle, Will was off.

He glanced at his watch as he hightailed down through the San

Diego streets—10:15—then he checked it once more as he skidded to a halt at the university campus—10:29.

He knew Professor Nathan James, Will's archaeology professor, had placed a deadline of 10:30am sharp on the assignment, and if Professor James had one rule, it was never be late.

"Mr. Hunter." Professor James was standing in the doorway of his office on the third floor of the faculty building, looking at his watch now. "You're overdue."

Will stood before him. With his assignment in one hand and sweat dripping down his brow after his mad dash across the campus grounds and up three flights of stairs, Will checked his own watch. "Three minutes, sir."

"Late is late."

Professor James started to close the door, but Will put his palm against it and stopped him. "Please, Professor."

Professor James sighed. He wasn't just your average archaeology professor; at only thirty-two, Nathan James was the youngest member of the History and Science faculty. Not only that, Will had always thought Professor James was kind of hot. Not only in an intellectual way, with his knowing eyes beaming behind his glasses and that quizzical expression on his face; but also because of the tan skin and somewhat manly exterior that had come from his years of field study.

He looked at Will now and shook his head. "You're my brightest student, Will. But the same rules apply to you as everybody else."

"I know, Professor, I'm not looking for any favors."

"Maybe you should be. Based on your attendance, favors are the only things that are going to get you through this course. And I'll be damned if I'm going to let a smart kid like you fail, not when it's my job to make sure you don't."

"What do you mean, sir?"

Professor James gestured for Will to enter his office, then closed the door behind him.

It was a small space, with a slender window at one end, a desk in the middle and tall shelves stacked with books encroaching from all sides. Will saw a stack of assignments on the desk.

Professor James took the ruffled papers out of Will's hand and threw them on the top of the pile. "I'm willing to put the time in to get your grades up to scratch, if you're willing to do the same. I'm talking about private tutoring, Will. Just one-on-one, you and me."

Will grinned from ear-to-ear. He knew his education was important; he also knew that offers like this didn't come along every day. "You'd do that? For me?"

"I'm not guaranteeing results. I'm not giving you an instant pass. You'll get out of this as much as you're prepared to put into it."

"I'm prepared to give it my all, sir! You can count on it."

Will was so thrilled, so relieved, so excited, that before he could stop himself—before he even realized what he was doing—he took Professor James' face in both hands and planted a long, lingering kiss smack on his lips.

Nathan gasped as Will's tongue entered his mouth. He flinched.

Will realized what he'd done and quickly pulled away. "Shit, I'm sorry, Professor! I wasn't thinking."

He quickly turned to go, but Nathan James caught him by the arm. "It's okay," was all he said. He didn't let go of Will's arm.

"Professor, I don't want you to think I did that just because of my grades, or your position."

For a moment Nathan said nothing. Then he smiled. "Tutoring can begin tomorrow. And perhaps right now, it's easier if you don't call me Professor."

Will and Nathan looked at each other for a moment longer. Suddenly Will could contain himself no more.

He lunged at Nathan James, pushing him back against his desk and tugging at the buttons on Nathan's shirt so fiercely that three of them popped off and scattered across the floor. He laid a hard smothering kiss on Nathan's lips, and their tongues twisted and locked together, pushing and thrusting in and out of each other's hungry mouths. Will hoisted the shirt off Nathan's shoulders. He was more muscular than Will had imagined. His pecs were firm and large, his shoulders round and strong. A thick, neatly trimmed forest of hair circled his brown chest and ran down his stomach before disappearing into his now bulging khaki pants.

Pulling out of the kiss Will tried to drop to his haunches, his mouth desperate to taste Nathan's chest, his nipples.

But Nathan caught him, grabbed his T-shirt and pulled it over his head before tossing it on the floor.

He stole a moment then, letting his eyes wander happily over Will's smooth muscled torso. "God, you're beautiful." He slipped his fingers inside the top of Will's jeans and yanked him closer. "How am I gonna teach you anything if I can't keep my hands off you?"

With his lips parted and his tongue searching for more, Will left of trail of wide open kisses down Nathan's chin, his throat, the top of his chest, breathing, "We'll find a way."

Will's tongue slid in circular patterns with the grain of hair on Nathan's right pectoral, slowly closing in on the nipple until his tongue encircled it completely. His lips caressed the small hard bud, his teeth twisting it gently.

At the same time, his fingers made their way down Nathan's rigid stomach and zeroed in on the buckle of Nathan's belt, swiftly undoing it.

Before unzipping the khaki pants, Will played in the area for a while, teasing Nathan before unleashing him. His fingers kneaded the massive bulge that squirmed and throbbed inside Nathan's pants, yearning to get out, torturing him with the promise of more.

But two could play that game.

Nathan's hands suddenly grabbed at the crotch of Will's jeans, taking Will's bulge in both fists and squeezing it, gently at first, then applying more and more pressure until he forced a loud groan from Will.

"Okay, you win!" Will breathed, suddenly pulling his hands away from Nathan, frantically undoing the zipper on his own jeans and letting loose his tall, hard cock. It swung free from his jeans so fast that three or four droplets of pre-cum landed on the hair of Nathan's stomach and glistened like dewdrops on a web.

Nathan grabbed the top of Will's unzipped jeans and jerked them all the way down to his ankles.

Will did a heel-toe maneuver with his feet, kicking off both shoes and flinging his jeans across the floor.

He stood before Nathan now completely naked and rock hard.

Nathan took one more moment to admire Will in all his youth and masculine glory. Then he took the young man's hands and guided them back to the zipper on his khaki pants.

Slowly, Will took the zip in his fingers and unlocked the treasure inside.

Nathan's cock was wide and hard and laced with thick bulging veins.

As soon as it was free—bouncing and pulsating, heavy with weight—Will moved quickly to touch it, to take it in his hands. But before his fingers could reach the stiff swollen cock, Nathan swung Will into an about-face position and pushed him hard against the desk.

Willingly, the young man bent across the desk, face-down.

Nathan leaned over him, pressing against him, and with one wide stroke, he swept all the books and assignments off the desk.

It was a dramatic gesture, full of urgent desire.

Papers fluttered into the air.

Will thought to himself—there goes Cleopatra, there goes Tut—but before another ancient icon could flash through his head, he felt Nathan's right index and forefinger part his ass cheeks and promptly slide inside his hot tight hole.

Will's breath snatched a short sharp breath of air.

He spread his legs wide and leaned further over the desk, as if inviting Nathan—no, daring him—to explore deeper.

Nathan accepted the challenge, pulled a bottle of lube and a condom from a drawer in his desk, greased up Will's crack, and pushed his fingers all the way inside Will, stroking the warm passage of his rectum, loosening him up, preparing him for a much larger load.

With his left hand, Nathan caressed Will's well-toned back, the muscles writhing and flinching under the skin as the ripples of pleasure shot up from his ass.

Leaning low over the desk, Will's hands ran down his own taut stomach till they found his own cock and balls.

With a gush of relief, he felt Nathan's fingers slide out of his hole, but he knew the real pressure—the real pleasure—was on its way. He squeezed his own cock in one hand and his balls in the other, pulling them down low as if to make way for Nathan's entry.

He felt the head of Nathan's large, sheathed, greased-up cock nestle between his cheeks, and then—

Will held his breath as Nathan pushed his way inside him, slowly at first, filling Will with the full length of his shaft. Once completely inside him, he lingered there a moment, letting Will's ass become accustomed to the intruder.

Then slowly he pulled back out, but not all the way, just far enough, before thrusting himself back inside Will, this time a little faster, and with more force.

Will's fingers felt his balls lift a little, but he pulled them back down, squeezing them hard. With his other hand he began to stroke and tease his own cock, twisting the bulbous head in his fist, turning pain into pleasure.

Nathan continued to pull back and push inside, gaining speed and force with each thrust.

With every entry, Will's sphincter tightened its grip on Nathan's cock, then released the tension a little as the massive shaft slid out of him before pushing inside him again and again.

Nathan took Will's hips in his hands now, riding him as the pace quickened.

Will let go of his balls and let them rise up into his body a little. He used his free hand to grab the edge of the desk, holding himself steady as the force of Nathan's body began to rock him back and forth.

With his other hand, Will continued to stroke his own cock, also picking up the pace.

Nathan began to groan. His khaki pants had slid down around his ankles now, and his glasses began to steam up. He knocked them off with one hand and they landed on the desk next to Will's grimacing, grinning face.

With Nathan's ever-hardening lunges, the desk inched along the floor, grinding against the old floorboards until it bumped hard up against a bookcase. The whole bookcase began to rock, the books collapsing on the shelves like dominos.

"I'm coming," Will heard Nathan breathe.

"Me, too," Will managed through clenched teeth.

The young man unlocked his jaw and let a loud moan escape him.

He felt that familiar hot rush inside his balls.

With three quick strokes of his fist, a blast of cum shot from his cock and splashed across Nathan's desk.

At the same time, Nathan threw his head back and pushed out a groan that came all the way from his loins. He thumped his hips hard against Will's ass one more time and held himself there as he unloaded a flood of his steaming cum inside the condom inside Will.

Will felt the burning flush inside him, and a second spurt shot from his own cock, flying even further than the first, this time slapping against the bookcase.

He cried out loudly, unable to stop himself, as he squeezed and stroked and teased the last tide of cum from his swollen spent dick.

Panting and heaving, Nathan fell against him and wrapped his arms around him. He laughed and placed one of his fingers against Will's moist, moaning lips.

"Sshh," Nathan breathed, smiling. "The whole Faculty will hear you."

Will smiled back, taking Nathan's finger into his mouth and sucking on it. Eventually, he let the finger slide from his lips, and with Nathan still inside him, he grinned and asked, "So, what's tomorrow's lesson?"

XX

TUSCANY, ITALY

The attic of the convent was chilly, the nuns were too old to maintain the building by themselves, so with planks of wood, a hammer in hand and nails clenched between his teeth, Luca climbed a rickety old ladder to the hole in the ceiling. He ducked as a pair of pigeons fluttered and flapped out through the hole into the bright Tuscan sky.

"They don't have a nest there, do they?" Sister Margarita worried, holding the ladder beneath Luca. "I wouldn't want to shoo them out of their home."

The attic was used for storage, and Luca had leaned the ladder against a bookcase filled with boxes, blankets and dusty old books. He took the nails from between his teeth now and set them down on the top shelf. "No, Sister Margarita. And this isn't their home. It's yours. Do you want to go through another winter like the last one? Look at these boxes. The rain has ruined—"

Luca stopped talking. He put down the planks of wood and hammer and was staring at something tucked behind a box on the top shelf.

"What is it?" Sister Margarita asked. "Are you alright?"

Luca reached to the back of the shelf and pulled out a frayed old basket. There was a baby's blanket in it, and lying beside that was something he had never seen before in his life, or at least could not recall. It was a small knitted child's toy.

A clown.

"Valentino?" Luca whispered, eyes wide.

Without realizing it, he touched his chest, and for the first time in his life, he couldn't feel his crucifix hanging there.

"Luca? Are you alright?"

Luca didn't answer straight away.

For a moment, he didn't even hear Sister Margarita say his name.

XXI

MUNICH, GERMANY

"You must walk a little more slowly," the Professor said. "I'm an old man, and I've been through something of an adventure lately."

"Yes," said Ernst, slowing his stride. "You've been most difficult to track down. And you know me. I never have any trouble finding things."

Herr Ernst Schroder was right. He was a man of many talents, but most of all, he could track down almost anything in the world, or at the very least, he was best place to start. From the rarest North Australian pearls to the whereabouts of the Heir to the British Throne after a friend's bachelor party, Herr Schroder had a knack. Or rather, he was very, very well-connected.

It was one of these contacts—currently a resident of a Siberian prison, no less—who had hired Herr Schroder to track down Professor Fathom, which he had finally managed.

They met here, in the Botanical Gardens on the grounds of the Nymphenburg Palace in Munich.

"Despite your rather colorful history together, he requests the pleasure of your company," Herr Schroder said as they strolled peacefully past a group of school children, smelling the flowers.

"Who?"

"Caro Sholtez."

The Professor stopped. It was a name he hadn't heard for a very long time. Caro Sholtez. No Mister or Monseiur or Signor or Herr. That's because nobody knew what nationality he was, including Sholtez himself. Or so he claimed.

Caro Sholtez was an enigma.

He was also one of the most dangerous men on the planet.

The Professor raised one eyebrow. "I don't often use the words pleasure and Siberia in the same context."

"According to Sholtez, he won't be in Siberia much longer."

"He's been imprisoned for life."

Herr Schroder smiled and shrugged. "I'm just the messenger."

"Of course," the Professor nodded. If nothing else, Professor Fathom and Herr Schroder had the utmost respect for a civil relationship. It would have been considered by many to be a friendship even, only Ernst Schroder made it his business not to have any friends.

The Professor sniffed at the air. "Ah, the blue cornflower," he smiled, turning to the left. "It's my favorite. Shall we?"

Herr Schroder looked to the left and saw a magnificent bank of blue cornflowers in full bloom. "I thought blue cornflowers had no scent."

The Professor smiled. "They don't—unless you're blind."

XXII

NEW YORK CITY, NEW YORK

Jake sat in the front seat of the cab, and when the driver asked him for the third time, "Left or right?" Jake still didn't respond. He didn't even hear him.

A car pulled up behind them and blared its horn.

The driver shouted one last time, "Sir, left or right?"

At the sound of the cab driver's frustrated voice Jake jolted back to life. "Left."

He tried to stay focused for the rest of the journey through Brooklyn, but his thoughts always strayed whenever he made this trip, as though the past was trying to pull him back, as though it had vowed to never let him forget what he had done. Soon however the cab pulled up outside the rehabilitation center.

"How are you, Jake?" asked the woman rising from her desk, as the duty nurse escorted him inside Mrs Beattie's small office.

Jake leaned across the desk, past a vase of white lilies, kissed Mrs. Beattie on the cheek then took a seat. "I'm doing okay. How are you, Mrs. Beattie?"

"Jake, after fifteen years I think you can call me Helen."

He smiled, a little embarrassed and nodded. "I have something for you." He reached into his pocket and pulled out a check. A check for one hundred thousand dollars. The money that Pierre Perron had deposited into his account before his journey to Kahna Toga.

He slid it across the desk to Helen now. "I was expecting more but things went a little pear-shaped."

Helen picked up the check and shook her head. "Jake, this kind of donation to the clinic is too much. I know you can't afford this! I'm sorry but I can't—"

But Jake just shook his head and plucked one of the lilies from the vase. "Consider it payment. For a flower."

*

The cemetery was cold. It was always cold. Jake was convinced it was God's way. To make happy places warm and sunny. And make sad places cold and gray.

He put his backpack down on the ground and knelt beside the grave.

The grave of Sarah Stone.

Died twenty-four years of age.

When Jake was only thirteen-years-old.

He laid the white lily from Helen's office at the foot of the gravestone now. God, even his tears felt cold as they raced down his cheeks.

Thankfully there were only two tears.

He refused to let any more go.

"Hey Sis. Sorry it's been so long. I've been kinda busy. Met some people who, I dunno, I kinda like. For once. Don't laugh, I know you're laughin' at me up there. I know for sure you'd like 'em. You always saw the best in people. You were always the strong one. The smart one."

He knew he was tired, but he must have been even more exhausted than he realized, for another three, four, five tears slid down his face. Jake pushed them away angrily with the back of his hand. "Shit, I'm sorry, I gotta go. I gotta go check on Sam."

He stood quickly, grabbed his backpack and started walking away. He turned back on last time.

"I'm sorry, Sarah."

*

Eighteen-year-old Sam staggered into the freight elevator, not having slept for three days. Everyone thought he was wired, and God knows Jake was always on his back about being high, but the fact was, Sam had never taken a drug in his life. The fact was he simply hated sleep. When you live on the streets for virtually your entire life, you go to sleep every night never knowing if you're going to open your eyes again the next day.

Which is why on the odd occasion he did actually sleep, he only ever slept at Jake's.

Sam loved Jake to death, he was the only one who looked out for him, but Jake was never around to talk to. And when he was around, sometimes he was so protective that the two ended up fighting.

And Sam ended up on the streets yet again.

But he knew today that Jake wasn't home, he had found the note he'd left days ago.

Sam's vision blurred now as he unlocked the door and stumbled into Jake's apartment. He was so tired, so hungry, he could barely walk. He headed for his mattress on the floor, but then thought twice about it. His head was spinning, but he hadn't had a shower in three days. And he knew he stank.

Sam kicked off his sneakers and stripped off his T-shirt, his jeans. He stumbled naked through the curtain to the bathroom, then pulled open the shower curtain and turned on the faucet.

Steam billowed.

Sam stepped under the water, and the calm instantly overwhelmed him.

He closed his eyes, and perhaps for a second, while standing in the shower, he fell asleep.

Even so, he suddenly sensed he wasn't alone.

Sam's eyes shot open in alarm.

He grabbed the shower curtain and ripped it aside, and took in a short sharp breath as he saw standing there in front of him a large black stranger.

The man smiled and spoke in a deep, thick French-Algerian accent. "My name is Ra. Monsieur Perron sent me. Tell Mr. Stone, there is an important message on his pillow."

And with that, the man raised a small straight pipe to his lips and blew into it as hard as he could.

Sam grunted as a dart hit him straight in the chest.

That's when his knees buckled, through exhaustion and shock more than anything else, and he slipped into the tub, tearing the shower curtain down on top of him.

*

On the street below, Jake got out of the cab, slung his backpack over his shoulder and entered the building. He started climbing the stairs to his apartment when he heard the clunk and rattle of the freight elevator descending. It passed down the middle of the stairwell as Jake ascended the stairs, and through the glass panels of the elevator, Jake could see a large black man inside—staring straight back at him.

Something told Jake to get upstairs as fast as he could.

The door to his apartment was open.

"Sam!"

He heard the shower running. He dropped his bag and raced across the warehouse floor, shoving aside the bathroom curtain to see Sam unconscious in the tub, the shower curtain pulled down over him and water splashing everywhere.

Jake dropped beside the tub, turned off the shower and scooped Sam up in his arms.

"Sam! Can you hear me?"

Sam's eyes blinked open. He looked around, stunned and dazed, then pointed to his chest.

"God!" Jake whispered, plucking the dart out as soon as he saw it.

"There was a guy," Sam gasped and panted in shock. "I never saw him before in my life. He said he left you a message. A message from some guy I never heard of. I swear to you Jake, I got no idea who he was."

"It's okay. Stay here. I'll get you a blanket."

He found a blanket. Wrapped Sam up in it. "You said this guy left a message?"

"Your pillow. It's on your pillow."

Jake lifted Sam out of the bath, laid him on the dry floor and rushed over to his mattress. There was an envelope on his pillow. He swooped down and ripped it open.

He immediately recognized the insignia at the top of the page.

Dear Mr. Stone,

It seems our dealings have reached terrifying new heights. You want your little friend to live, and I want a new treasure to replace the mansion you sent to the bottom of the Grand Canal as well as the finger I've lost! Your precious Sam has a rare poison called Deldah-sha running through his veins. It is slow and lethal. He will die in precisely 120 hours, roughly five days, unless of course he receives the antidote, the only known bottle of which is in my possession. It is something I will happily trade for one thing: the location of the Lost Pyramid of Imhotep.

Yours truly, P. Perron

XXIII

PALERMO, SICILY

The surgeons stared at each other and said in Italian:

"Is that what I think it is?"

"It's a flare, embedded in his stomach. And there's another one, here, in his side. We assume that's what's caused the third degree burns on his face and body."

The head surgeon shook his head in disbelief at the heart-rate monitor. "This man shouldn't be alive. Who brought him in?"

"Some fishermen. They found him tangled in their nets."

"What happened to his arm?"

"Evidently it was already missing."

The head surgeon lifted the sheet and looked at the twisted mangled stump that protruded from the man's left shoulder. "That would've hurt—a lot. He's obviously no stranger to pain. And nobody knows who he is?"

The assistant surgeon checked the file and shook his head. "No ID. No reports of a missing person. No eyewitnesses to any accidents. It's as if he fell straight out of the heavens."

At that moment, there was a blip on the heart-rate monitor. "Did you see that?" the head surgeon asked suddenly, looking strangely at the patient.

"See what? Doctor? Are you alright? What was it?"

With a shake of his head, the surgeon said, "Nothing, I'm fine. It's just that, when you said he'd fallen from heaven, for a second there, I could have sworn he just—smiled."

the adventure continues...

THE RIDDLE OF THE SANDS

available now...

www.fathomsfive.com

GEOFFREY KNIGHT

The Amazing Adventures of Elsa Strauss:

THE DAME OF NOTRE DAME

Paris, France

It wasn't thier intention to steal the tapestry
And it certainly wasn't their intention to get caught.
All they had to do was take a photo of the Tapisserie de l'Arc—click one clear, hi-res snap of the tapestry—and upload it to the Professor's files. Then get the hell outta there!

But things didn't run quite as smoothly as the Professor and his men had hoped.

American businessman Lawrence Vanderbilt had owned the Palais d'Automne—located twenty minutes south of Paris—for almost a decade now, and had adorned his 16th century, 48-room French residence with a priceless array of French art, both old and contemporary, including the Tapisserie de l'Arc, an intricate tapestry depicting the last battle of Joan of Arc. Hanging now on a wall of the palace library, the tapestry was 6 feet high and 14 feet long, woven in the year 1585 and said by some to contain a map leading to a place lost in history—

—the true location of the sword of Joan of Arc.

A symbol of righteousness, faith and courage against all odds and expectations. A weapon that defied both tradition and tyranny.

According to the Duke of Alencon, the sword was destroyed in Saint Denis, and over the years the story of the map woven into the tapestry became just that. A story. A legend. A myth. Until—

Dressed in tuxedoes and bowties, Jake Stone, Eden Santiago, Shane Houston, Luca da Roma, Will Hunter and Professor Maximilian Fathom handed their invitations to one of the many suited guards manning the palace, then made their way through the exquisitely-attired, champagne-sipping crowd filling the Palais d'Automne to attend Lawrence Vanderbilt's annual Autumn Ball.

As Jake and Shane took six champagne flutes from a passing waiter and handed them to the others, the Professor spoke softly to his men, the sound of a nearby string quartet preventing anyone else from hearing his voice.

"According to Herr Schroder, the tapestry is in the library in the east wing. There is a single gold thread running through the tapestry. That's the map. If we can get a clear shot, digitally we can wipe out everything else and all we'll be left with—"

"—will be the sword of Joan of Arc," Jake smiled.

The Professor turned to his men and said, "Go now."

As they quickly dispersed, the Professor heard a voice behind him.

"Max!"

He turned and a hand reached for his, shaking it firmly.

"Lawrence, how good to hear your voice."

"It's damn well time you finally accepted one of my invitations, Max!" said Lawrence Vanderbilt, a distinguished gentleman in his early fifties.

"Oh, you know me. Always waiting for the right moment to leave my mark."

Vanderbilt gave a mock laugh, then took the Professor by the shoulder and leaned in close to his ear. "And you know me. Art everywhere. Guards everywhere. If you're thinking of trying anything, Max, I have a dungeon in the basement that could use a little company." At that moment, Vanderbilt became curious and looked around him. "Speaking of company, where did your friends go?"

*

The five boys had made it to the library and found the tapestry hanging on the wall. They had one digital camera between them.

There was nobody else in the room.

Meanwhile, all five boys tussled over who would take the photo.

Jake was the first to try to snap the tapestry.

"You missed the edge of it," Eden told him.

"It's a good shot," Jake defended himself.

Eden grabbed his hand, trying to pull the camera free. "No, Jake, it's not! Do you want to trace the map or not?"

"Here, give it to me," Luca stepped in. "I know art—"

"—and none of you guys know how to use a camera properly," Will interjected, grabbing it from Luca. "No offence, but you're all too old. Not enough Facebook time. The way to capture a moment is to—"

The flash went off.

A split second later, outside the stained glass windows of the library, thunder clapped and lightning cracked open the sky. Rain began to pour down.

Shane, who was keeping guard at the door, quickly turned to the others. "Guys! We got company!"

But he was too late.

A guard suddenly hurried into the room. He instantly saw the camera in Will's hand.

"Gentlemen. I'll have to ask you to hand that camera over immediately. And then to please leave this room and return to the—"

CRASH!

Shane, who was now behind the guard, suddenly smashed a vase over the top of the guard's head.

As the man collapsed to the floor, Shane grimaced at Jake. "That was Ming, wasn't it."

Jake bit his bottom lip and nodded back. "Never mind! Forget the damn camera anyway!"

He raced up to the tapestry, grabbed the edge of it, then pulled it from the wall.

Eden's eyes shot open in shock. "Jake! What are you doing!"

"We're taking the fucking thing with us."

"What?"

Jake kept pulling the ancient tapestry off the wall. "I said we're stealing it! Now are you gonna help me or what?"

"I'll help you!" boomed a voice from the library doorway.

All five boys, including Jake, turned to see Lawrence Vanderbilt standing in the doorway—with no less that twelve armed guards.

"Gentlemen, seize the camera. Then please escort Max's men to the dungeon! Before they try to steal anything else!"

*

The second Lawrence had walked away in search of the boys, the Professor pulled the phone from his jacket.

In their suite at the Hotel Descartes back in Paris, Elsa jumped up as soon as the phone rang.

She had been fussing and fretting, cooking in the large suite's kitchenette, washing and cleaning, unfolding and folding all of the Professor's clothes, when suddenly the Professor himself was on the other end of the phone line.

The second she heard his voice she began to melt into hysteria. "Oh, Professor! You know how much I worry about these excursions of yours! *Mein Himmel*! I've been so stressed I've baked strudels to last a lifetime! Please tell me you and the boys are alright!"

"Actually, no. Elsa, I need you to listen very carefully. I fear the boys may have been caught trying to find the tapestry. Lawrence Vanderbilt has gone in search of them, and he—"

The Professor paused.

Elsa panicked. "He what?"

"He intimated that he has a dungeon ready for us."

Elsa shrieked down the line. "*Mein Gott*! I need to bake more strudels!"

"No, Elsa. You need to do something more important than that. If we are to be put in Lawrence's dungeon, you need to get us out!"

"How!"

"The main entrance is covered with guards, you'll never get past them. I need you to find another way in, you have to find the dungeon."

"Find the dungeon!"

"Yes, but the only way you can do that is to get your hands on the original blueprints of the palace. This place is 16th century. France was a bloody place back then. No church or monastery or palace in France was built without a tunnel system, everyone had an escape plan up their sleeve. I need you to get inside the Notre Dame Archives, it's a chamber beneath the cathedral. That's where all the hidden architectural records of France's cathedrals and palaces are kept. Look for the Palais d'Automne and you'll find another way in."

"Professor, are you crazy!" Elsa was sitting on the bed in a state of distress now, clutching the phone with one hand and fanning herself frantically with the other.

"Elsa, you can do this. The archives chamber will be manned. All you have to do is distract the attendant with—" The Professor faltered.

"With what!" Elsa asked, incredulous. "Beef goulash!?"

Elsa could almost hear the Professor shrug over the phone. "I was thinking more along the lines of using your feminine charm."

Elsa shrieked.

Suddenly she heard a stern American voice down the line. "Max! I think you'd better come with me! I intend to enjoy my party. You on the other hand, will enjoy a night in—"

Suddenly the phone went dead.

"The dungeon!" Elsa gasped in fear.

She didn't know what to do.

All she knew was the Professor needed her.

The boys needed her.

And strudels were burning in the oven!

*

Ten minutes later, Elsa Strauss was anxiously muttering to herself in the backseat of a cab that raced through the stormy Parisian night. As the driver pulled up outside Notre Dame Cathedral, Elsa peered timidly out the window.

A bolt of lightning shot across the sky, illuminating the bell towers, accompanied by a gothic chorus of thunder.

For a moment, Elsa thought of staying in the cab. She was seconds away from telling the driver to keep driving.

Instead she took a deep breath, stepped out of the cab and watched as her umbrella instantly turned inside out with a blast of wind. Rain pelted down. The cab sped off, leaving her alone to face the storm. Thunder rocked the night again, and Elsa battled forward, using her inside-out umbrella as a shield against the wind.

She reached the relative safety of the doorway to the cathedral and stopped a moment to catch her breath. Through the pouring rain she saw a small sign that read Notre Dame de Paris Archives pointing around to the side of the building.

With a single step back out into the tempest, Elsa's umbrella twisted into a modern French sculpture and was snatched from her hands. She shrieked as it became a spindly wire tumbleweed before disappearing into the Seine.

It didn't matter, she supposed. She was already drenched and too anxious and terrified to care anymore. With all the speed she could muster, she hightailed it around the side of Notre Dame until she found a small concealed door halfway along the north wing of the cathedral.

"Oh, thank Heaven!" she breathed, relieved to find the door was unlocked.

She ducked inside quickly, her clothes dripping, and cautiously made her way down a stone spiral stairway that led her deeper and deeper into the bowels of the cathedral.

Elsa descended the stairs for what seemed like an eternity.

Finally they leveled off into a corridor, at the end of which was a door simply marked: Archives.

Warily she opened it.

The door squeaked as it swung, beckoning her inside.

The first thing she saw was a little bald man with a pencil thin moustache in what looked like a cage.

"Can I help you!" he demanded sternly. He seemed just as

surprised to see Elsa as she was to be here, as though he didn't get many visitors down here in the Archives chamber.

Quickly realizing that the little man was not in a cage but was in fact shut inside an attendant's booth, Elsa smiled, putting on as much charm as she could manage. "Bonsoir!" Her eyelids fluttered. "Is this the Notre Dame Archives?" She had already noticed the padlocked door to her left with a sign that read Archives Entrée.

"Oui, can I help you!" The little man eyed Elsa narrowly. Suspiciously. "This department is not open to the public."

"I'm looking for some information," Elsa said, stepping closer to the little man's cage.

"If you want to access any of the archives, you'll need papers. I need to see signatures. It takes at least three weeks to get everything processed through the Cathedral archives, and after that there are numerous approvals and forms of consent that will need to be stamped and verified and—" The man's annoying, prattling voice trailed away for a moment as Elsa leaned forward and peeled off her coat.

"Oh, I hope you don't mind, I'm dripping wet. I'll catch cold if I don't get rid of these wretched clothes."

The little bald man with the pencil thin moustache cleared his throat, distractedly staring at Elsa's ample bosom as she let her coat fall to the stone floor.

"I wouldn't want to be responsible for you falling ill," he muttered, eyes fixed on her plunging neckline now. "But as I said, before I can let you in, I'll need verification of… various… forms of… verification…"

Elsa started popping open several buttons on her sticky wet blouse. Cleavage suddenly appeared like a holy revelation.

The little man gasped and an involuntary smile appeared on his face.

"My name is Elsa. What's yours?" she asked, leaning in even closer.

The little man swallowed hard, his throat suddenly so dry it made him splutter. "Gaspard," he breathed.

"Gaspard! Such a strong name."

The little man grinned from ear to ear and his chest puffed out, just a little. "Do you think so? It means wealthy man."

"And are you? Wealthy, I mean?"

Gaspard shrugged. "Not really. But I like my job. It's peaceful and quiet and…"

"Lonely?"

Gaspard sighed and his chest deflated. "I suppose. Just a little."

"Don't you long for a little thrill? Just once in a while?"

Not one to own up to his boyhood dream of one day becoming a crime solver, Gaspard shook his head. "No. I get a lot of reading done." He held up a paperback thriller about age-old secrets hidden in the works of a Renaissance artist, now located in the most famous museum in Paris, as if to prove his point. Then he stood and pointed to his holster. "Plus they let me carry a gun. In case of emergencies."

"Oh," Elsa said, her voice turning from sultry to sickly as her nervousness sank in again. "Perhaps I should be going then."

She turned, but Gaspard called after her before she could leave. "Wait! Please don't go!"

Elsa hesitated. She thought about the gun in Gaspard's holster. Then she thought about the Professor.

She turned and forced a smile onto her face.

Gaspard was looking at her with begging, hopeful eyes. "I have a secret little cellar hidden under the stairs. There's a beautiful bottle of 1969 Bordeaux just waiting for a special occasion." His pencil thin moustache curved upward in a little smile. "Will you share it with me?"

Elsa let out a nervous giggle, "Ha! But of course."

Gaspard smiled excitedly.

He quickly opened the door to his booth and released himself from his cage. Trembling nervously, he scuttled around the rim of Elsa's buxom form, squeezing past her as he headed down the corridor that led to the spiral stairs down which Elsa had descended only moments ago.

"Please don't go anywhere!" his voice echoed back to her. "I'll be back in just a moment."

"Where could I possibly go?" Elsa called back, watching as his little shadow disappeared down the corridor.

As soon as he was out of sight, sexy Elsa turned to panicked Elsa as she swiftly made her move.

"*Mein Gott*! What am I doing!" she babbled anxiously to herself as she tried the door handle labelled Archives Entrée. There was no getting past that padlock without a key.

Elsa raced into Gaspard's little booth and began rummaging through drawers. She emptied everything—paperclip boxes, loose change jars, crumpled used envelopes filled with receipts—until she finally found a key hidden in a box of old mints.

She jiggled it in the padlock.

It popped open.

The door gave a cranky groan and Elsa raced into the archives chamber before stopping dead in her tracks, her face suddenly besieged with fear. "Oh my," was all she could manage.

The Professor my have told her where the little-known archives were located, but he failed to mention how big they were!

Suddenly, Elsa found herself standing in a massive stone cavern carved out beneath Notre Dame Cathedral, staring at row after row after row of endless shelves all stacked to a ceiling at least twenty feet high. Each shelf was crammed full of badly labelled archive boxes, half of them falling apart, their contents already spilled across the floor and collecting dust.

Elsa was not an overly religious woman, but she crossed herself nonetheless. She figured if she was in a house of God—or at least, underneath one—any assistance she could get right now would help.

She raced up to the nearest shelf and looked at the label on the first box she laid eyes on. It was difficult to read, but she managed to decipher the first letter. A. She pieced together the other letters on the scribbled label—Avignon Cour.

Quickly she realized that the entire archive was alphabetized. And there was no denying, given the size of the chamber, that Palais d'Automne was a long, long way from here.

Elsa started running.

By the time she found the Ps, she heard the creaky archive door groan open.

Gaspard's voice called out, sounding a little uncertain and

betrayed. "Madame? You should not be in here!"

Elsa ignored him, her eyes desperately scanning the tower of boxes in front of her.

Suddenly she saw one labelled Palais d'Automne several feet above her head, stacked high on dozens upon dozens of other Palais boxes. She stepped up onto the edge of a box, trying to climb the stack like a ladder, digging her toes into one tight gap after another, hoisting herself precariously up the side of the towering shelf.

She managed to hook her finger under the box she wanted.

It wouldn't budge.

"Elsa!" Gaspard's voice echoed loudly through the chamber, clearly angry now. "I cannot allow you to be in here without the proper authority! You need verification! And signatures!"

Elsa ignored him still, her fingers trying to inch the box out from above her head. It edged out a little... A little more... Then suddenly—

The box gave way.

Elsa's footing gave way.

She let out a shrill scream.

In a thunderous landslide, Elsa, along with four dozen boxes, came crashing to the ground.

At the same time, a short distance away, a bottle smashed against the floor and rich red wine spilled across the stones. Gaspard was no longer holding his Bordeaux, but was instead clutching the gun he had never used.

As Elsa pushed the broken boxes and mountains of paper off the top of her with a "Pssh-Pssh!", the sound of running footsteps echoed closer and closer.

She panicked, pulling herself out of the wreckage before sifting frantically through the files surrounding her. Her hands rummaged desperately and found the now broken box labelled Palais d'Automne. She flicked through papers like a starving dog digging for a bone, looking for anything that remotely resembled an old blueprint.

The sound of running footsteps grew closer and closer.

Elsa looked up and saw Gaspard charging out of the darkness, his gun drawn.

"Freeze!" he shouted the moment he spotted her scratching through her mountain of paper—in what was undeniably the little Frenchman's best attempt at an American movie star accent.

Elsa gasped.

That's when she saw the blueprint.

The Palais d'Automne.

The cross-sectioned estate.

An underground tunnel system.

She snatched up the blueprint and scrunched it down her blouse, just as Gaspard fired off his first shot.

Elsa screamed.

The bullet missed by a mile, but slammed into another tower of boxes and caused a second archive avalanche.

Elsa jumped to her feet and leapt out of the way before being crushed by another landslide of centuries-old records.

A loud boom echoed through the chamber as the boxes exploded on the stone floor and random pages flew high into the air, covering Elsa's escape to God only knows where.

Running as fast as she could, Elsa steered aimlessly through the giant chamber, until suddenly—

—she reached the end of the Archives Department and realized she was as far from the entrance as she could possibly be. From here, getting past Gaspard was near to impossible. She would have to find another way out.

The far wall was lined with shelves and Elsa gasped in horror as all hope seemed lost. Suddenly she remembered the Professor's words.

No church or monastery or palace in Europe was built without a tunnel system, everyone had an escape plan up their sleeve.

Desperately, Elsa began pushing on every shelf she could find. She shoved on boxes, she plucked file after file off the shelves and threw them in the air.

Suddenly she stopped and stared.

Sitting on the shelf in front of her, amongst the dozens and dozens of badly labelled boxes, was a Bible. A fat, dusty old Bible.

A gunshot went off behind her.

Elsa ducked, and the ceiling light above her exploded in a shower of sparks.

She grabbed the Bible and pulled at it.

With a rumbling of stone, the shelf in front of which she was standing—in fact, the floor on which she was standing—began rotating ninety degrees, and a dark stone escape passage opened before her.

Another gunshot was enough to send Elsa sprinting down the mystery passage.

She couldn't see where she was going, she had no idea where the escape route was taking her. All she could hear was her own nervous panting and the sound of Gaspard's relentless footsteps racing after her.

Running blindly along the passage, Elsa shrieked when she suddenly charged headlong into a spiral staircase leading upward.

She picked herself up and began to climb—

—and climb—

—and climb!

Her feet didn't falter as she raced upward and upward, but she feared her heart would. Elsa's pulse had never pounded so hard and heavy in all her days.

The staircase eventually spat her out into a tower with more stairs, and in her panic Elsa kept climbing, unaware she was now heading all the way up the north bell tower of Notre Dame.

Windows came into view.

Lightning flashed.

Gaspard continued his chase upward and upward, and Elsa continued climbing higher and higher until she came face to face with the biggest bell she had ever seen in her life.

Thunder cracked across the Parisian night.

Another flare of lightning lit up the bell tower.

And the almighty Emmanuel—the thirteen-ton bell of Notre Dame—began to slowly tilt to one side.

Elsa's penny dropped.

She looked at her watch.

It was nine o'clock—sharp!

Emmanuel lifted to her full height, and then—

254

—the bell dropped in utter silence, swinging towards the most deafening noise on Earth.

Elsa covered her ears.

The bell *CLAAAAAANGED*!

It was a sound so loud, all of Paris heard it.

Elsa screamed and reeled, still holding her ringing ears as she stumbled backward and fell straight out of the tower window.

She screamed again as she plunged twenty feet from the tower window onto the sloping roof of the cathedral, landing so hard that several original thirteenth century tiles snapped loose and fell to their deaths below.

The rain was pummeling down more fiercely than ever.

Elsa felt herself begin to slide down the steep roof.

Her fingers tried to grab at anything they could snag, but there was nothing to hold.

She slid faster and faster down the slippery wet roof.

The tiles were like glass beneath her.

There was nothing to save her, nothing to stop her—

—until she slid straight over the edge of the cathedral's roof and her fingers miraculously hooked onto the guttering.

A high-pitched scream filled the night and competed with the clanging of the bells above, but somehow Elsa had saved herself—for the moment.

Precariously she dangled from the edge of the guttering.

She screamed for help, but the only reply she got was a clap of thunder and a blinding blast of lightning.

Drenched and terrified, Elsa knew she had two choices: either pull herself up, or fall to her death. And although letting go of the guttering and saying goodbye to the world was probably the easier option at this stage, the thought of never stuffing another blargenwurst again was enough for her to muster the strength to pull herself back onto the roof—one determined breath after another, one hand over the other, one leg up at a time.

The bells continued to sweep and toll as Elsa strenuously hauled herself up onto the edge of the guttering. At that moment, the sound of gunfire continued.

One bullet ricocheted off the tiles.

Then another.

Elsa screamed again.

She glanced up and saw Gaspard now leaning out of a tower window, firing random shots into the thundering rain.

Elsa tried to scramble to her feet on the slippery, slanted roof.

"Stop! Stop! I thought you liked me! I thought you wanted to get me drunk and make love to me!"

Gaspard took another random shot through the deluge. "Love! War! To we French it's all the same!"

Elsa shrieked and began running across the slanted roof of Notre Dame, her back hunched and her arms covering her head from the gunfire. The bullets continued to snap tiles and ricochet off the roof. The bells continued to clang and boom through the night. They rocked her already shattered balance and Elsa couldn't help but howl, "The bells! The bells!"

Huddling beneath an umbrella on the other side of the Seine, a newlywed Japanese couple honeymooning in Paris heard the cry over the thunder and looked up. The young man let go of his umbrella. In the pouring rain he pointed in astonishment and fumbled desperately for his camera, choking in shock on the words, "Hunchback! Hunchback!"

Elsa reached the eastern end of the cathedral and saw the flying buttresses extending down from the roof in all directions, sloping toward the ground.

As the bullets continued to flip tiles from their resting place, Elsa desperately jumped through the rain, leaping from the rooftop and landing with a heavy thud on one of the flying buttresses. With a scream and a squeal and a grunt and a foul German curse she would never use in front of the Professor, she slid gracelessly down the slippery slope of the buttress. Then, like a champion sky-jumper, she flew rump-first off the end of the buttress, bounced off the lower roof of the cathedral and landed with a loud smack in a puddle on the ground.

Across the Seine she saw a camera flashing madly.

Elsa didn't care.

She was alive.

She had the blueprint.

And before Gaspard could find her, she picked herself up and limped hurriedly away into the stormy Parisian night.

Back in the bell tower, Gaspard smiled and proudly blew the smoke from the snout of his gun. From now on, he'd read those thriller novels in a whole new light. He may have intentionally misfired every bullet from his pistol, but that night, the mysterious femme fatale called Elsa, that dangerous dame of Notre Dame, had made him a man!

*

"And whose ingenius idea was it to try to steal the tapestry in the first place?"

Arms crossed, the Professor was pacing back and forth in front of his boys who were sitting on the stone floor of the dungeon, their backs to the cold rock wall. At first none of them said a word, they merely exchanged glances like boarding school boys who had been caught smoking behind the bicycle shed.

Then with a heavy sigh Jake stood.
"I can't tell a lie." He pointed. "It was Will."

"What!" Will shrieked. "It was him!"

Jake shook his head. "Will, one day you'll be old enough to admit you were wrong and take some responsibility for your actions."

"Professor! Don't listen to him!"

Shane joined in the joke. "Will, its okay to make mistakes sometimes."

"Hey, at least I didn't smash a Ming vase!"

The Professor gasped. "A Ming vase!"

Suddenly over the yelling and mud-slinging that quickly escalated, Eden heard a clang on the other side of the dungeon wall. "Shh! Shh! Did you guys hear that?"

Everyone fell silent and listened to the unmistakable sound of a latch turning, a bolt sliding, then the heavy sound of rock scraping against rock. Suddenly—

—a section of the dungeon wall slid open to reveal a secret

doorway.

And standing in that doorway, her eyes bug-wide, skin bruised, mud up to her knees and her clothes drenched and tattered, stood a heaving, frazzled Elsa Strauss.

The boys jumped up and rushed to hug her.

"Elsa, we are glad to see you!"

"What happened to your clothes?"

"How'd you find us?"

To which Elsa's only reply was, "What?"

The Professor made his way over to her. "Elsa, are you alright?"

Elsa stared at him blankly and shouted, "What did you say?"

The Professor shouted back. "I said you look terrible! Are you alright?"

With her wide dazed eyes, Elsa replied loudly, "Did you say something? All I can hear is bells."

"Oh dear," the Professor muttered. "Gentlemen, I think we've overstayed our welcome here. The tapestry will have to wait for another day. In the meantime, I suggest we make our exit now, before Mr Vanderbilt returns."

Gently, Luca and Shane took Elsa by the arms and all seven of them made their way back down the secret tunnel that Elsa had located. Their feet splashed through puddles as they headed for the flares of lightning at the end of the passage. And all the while Elsa's bellowing voice echoed off the stone walls.

"Who's ringing the bells?"

"Nobody's ringing the bells, Elsa."

"When will they stop ringing the bells?"

"Nobody's ringing the bells," the Professor told her. "And try to keep your voice down."

"What?" Elsa shouted.

"I said—oh, never mind."

FROM THE SECRET FILES OF FATHOM'S FIVE

WHO IS JAKE STONE?

Although born and bred in New York, the World is now Jake Stone's playground of mystery and trouble!

At 28 years of age, Jake has scoured the planet uncovering ancient relics and rare artifacts, hired by merciless millionaires to build their own personal collections, expanding the wealth of their priceless belongings. But now, under the guidance and wisdom of Professor Fathom, Jake is about to understand the true value of belonging.

With a furrowed brow of bravery, a glint of glory in his piercing blue eyes and one determined hand clawing at his spiky black hair, Jake Stone is always ready to plunge headlong into action and adventure—and if Professor Fathom has anything to do with it, he'll be the latest addition to Fathom's Five!

But what exactly is Jake's true motive~self-preservation, money, or love?

And who is Sarah Stone?

WHO IS DR. EDEN SANTIAGO?

Born and raised in the slums of Rio de Janeiro, Brazil, 27-year-old Eden Santiago rejected a life of crime and corruption on the streets to put himself through college, becoming a doctor in not only biology, but also genetics and forensics. His studies also make him an expert in botany and toxicology.

Sensible and sexy, grounded and gorgeous, Eden has proven himself time and time again as Professor Fathom's right-hand man. Professor Fathom entrusts Eden to keep the team together; he has often considered Eden a younger version of himself—calm, collected, clever and calculated in his approach to their missions. Yet Eden possesses a compassion that may one day be his downfall.

With his shimmering brown skin, his heart-melting Latino tongue, his trim shaved head and his perfect body, Dr. Eden Santiago is the cornerstone of Professor Fathom's team.

WHO IS SHANE HOUSTON?

His short-cropped blond hair peeks out from under his cowboy hat, his mouth is always twirled in a cheeky grin, and his manners are impeccable: Shane Houston is the essential Texas gentlemen and animal lover—with a bad boy's love of action and adventure!

At 25 years of age, Shane is a renowned cartographer with a sense of space and distance considered uncanny by many—but handy to the Fathom's Five team. After leaving his family ranch (and his beloved mother, Gertrude) at the age of 18, Shane moved from one ranch-hand's job to another until Professor Fathom caught wind of his unparalleled cartography skills.

With a heart as big as Texas—and a sense of fun and adventure to match—Shane Houston is Fathom's Five's untamed cowboy with compassion! It's time to hold on tight for a wild, wild ride!

WHO IS LUCA DA ROMA?

Twenty-six years ago, a baby boy was left in a basket on the doorstep of the convent of Santa Maria del Mare in Tuscany. There was a note pinned to the baby's blanket explaining that he had no name and was a bastard child, born in the ghettoes of Rome. Around his neck was a small crucifix on a silver chain. No markings. No engraving. No clue as to who this child could be.

When the kindly Sister Eva discovered the baby on the doorstep, the morning sun was shining on the child's face. She took him in, and the three nuns living at the convent named him Luca da Roma—the Light of Rome.

Now, with his tousled brown hair, his catwalk looks and his timelessly beautiful Italian Renaissance body, Luca da Roma is himself a work of art, as well as being an expert on the subject—both ancient and modern—and as such is one of the greatest assets in Professor Fathom's team.

But Luca will not rest until he discovers the secrets of his past:

Who were his parents?

Why did they abandon him?

And who is the clown known only as Valentino?

WHO IS WILL HUNTER?

College is a bore... Unless it helps 19-year-old Will Hunter solve some of the deadliest secrets in Archeological History. When he's not on the field earning his stripes as a college quarterback, Will is being tutored by his hunky Ancient History Professor, Nathan James. And what he learns behind the closed doors of Professor James' office—with his pants down and his legs spread—Will puts into practice, solving deadly mysteries and finding the clues to ancient relics lost or hidden for thousands of years.

Always ready for action, the blond tousle-haired student is the son of a wealthy diplomat—Charles Hunter—who has left Will to grow up under the guidance of his loyal butler: the prim, proper and much-loved Felix Fraser.

Born with a need for speed and undeniably the bad boy of this sexy bunch, Will Hunter is without a doubt the wild child of Fathom's Five!

WHO IS PROFESSOR FATHOM?

Professor Fathom is a man with a dream: a dream that all gay men and women will one day share the same rights and respect as everyone else. It is a dream realized through his quest to obtain ancient treasures, right age-old wrongs, and uncover the truth behind some of the most dangerous mysteries of all time.

Now in his sixties—and rendered blind by an accident some 40 years ago—the fate of Professor Fathom's quest lies in the hands of five daring gay thrill-seekers: Luca da Roma, an Italian model and art expert; Dr. Eden Santiago, a Brazilian biologist; Shane Houston, a Texas cowboy and skilled cartography; Will Hunter, college quarterback and ancient history major; and hunky New Yorker Jake Stone, adventurer-for-hire.

Steered by Professor Fathom's wisdom and driven by his passion to uncover the deadliest of secrets, Fathom's Five—as they have become known—will stop at nothing to solve these ancient mysteries, unearth vital treasures, follow the clues and bring justice to the world!

available now

THE RIDDLE OF THE SANDS

THE CLOCK IS TICKING!

A rare and deadly poison is slowly threading its way through Sam's bloodstream and his only hope of survival lies with Fathom's Five.

Blackmailed by the vengeful Pierre Perron, Professor Fathom's team of gay adventure-hunters must use all their knowledge, wit, strength and skills to uncover the legendary Riddle of the Sands to save Sam's life.

But what is the Riddle of the Sands? Where are the long-lost clues and hidden maps that lead to its whereabouts? Is it a myth, a mirage, or the greatest engineering feat in the history of ancient Egypt?

From Paris to Brazil, from the icy plains of Siberia to the dusty streets of Cairo, from the valleys of the Nile to the deepest, darkest secrets of the Amazon, join New York adventurer Jake Stone, Brazilian biologist Eden Santiago, Texas cowboy Shane Houston, Italian art expert Luca da Roma, and Californian college quarterback Will Hunter in the heroic adventures, hunky sex and hot, high-octane action of The Riddle of the Sands.

coming soon

THE CURSE OF THE DRAGON GOD

China - a land of ancient wonders, a history filled with tradition, triumph and tyranny. And now, as it casts a shadow across the entire globe, this once forbidden country will awaken as the dominant force in a new world economy.

Business empires will rise, deals will be made, lives will be lost as money changes hands, but one treasure will remain the most precious in all of China: a diamond known as the Eye of Fucanglong, the Dragon God of lost jewels and buried treasures. The diamond is flawless. It is priceless. It is cursed. And it is about to be stolen in the heist of the century.

Can Professor Fathom's team of gay adventure-seekers find the diamond before this perfectly-executed crime leads to a cataclysmic event of mass destruction?

From the towers of Hong Kong to the diamond mines of Shandong; from the streets of San Francisco to the deserts of Dubai to the male stripclubs of Beijing; from China's mystical past, to the boardrooms and backrooms of a modern industrial giant, take the high road to China and join in the sizzling action and page-turning adventure of The Curse of the Dragon God.

coming soon

THE TEMPLE OF TIME

There is a civilization that once vanished trace. There is a calendar that predicts the end of time. There is a fragile fraternity that protects the most important secret in human history. And there is one man who will destroy everything and anyone to know the truth—his name is Caro Sholtez.

He has the first piece of the most powerful mythical clock in the world, and the only person who can stop him from reaching his lifetime's goal is Professor Fathom. And so it seems to Caro Sholtez that distractions, kidnappings, killings, are necessary to disperse the Professor's men to prevent them from stopping him from finding the one thing he wants— the power to control the passage of Time.

From the landmarks of London to the cobblestoned streets of Prague, from the markets of Marrakesh to the pot parlors of Amsterdam, from the chaotic crowds of Mexico City to the very cradle of Mayan civilization, join New York adventurer Jake Stone, Brazilian biologist Eden Santiago, Texas cowboy Shane Houston, Italian art expert Luca da Roma, and Californian college quarterback Will Hunter on their greatest adventure yet— The Temple of Time.

One will be betrayed.

One will turn his back on everyone he loves.

And for one, the Fathom's Five journey will end—forever.

ABOUT THE AUTHOR
GEOFFREY KNIGHT

From palace hopping across the Rajasthan Desert to sleeping in train stations in Bulgaria, from spinning prayer wheels in Kathmandu to exploring the skull-gated graveyards of the indigenous Balinese tribes, Geoffrey Knight has been a traveler ever since he could scrape together enough money to buy a plane ticket. Born in Melbourne but raised and educated in cities and towns across Australia, Geoffrey was a nomadic boy who grew into a nomadic gay writer. His books are the result of too many matinee movies in small-town cinemas as a child, reading too many Hardy Boys adventures, and wandering penniless across too many borders in his early adult life. He currently works in advertising and lives in Paddington, Sydney. And can't wait to buy his next plane ticket.

COMING SOON

FROM

GEOFFREY KNIGHT

IN ASSOCIATION WITH

DARE EMPIRE EMEDIA PRODUCTIONS

DRIVE SHAFT

Jensen Rivers wasn't looking for trouble. As the new kid on the block at Clyde's Body Shop, all Jensen wanted was a job, a place where he could put his head down and ass up. Young and handsome, he was the kind of simple, honest guy who was happiest when he was working hard, with oil smeared across his chest and grease up to his elbows.

But Dean 'Hutch' Hutchinson plans on getting more than just Jensen's hands dirty!

Reckless and arrogant, drenched in sweat and dripping with a masculinity that cannot be tamed, Hutch challenges Jensen to a series of perilous night races. The prize: sexual domination!

Night after night, wheels burn, passions flare and the no-holds-barred lust between two testosterone-fuelled daredevils ignites. But losing a race is one thing. Losing your heart is something altogether more dangerous.

Will Jensen risk everything to find the love trapped behind Hutch's fearless façade? Will Hutch bury the secret tragedy of his past before he throws away his last chance at a future?

Kickstart your need for speed, fire up your lust for life and buckle up for hottest thrill-ride of the year—*Drive Shaft*.

SCOTT SAPPHIRE AND THE EMERALD ORCHID

"a new gay adventure hero is born..."

Meet Scott Sapphire—lover of French champagne, Belgian chocolate and dangerous men. He is suave. He is sexy. He is a man of the world—and a man that the world desperately wants to catch.

For Scott Sapphire is the greatest jewel thief of our time. Dashing. Daring. And always neck-deep in trouble.

When Scott's latest heist lands him in possession of a map to a rare and precious orchid, it'll take more than bedroom eyes and a charming smile to stay one step ahead of the world's deadliest drug baron, as well as keep the CIA off Scott's back and a handsome special agent out of his pants—or maybe not.

From New York City to the Amazon jungle, from Rio de Janeiro to the French Riviera—and from the writer of the world's Number #1 gay adventure series, Fathom's Five—comes a brand new hero as irresistible as diamonds and pearls.

Adventure has a new name!

And that name is Scott Sapphire.

Made in the USA
Lexington, KY
25 July 2011